THE WALLED CITY

THE
WALLED
CITY

by Marcel Clouzot

Translated by June P. Wilson
and Walter B. Michaels

M. EVANS AND COMPANY, INC.
NEW YORK, N.Y. 10017

M. Evans and Company titles are distributed in
the United States by the J. B. Lippincott Company,
East Washington Square, Philadelphia, Pa. 19105
and in Canada by McClelland & Stewart, Ltd., 25
Hollinger Road, Toronto 374, Ontario

1

HIS BACK against the rampart wall, Robert Baudruche watched the flood of refugees crowding through the gates below. There was no end to them. At first, weeks ago, there had been only five or six a day—no one paid any attention then—but then there were twelve, twenty, fifty. That's when Baudruche began to worry. And the number kept increasing. Now it was a thousand a day.

He had asked them questions at the beginning. But their answers were vague, evasive. They didn't know, really. If pressed, they panicked, cowering before him. All he could worm out of them was that there would be more, many more, until all the villages were empty. They admitted to a vague sense of fear, but they could not explain its origin. They knew only that they had to come back to the shelter of the City as quickly as possible. They had brought little—whatever a suit-case or knapsack would hold—and what they had left behind, they burned.

Baudruche turned and peered at the horizon through a spy

hole. He couldn't see a thing. He put on a pair of thick, horn-rimmed glasses, and the farthest reaches came into focus.

In the distance, everything was in flames, sad wisps of smoke rising straight into the sky.

"They've burned everything. There won't be a damn thing left," Baudruche said, shaking his head.

It broke his heart to see all those villages in flames. They had been built at such cost, the land so hard to come by. He had known those villages, visited them, inspected them in those distant days when he was only a minor official. Often he had regretted not being able to go back, look around, have a chat with the people he had come to know. They would be his age now; some even older.

He had recognized a few among the refugees, but they didn't seem to recognize him. They just stammered: "Yes, Mr. Commissioner," or "No, Mr. Commissioner." Fear!

They must be sick! How is it possible?

A strange sickness, this flight, this cringing need for refuge behind the City's high walls. Refuge from what? No one had attacked them. The enemy had never come close; they had been particularly well protected.

Yet panic had swept through the villages. It had spread like a grass fire until all the villages were burning.

What were they so afraid of? The wars were very far away, and nobody discussed them anyway. It was bad luck.

Tiny columns were winding over the land as far as the eye could see; Baudruche knew they were men even though he couldn't distinguish them. They came from every direction, converging at the main gate, the only one open in the City. More than one gate open to the outside would have terrified the populace. The Prefect was adamant: only one gate open—the main one—from sunup to sundown.

The smoke spread to the City and it stung Baudruche's eyes. A long gray veil, it followed the refugees like a reproach.

Baudruche looked down. It was less painful to watch what

6

was going on inside the City. Everything appeared to be normal, as ordained by the Prefect. Baudruche's men stood in double file, channeling the flow of arrivals. Most of the families were complete, their members clinging to each other. Social Service employees directed them to welcome centers.

The refugees were submissive, some even obsequious. No complaints, no arguments—no songs or laughter either.

Baudruche removed his glasses and walked down the wide stone steps. The crowd made way as he approached. He took up his position next to the Chief Medical Officer who had been watching the refugees file by.

"What do you think is the matter?" Baudruche asked.

"Nothing, as far as I can see. They seem normal enough."

"Normal? Look at them!"

"They correspond exactly to the current rational type. No difference at all. We could test them out but I don't think it would tell us much."

"We could do what?"

"Test them . . . give them an examination."

"Out of the question. The Prefect has forbidden any more interrogation. They won't answer anyway. But is there nothing else we can do? Do we have to leave them in this condition? You're a doctor!"

"Yes, but I'm not a veterinarian."

"You're all alike. You don't give a damn!"

The doctor went pale and answered dryly, "I am here by order of the Prefect and that is all, Mr. Commissioner. He asked me to look over the refugees to see if any were sick. I have seen no one sick, and that's that. Beyond that there is nothing to say."

"Then there's no point in your staying. I'll include what you've just said in my report."

The doctor raised his hat and headed off.

The crowds from the City had been thinning out during the preceding weeks. At first, curiosity had led them to see if these distant relatives, gone so long ago, would be different from themselves. To their disappointment, they found the refugees were not. Three days after their arrival, no one even remembered they'd come from the villages.

Baudruche returned to the steps and climbed them slowly. He reached the sentry walk and surveyed the countryside.

The last groups were hurrying to make it to the gates before sundown. Baudruche looked at his watch, tapped his foot nervously and ordered the gates closed. It was already past the hour.

An uneasy conscience drove him to take a last look beyond the walls. A solitary man was approaching at a leisurely pace. Baudruche was about to call to him to hurry when he remembered his orders: never do anything that might in any way frighten the refugees. So instead he blew his whistle. "Don't close up yet. There's still one coming."

This was most unusual. No one had ever seen a man come alone. It was most disturbing. He must watch the man closely. Baudruche blew his whistle again and called down, "Heh, Bicard! Come here for a minute, will you?"

Bicard climbed up.

"Bicard, a solitary man just went through the gates. Find out who he is and where he is to live."

"Yes, Mr. Commissioner."

Bicard disappeared from sight. The gates closed, the last refugees scattered and the few remaining townspeople dispersed. Baudruche's men broke ranks and waited for him at the bottom of the steps. With a wave of the hand, he sent them all home.

Night was falling fast. Baudruche glanced at the horizon: all that remained was a reddish glow. He walked to the first small turret and asked the man inside, "Aren't you cold?"

"No, Mr. Commissioner."

"Right. Wait for winter to feel the cold. Call out to the left tonight."

8

The sentry called to his neighbor in the next turret, which was barely visible in the dark. The call was repeated by the neighbor and then by another voice farther to the left. It grew fainter and fainter, then picked up strength and returned clear and sharp to the right.

"O.K. Everybody's here. The City will sleep soundly tonight. I should know you. What's your name?"

"Shell, Mr. Commissioner."

"Shell . . . Wasn't your grandfather a carpenter? Mine had a helper by that name."

"I don't know, Mr. Commissioner."

"You don't know your grandfather?"

"No, Mr. Commissioner, I only know my orders."

Baudruche shrugged, then worried that the man had noticed. He reached in his pocket for his packet of tobacco, but it was empty. The tobacco, as usual, had leaked out. "Damn this system! Can't they give us any decent paper! God knows they charge enough for the tobacco."

"Oh, Mr. Commissioner, what if somebody heard you!"

"So what! Show me anybody who'll say this is good paper."

Baudruche dug into his pocket, came up with a few shreds of tobacco and placed them in the hollow of his left palm. Then he took out a pad of cigarette wrappers and rolled a cigarette. The sentry rushed to him with his cigarette case.

"Please take one of mine, Mr. Commissioner. You shouldn't be rolling your own cigarettes!"

"They taste better this way. Try one, you'll see." Baudruche handed him a wrapper.

"I don't know how."

"Can't you do anything for yourself? Does someone hold your hand when you screw your wife?"

"Surely Mr. Commissioner is joking."

"Nothing sure about it. . . . Come, hold your lantern up."

The man held it out to him. Baudruche opened the tiny door, drew on his cigarette and walked away.

9

He went down the steps and headed for the main street. It was empty now. Baudruche liked to go home alone in the evening, through the deserted streets, without escort. He knew he had nothing to fear. No one in the City would dream of doing him harm.

Fifteen minutes later, he was in his office facing the belfrey of City Hall. He was astonished to find Miss Bourrot still there.

For twenty years, he'd been astonished to find her there in the evening. Why the devil didn't she go home? She wasn't indispensable. She carried work to the point of a vice. Her only vice: that was clear by looking at her. Oh, well, he was grateful to her. Not for her looks God knows, but for her character. In her presence, Baudruche could say what he didn't dare say elsewhere. She would just look down and pretend not to hear. Nothing had ever leaked out. He would have known after all these years.

For eleven years, she had belabored him with "Yes, Mr. High Commissioner," and "No, Mr. High Commissioner," until one day, exasperated, he asked her for God's sake to stop using his formal title: all it did was remind him of his exhausting duties. Ever since, she had kept it to a simple "Mr. Commissioner," but he could see that her heart wasn't in it.

"Miss Bourrot, is Bicard back?"

"Yes, Mr. . . . Commissioner, he's in the waiting room. He wouldn't leave without seeing you. I tried to tell him . . ."

"You have nothing to tell him but to come in—immediately."

She shuffled to the door and Bicard entered.

"So . . . did you find out who the man is?"

"Mr. Commissioner, I have to tell you . . ."

"I'm sure you do."

"What I wanted to explain was . . ."

"Explain what? That you let him get away?"

Bicard's head drooped.

"Ah, splendid! I give you a simple assignment and . . . Did anyone see him?"

"Of course, Mr. Commissioner. A man all by himself like that."

"O.K. I don't care how you do it, but by noon tomorrow, I want to know where he is. Understand? You find out or I'll have you recycled to the Factory."

"Yes, Mr. Commissioner," Bicard mumbled and backed out the door.

Baudruche dropped his hands on the arms of his chair. "What am I to do with men like that! There's only you and me, Miss Bourrot. But don't look at me with those calflike eyes."

Miss Bourrot stammered, "I just wanted to know if everything went all right today."

"You're about to find out. I shall now dictate my report to the Prefect:

"Sir:

"In accordance with your instructions, I went to the main gate of the City to observe those arriving from the villages.

"Their *physical* condition seemed excellent. The malaise they feel—as with the City's populace—appears to have no visible effect on their physical condition, according to the Chief Medical Officer.

"Our welcome services directed the refugees in groups of twenty to the housing which had been prepared for them in line with your instructions.

"As night fell, I made a last trip to the ramparts and examined the environs. As far as the eye could see, there was no movement, and the villages had burned to the ground.

"I was about to give the order to close the gate when a solitary individual presented himself at the gate. I did not interrogate him, just as I have stopped interrogating other refugees at your request. But I noticed that he was well dressed, of medium height, and carried one suitcase. Once inside the City, he did not join a group and avoided our welcome services along the main street. At that point, I lost sight of him.

"A few minutes after the gate was closed, the main arteries of the City were empty and all lights in the refugees' quarters were extinguished."

Baudruche stopped. He had nothing more to say. Miss Bour-rot watched him, then said in a timid voice:

"What about the weather, Mr. Commissioner?"

"The weather? Why, the same as usual, Miss Bourrot. Do I have to remind you?

"No change in the weather is predicted. It will remain without sun, because of the cloud cover over the City. Our sentries report no unusual noise outside the City, nor has the enemy appeared on the horizon.

"That's all. Give me a sheet of paper and I'll sign it. You can type the text above it."

Baudruche got to his feet, took his hat and headed for the door. As he was closing it, he felt a pang of remorse. So he added:

"Good night, my pet."

He closed the door without waiting to see the shock on his secretary's face. But he could visualize it.

Baudruche was in a hurry to get home. Home was where he renewed his oxygen supply every evening; home was what made it possible for him to face the next day.

His house had belonged to his grandfather, the carpenter in chief. Baudruche had refused to give it up for the official residence offered him as High Commissioner.

"Live in that dump! I wouldn't put my rabbits in it! My house was built of stone and I know who built it. He was a good man and I know it will hold together."

His house opened onto the street, which frightened Martha. The front door was too accessible, she thought. He laughed.

"Who would think of harming me beside you, my dear? Anyway, I still have enough strength to defend myself."

"But, Robert, some madman . . ."

"We no longer have madmen in the City. The worst we have are bureaucrats. They may have evil thoughts but they're not dangerous."

Once he was inside his own house, Baudruche forgot the bureaucrats as well as his own troubles—everything except the Prefect.

That night, Baudruche flopped as usual into his deep chair next to the fireplace, unlaced his shoes and said:

"Martha, hand me my slippers."

"They're on the floor right next to you. You poor dear, are your eyes getting worse?"

"Don't tease. Just wait ten years, until you're my age."

"Fifteen years, Robert."

"Forgive me, dear. My mistake. It's only that you haven't been looking all that young recently."

"If you can find anyone else who'll put up with you, I won't be jealous."

"I've found her already."

"Who is she, dear?"

"I'm going to divorce you and marry Miss Bourrot."

"I must say she deserves it."

They played that game every night: the game of disguised love.

2

BAUDRUCHE started each day with a visit to the ramparts. The walls had been one of the City's main concerns for a long time. No one could have slept without knowing they were there. People talked about them often just to reassure themselves. Who else had such ramparts? Who would dare attack them? Yet everyone trembled, and the condition of the walls was under constant scrutiny.

Baudruche loved the ramparts but not because they gave him reassurance; a military attack, he knew, was highly unlikely. No, he loved them for themselves. He'd been climbing them since he was a child. His father had loved them too; even his grandfather had taken him there sometimes.

"Who built them, Grandpa?"

"I don't know. They're very old. *My* grandfather didn't know."

The Prefect knew only too well how important the ramparts were to the populace and ordered them carefully examined every morning by the City's chief architect under Baudruche's supervision. So together Baudruche and Labrique made sure the ramparts hadn't disappeared during the night.

"How are you this morning, Labrique?" Baudruche asked when they met in front of the main gate.

"Better than the people here, or anywhere else for that matter. Are we through with the new arrivals? It looks that way. They haven't opened the gate this morning."

Baudruche went up to one of the guards. "Why haven't you opened up? No more refugees?"

The guard stood at attention. "No, Mr. Commissioner."

Baudruche walked up to the gate and looked through a spy hole.

"Who's that man sitting out there?"

The guard looked uncomfortable. "We don't know, Mr. Commissioner. He didn't come to the gate. He just sat down there and turned his back."

"Is he a refugee?"

"We don't think so, Mr. Commissioner. He isn't dressed like they were."

Baudruche peered again, then took out his glasses. One glance was enough. He knew what they were dealing with. "He didn't ask to enter?"

"No, Mr. Commissioner."

"And you didn't go out to him?"

"Leave the City? Never! It's against orders."

"You didn't talk to him? You didn't ask him what he's doing there?"

"You know better than us that it's forbidden now, Mr. Commissioner."

Baudruche left him and joined Labrique. "Do you know who that man is sitting outside the gate?"

"No, and I don't give a damn."

"You don't give a damn about anything."

"I'm a reasonable man, my friend."

"Well, I'll tell you who's sitting out there. I recognized him right away. It's a soldier."

Labrique let out a dry laugh. "Wouldn't it be funny if they were coming back!"

Baudruche grabbed him by the lapels. "You shut up. You don't know what you're saying." He let go of Labrique. "I have to find out what he wants. Wait for me here."

Baudruche climbed the eighty stone steps (he knew the number by heart, he had climbed them so often) and leaned through a spy hole. He was right. He recognized the man as a soldier because he remembered how they had looked when he was a boy. He called to him softly. "Hey! Soldier!"

The soldier turned and looked at him. Baudruche continued. "Do you want to enter the City?"

The soldier shook his head. Baudruche wanted to ask him more questions. It had been such a long time since anyone had talked of them. But he must be careful—even he, Baudruche. It would be bad if word got around that he'd spoken to someone like this. A group of people were approaching in the distance. He left and rejoined Labrique.

The architect asked, "Don't we do our tour of the ramparts today, Baudruche?"

"No. I'm worried about this soldier."

Labrique shrugged.

Baudruche asked, "You have nothing to report about the ramparts today?"

"I certainly do! I wish to report that the ramparts haven't budged."

"You'll never die of overwork."

"What is there to get worked up about?"

"So long, Labrique."

"See you tonight, Baudruche."

No doubt about it: strange things were going on in the City. First the flood of refugees, then yesterday the solitary man, and today, the soldier. Why was he back? What would happen if the others came back? The City's inhabitants had assumed they were far away, beyond the farthest villages, and had hoped they would never return. A soldier smelled of war and that smell caused fear in the City.

Baudruche looked at his watch. It was time to go to the Factory, his daily agony. Everything there got under his skin: the noise, the atmosphere, the people. The worst place in the City—and the most important—for it made all the machines. He had to admit it: the Factory was the very heart of the City, a heart that beat harder and faster every year. The City's whole life depended on the vast building that stretched endlessly, swallowing up houses and gardens as it spread.

But the people in the Factory talked a language Baudruche didn't understand, or, rather, understood too well. It was vague yet full of lies, fuzzy while it pretended to be precise. They manufacture more words than they do machines, he thought to himself.

The Director of the Factory was an engineer named Leponte. His was an enviable job, but a very dangerous one. There could be no interruption in the increase of "productivity." The smallest slowdown, for whatever reason, would mean his forced retirement, or a transfer to a lesser position. But right now, only the Prefect and Baudruche stood above him.

"Well, what have you to report today?"

"Mr. Commissioner, everything is going admirably. The flood of refugees is bringing us a vast new source of manpower. Totally unexpected, a real windfall. It's a miracle, Mr. Baudruche! They all came to the Factory and, in a manner of speaking, recycled themselves. The work is simple enough: just a few motions to learn. . . ."

"I know, I know. You think of the Factory and nothing more. My main concern is the morale of the refugees."

"Magnificent! They are in seventh heaven. So far as productivity and technical know-how are concerned, I believe I can tell you in a few words . . ."

"Don't. If you get started, I'll be here two hours. You won't know what you're saying, and I won't understand a word. Just take a piece of paper and write down what I'm to report to the Prefect and print in the newspaper. That will be much quicker. And I'll try to do a passable translation."

Ah, Leponte fumed, if only he could strangle Baudruche with his own hands, right here in the office. Why did this man humiliate him every day, show such contempt for science, technology, progress—in a word, for the future? It was beyond comprehension.

"I'm waiting."

"Forgive me, Mr. Commissioner. I was going over the figures in my head. I'll give you the report right away. I'll dictate it and then it can be typed up."

"You've forgotten how to write?"

"Forgive me, Mr. Commissioner. I must admit I have more facility with figures than with letters."

A young secretary who amply filled her metallic blue uniform came in. As Baudruche watched her take dictation, his mind wandered back to Miss Bourrot. The comparison annoyed him and increased his dislike for Leponte. He sat motionless in his chair, thumbs crossed, his eyes on the ceiling.

"Mr. Commissioner, excuse me for interrupting your daydreams . . ."

"I was not daydreaming, Mr. Leponte. I was meditating."

"Miss Niquel will bring you the report in five minutes."

"That won't be necessary. I'll pick it up on my way out."

In the adjoining office, Baudruche watched the secretary's game with amusement. "Are you sure you're comfortable? Wouldn't you like a cigarette?" and she rushed up to him with a lighter. He smiled smugly, thinking of the welcome that ass of a technocrat would have gotten from Miss Bourrot. She would have bitten him by now.

The secretary handed him the sheet of paper, her fingers lingering in his for a moment. Baudruche hesitated. This would put him one up in his game with Leponte. But he'd

19

better skip it. Everything to do with the Factory was to be kept at arm's length. No human relationships with people of that sort—only official ones.

Baudruche stuffed the paper in his pocket and walked out, looking neither left nor right.

As soon as he reached his office, he gave Miss Bourrot the piece of paper.

"Take this thing and do up a piece for the newspaper, and tell Bicard I want to see him."

"But, Mr. Commissioner, the Director of Residences is waiting to see you. He says you summoned him."

"True enough, I did. Tell him to come in."

The Director of Residences was small and thin. He stood very straight in front of Baudruche.

"Do all the refugees have lodgings now, Mr. Parpins?"

"Every last one, Mr. Commissioner. No trouble at all. Each one has the sixteen square yards allotted to all our citizens. And hygienic conditions and livability have been strictly observed."

"Are they happy?"

"Absolutely. From the moment they realized that each lodging had its own machine. They turned it on right away and were thrilled. They'd never seen one before. They all agreed to the monthly charge for the machine. The Factory Director will withhold it from their wages."

"Fine, fine. But do they show any signs of life, any spirit?"

"Oh, no, Mr. Commissioner. Rest assured, all is perfectly calm. They're too busy with their machines."

"Did you by any chance come across a solitary man among the refugees?"

Parpins started with surprise.

"Certainly not, Mr. Commissioner! I wouldn't have admitted him."

Baudruche dropped his arms with discouragement.

"All right, Parpins. You can go now."

Parpins backed out. Baudruche buzzed and Bicard walked in.

He announced, "I have found our man, Mr. Commissioner. He is staying at the Hotel. Alone, in a room."

"I didn't suppose he'd sleep in the kitchen. Who the devil is he?"

"No one knows, Mr. Commissioner. He didn't give his name. But I did find out what you wanted to know, didn't I?"

"That hardly took a magician. It was more than likely he'd stay at the Hotel."

"Not really, sir. With a lone man, you never know. Should I continue to watch him? Do you want him arrested?"

"Arrested? What for?"

"I don't know. His being alone would be enough. . . ."

"You can go. Don't you bother with this anymore. I'll handle it from now on."

Baudruche looked at his watch. It was past noon. He told Miss Bourrot he was going to lunch.

"But, Mr. Commissioner, they're waiting for orders to put up the posters."

"What posters?"

"The prohibition against feeding the birds."

"But I told the Prefect there was no need to fear a drain on our provisions. Our stocks are more than ample."

"He wouldn't listen, and the people are beginning to talk. They say it's wasting food; it's taking bread from the mouths of the workers. The Prefect has signed the posters. He wants you to sign them too."

"Show me one."

Miss Bourrot left and returned with a long tube of paper which she unrolled on his desk. He read it over slowly.

"You may send out orders to have them put up, but I refuse to sign them. Wait a minute. I've got an idea. Have another one printed immediately. Take this down.

"We wish to inform the people of the City that the gates will henceforth be closed only as a security measure. They will be opened for anyone desiring to leave the City for whatever reason.

"That's all. Take it to the Prefect for his authorization. Then have them pasted up. These I want to sign with my own name."

"You don't think this will disturb the people?"

"For God's sake, why? I've said nothing threatening."

Baudruche walked out. He was in a hurry to get home, first because he was hungry, second because he needed to relax. But he didn't want to tell Martha about the City's problems. They were men's problems. Besides, things were not going to his liking, and he didn't want to talk about them.

"Anything new, Robert?"

"No, Martha, nothing. Just the usual. . . ."

After lunch, he left the house sooner than usual. He needed to think, and he didn't think well at home. On the other hand, it was where he did his best debating. . . .

As he was walking, one of his men stopped him.

"The Public Library didn't open this morning, Mr. Commissioner. I rang the bell but there was no answer. What should I do?"

"Can't I be left in peace during the lunch hour? Why not open the door?"

"We thought of that, but we were waiting for orders. We didn't want to do anything without asking you first."

Always the need for orders! Don't do anything until you're thoroughly protected! What would they do without him as their umbrella?

"All right. I'll go."

"You'll go yourself, Mr. Commissioner?"

"Yes, I, myself, as you see."

He had to go himself if he wanted to find out anything. Besides, he had known for some time that he must get more involved in the City's affairs. The City was sick. He knew it as if he were a doctor. To the ordinary man, it looked healthy, strong and prosperous. But he had noticed the slack motions, the somnolence. Something was happening to the City, and he had to watch.

"Let's go," he said, prodding his man from the rear.

He was concerned about the Librarian; he was very fond of Mr. Pholio.

Pholio was a former professor of literature who had been forced to retire for lack of students. With considerable spunk, he had complained all the way up to Baudruche. He held that he had made a moral contract with the City and the City with him.

"But, Mr. Pholio, you have no students!"

"The fact that I have no students is the City's problem. It owes them to me. All it has to do is furnish them."

In the end, Baudruche became convinced that the City did indeed have a responsibility. It was obligated to provide Pholio with students just as he was obligated to teach them. All the same, Baudruche tried to argue with him, devoting an hour of his precious time to it, but in vain. The old man would have none of it.

By the same token, Pholio knew perfectly well that there was nothing Baudruche could do about it. God and the Prefect stood above him.

Baudruche solved the problem by giving him the job of Librarian, and Pholio had resigned himself both to the lack of students and the lack of readers. He had shut himself up with his books, abandoned the house the City had put at his disposal and slept on an iron cot between the stacks. He ate hurriedly at a corner of the main reading table. A loyal old neighbor brought him his food twice a day.

It was she who had found the door locked and alerted the police.

As Baudruche had feared, they found Pholio lying pale and motionless on the floor.

"Carry him away," he told his men.

Four men bent to the task, although two would have been ample. Baudruche watched Pholio go, his eyes staring fixedly in Baudruche's direction. He followed his men to the door. "I'll join you in a moment."

He locked the door and stood alone in the enormous room.

The books stood on symmetrical shelves from floor to ceiling. He approached a shelf and read a few titles. He didn't recognize one. Stubbornly, he read more titles, but without success. He was in unknown territory, another world.

Of course he read from time to time, whatever he found at the bottom of a closet. Sometimes he read the same book several times. He would get to page 50 or 60, stop abruptly, laugh at himself and say out loud:

"God, I'm stupid, Martha! I've already read this damn book."

Was reading necessary? He didn't know. They had insisted on it, back in elementary school, but he'd paid no attention to them. Necessary? He wondered. Hadn't he managed without it, and better than most?

Baudruche pulled a book out at random. The title attracted him: *Considerations of the Causes of Rome's Grandeur and Decadence.* He opened the book, sat down and ran his eyes over the pages. He was struck by several sentences:

The houses were small and scattered, without visible plan, for the men were hardly ever home, being always at work or in the public square. But Rome's grandeur was obvious in its public buildings. The works which conveyed, still convey today, the best indication of its power were accomplished under the kings.

Baudruche thought of the City and how its small houses were disappearing fast while the ramparts remained.

Eventually, the benevolence of the early emperors—their only means of understanding their situation—came to an end. The prince knew only what he was told by his few confidants.

Baudruche couldn't help thinking of the Prefect.

This then is the history of the Romans: they conquered every people by their maxims, but the republic could not survive its success. The government had to be changed. But the maxims used by the new government were the opposite of the original ones and so its grandeur collapsed.

24

He thought of the City he had known as a child, compared to the one he knew today, and it frightened him.

He noticed a large ledger on the table with the word "Loans" on the cover. He opened it, took out his pen and wrote his name and the title in large, energetic letters.

He left the library, carefully locked the door and put the key in his pocket. Then he walked away, clutching his book. "You're reverting to your childhood, Baudruche! You look as if you were going back to school. . . ."

He was angry with himself. Why had he neglected Pholio? Of course no one had ever told him that such an insignificant-looking person could occasionally be useful to a man in his position.

Pholio must have read a lot, not just books found in closets. And now he was dead. There was nothing for Baudruche to do but work things out for himself.

His greeting to Miss Bourrot was distracted. He looked at the clock. It was too late to go to the Hotel and check on the solitary man, and it was too early to make his report. He dropped into his chair and cast a weary look at the book he had placed on the table. No, he'd read enough for one day. Exhausted, he soon fell asleep.

When he woke up, it was almost dark. Time for his report. He rang for Miss Bourrot.

She had already prepared the daily newspaper release. He glanced at it. It was brilliantly done: vague, imprecise, artful. No doubt about it: Miss Bourrot was better at it than he was. He thanked her and suggested they turn their attention to the Prefect's report—that wretched report that made him sweat blood every night.

"Mr. Prefect:

"The gates of the City have not been opened since last night, as no refugee has asked to come in and no inhabitant of the City has asked to leave.

25

"As usual, the City's architect inspected the ramparts and found them to be in perfect condition.

"While I was on the ramparts, I noticed a man sitting outside the walls, his back turned to the City. I realized that we were dealing with a soldier. I asked him if he wanted to enter the City. He shook his head. Of course, I would not have permitted a soldier to enter the City without first informing you, and would have kept him under the strictest observation while awaiting your decision.

"There are no more fires in the villages, the houses having burned to the ground.

"During my daily visit to the Factory, Director Leponte expressed great satisfaction with the refugees, all of whom had applied for work."

Baudruche stopped and addressed Miss Bourrot:

"Hand me the paper they gave me at the Factory this morning. I must try to make it out before I continue."

"Mr. Commissioner, I've done it already. I condensed it into a few words."

Baudruche took the sheet and sat down.

"Good; this will help a lot. Where were we? Oh, yes, the refugees.

"Due to this increase in our labor force, we can look forward to a productivity growth in the area of seventeen to seventeen point four percent. I quote the Factory Director.

"Another extremely encouraging piece of news: a young engineer turned up among the refugees who, upon examining the machines, suggested a slight modification which would increase production in the neighborhood of eight point fourteen percent."

Baudruche breathed hard for a moment, stood up and resumed his pacing.

"I must inform you of the sudden death of the City's Librarian, Mr. Pholio. I have locked the library doors until such time as another librarian is appointed.

"Following your instructions, I had a detailed inventory made of our food supplies. The results show that they are more than ample, which is very reassuring. Nevertheless, in line with your orders, I instructed that the posters forbidding the feeding of birds be put up.

"Again in line with your orders, I instituted a search for the solitary man whose whereabouts were lost track of yesterday. Not unexpectedly, he had taken a room at the Hotel. Anything else would have been . . . hmmm . . . quite irrational, therefore unthinkable."

"You want me to write 'irrational therefore unthinkable,' Mr. Commissioner?"

"Of course, Miss Bourrot. You have to have meaningless words in official reports. It makes them sound more serious. Come, let's get to the end of this.

"May I assure you, Mr. Prefect, that my colleagues and I will not lose track of this man a second time.

"There. Finish up with the usual weather report: no sun, no rain, no change predicted. Same for the sentries: no sign of anyone outside the walls. Send it to the Prefect while it's still warm. I've got to go. As soon as you've finished, you do the same."

At home, he saw that Labrique had preceded him.

"Are you still hanging around, you miserable parasite! Isn't there anything to eat in your house?"

"Sure. But supper is one long argument. Besides, the food is better here or I wouldn't honor your table with my presence."

Labrique paid them this honor three or four times a week.

When the meal was finished and the dishes cleared away, Martha took out the cards and placed them between the two men. This had become a ritual. The game was slow and frequently interrupted. They chatted between hands and Baudruche always lost. "I couldn't keep my mind on the cards tonight," he said every night as he paid up.

Tonight, he gave himself wholeheartedly to the game. Again he lost. But something caught his attention.

"Labrique, you cheat, you bastard!"

The architect spread his cards on the table without a sign of emotion.

"Of course I do. I always have."

"Have you no shame?"

"A little. But at least this way I win."

3

THE CHEATING business annoyed Baudruche. He was still brooding about it when he went to bed. He spoke of it to Martha the next day, but he masked his anger, not daring to say what he really thought of his friend. It made Martha laugh. She had known about the cheating for a long time and often joked about it with Labrique. It was so funny, swindling the Commissioner in his own house for all these years!

"Good morning, Baudruche," Labrique said at the base of the ramparts and held out his hand. They shook.

"So we're shaking hands today? Yesterday you refused."

"I don't like to shake hands with crooks."

"You do nothing but."

"That's a professional obligation. In my own house, it's different. I want my house respected."

"O.K. I won't set foot in it again."

"I'm sure you'll have no trouble finding a house that feeds you as well as mine. And where you can steal to your heart's content."

If Labrique answered him, Baudruche didn't hear. He went to examine the large bulletin board near the gates. Among the official anouncements were the two new ones, the one about the birds, and the other telling the inhabitants they were free to ask that the gates be opened. Some people were standing around discussing them, but they moved away as Baudruche approached. He asked one of the guards, "What do people say when they read these bulletins?"

"I don't know, Mr. Commissioner. I haven't been listening."

"What about you? Have you read them?"

The man hesitated. If he said he hadn't read them, he'd be accused of showing no interest in the City's affairs; if he had, he would be asked his opinion.

"Yes, Mr. High Commissioner, I've read them."

"What do you think of them?"

"I think that if they came from City Hall, it's not for me to have an opinion. It must be good for the City."

"Do you want to get out of the City?"

This was clearly a trap. He must be very careful.

"I have no need to leave the City, Mr. High Commissioner."

Baudruche gave up and returned to Labrique.

"Come on. Let's make the rounds."

Climbing the steps ahead of Labrique, he asked, "What did you do with the money?"

"What money?"

"The money you've been stealing from me all this time."

"I buy presents for your wife. You never do."

From the top of the walls, Baudruche looked outside. Yes, the soldier was still there, sitting in the same place. He had put up a small tent and made a tiny fire which was almost out. He faced the horizon.

"Labrique, look and see if anyone is watching me."

Labrique scanned the ramparts. They were empty. But at the base of the walls, some of the guards had their eyes on Baudruche.

"The guards are watching you."

Baudruche snapped his fingers in irritation.

"Damn. I wanted to know so badly . . ."

"Know what?"

"What he's doing there, what he intends to do, what the rest of them are up to."

"Better you shouldn't find out. Come on, let's go."

Labrique dragged Baudruche away by the arm. But they had taken only a few steps when he stopped and asked Baudruche to lean over the ramparts.

"Look, there, at the bottom of the wall."

Baudruche leaned but saw nothing.

"Look again. Don't you see that long gray line?"

"Sure. What of it?"

"Those are ants."

"So what?"

"I don't know, but it's not normal. No ants have ever dared to climb these walls."

"I have more important things to worry about than ants."

"I wouldn't be so sure, Baudruche. Believe me, I'd do something about them. At least bring it to the Prefect's attention."

Was Labrique trying to make him look ridiculous before the Prefect, just as he'd been making him look ridiculous three times a week, year after year, in his own house, before his own wife? Baudruche blushed as a dull anger rose inside him, but the anger was mixed with so much affection that it quickly collapsed. He'd catch up with Labrique someday.

Baudruche brooded as he walked, his mind turning over the nonsense about the ants. For all that he tried to chase them away and think of something else, back they came.

"Labrique has shrewd instincts sometimes," Baudruche would say to Martha by way of concession. So which was it this time? A stupid joke or a judicious warning? It was too bad he'd left him so abruptly. He should have shaken it out of him.

"If I had him here . . .!" And Baudruche caught himself going through the motions in the middle of the street. Passersby looked at him startled, and he walked faster, brushing his shoulder as if he were trying to shake away foolish notions.

But he couldn't escape the ants. They were climbing his shoes, about to scale his ankles. He had to keep himself from scratching. He was saved by the great white facade of the Hotel which loomed before him. He glanced at his watch. Yes, he had time to go in. "Let's have a look at the man. He's a lot more important than a bunch of ants."

Mr. Baidroume bowed deeply and asked what had earned him the honor of this visit.

"Let's go into your office. I want to talk to you."

The Manager bowed sideways. It must be serious. In the office, he remained standing as Baudruche sat down.

"What fair wind brings you here, Mr. High Commissioner?"

"We've had no wind for years. What brought me here is a man."

The Manager breathed again. So it wasn't serious after all.

"You mean the guest on whose behalf Inspector Bricard came to seek information?"

"Nothing gets by you, does it? When you've reached retirement age, come join my staff. Who is this man? Show me his registration."

"Here it is, Mr. Commissioner. We removed it from his room this morning."

He handed Baudruche an unmarked card.

"Why hasn't he filled it out?"

"It isn't our fault, Mr. Commissioner. We told him we had very strict rules. You know how careful we are about following regulations, Mr. Commissioner!"

"Sometimes, Mr. Baidroume." Baudruche placed the form on the desk. "Tell me about him. Have you noticed anything unusual about him?"

"Absolutely nothing at first glance. He's not a talker, Mr. Commissioner. Do you want me to make him talk?"

"Under no circumstances. You take care of your hotel and nothing else. Is he in now?"

"Yes, Mr. Commissioner."

"What's the number of his room?"

"Twenty-three."

Baudruche got up, opened the door and went out. He had just reached the main lobby when the Manager touched his arm.

"Look. There he is."

A thin man was disappearing through the revolving door. Baudruche followed.

Baudruche found himself walking along the same street he had taken earlier. When the man reached the main gate, he started to climb the steps. Baudruche gave him time to disappear along the sentry walk before starting after him.

Once on top of the ramparts, Baudruche hid in one of the sentry turrets which were empty at this time of day. Through its spy hole, he could see the entire length of the ramparts. A group of idlers were watching the soldier from a position above the main gate. He spotted his man among them. Baudruche saw him cup his hands to his mouth and call out:

"Hey, soldier!"

The soldier turned his head and looked up. The group scattered in terror. The soldier shrugged. The man was alone now. The soldier gave him a friendly wave. Baudruche strained his ears.

"What are you doing down there, soldier?"

"What does a soldier do when he's not fighting? He waits."

"Have you fought a lot?"

"Yes. When they told me to fight, I fought."

"What did you fight for?"

"It wasn't for me to ask. I'm a soldier."

"Why are you alone?"

"That's a stupid question. I'm alone because there aren't any other soldiers."

"What happened to them?"

"Some died, some gave up the profession."

"Why don't you come into the City?"

"A soldier's place is outside the City. Besides, I have an idea they wouldn't understand me in the City now. The people on the ramparts look at me oddly. I don't know why but I scare them. Don't they see I'm a City soldier?"

"I do."

"Will you go and tell them?"

"I can't. They wouldn't understand."

"What do they do in there?"

"They make a machine."

"What kind of a machine? Only one machine?"

"Yes. And just one model of the one machine."

"What do they do with it?"

"They sell it to the people who make it."

"What do they do with it?"

"They turn it on at home at night, and all day Sunday."

"It sounds crazy."

"It's worse than that, soldier."

"They think things can go on like that forever?"

"They do, but I don't. They can't last much longer because they have no reason to exist and there's no reason why they should."

"My reason to exist is war, whether there's a war or not."

"Do you think the enemy will come?"

"I don't know. I just wait in case they do. I can't retreat any farther; I'm already at the gates of the City."

"I think the enemy is going to come. But it won't necessarily come from the outside. Tell me, soldier, what do you eat?"

"I'm on my last rations now."

"What will you do after that?"

"I don't know, but I'm not worried. A soldier's destiny isn't to die of hunger."

34

Baudruche watched as the man waved a friendly good-bye to the soldier. He had listened to every syllable, but what had he learned? Well, one thing of great importance: this was the last soldier and there weren't likely to be any more. Baudruche knew why the people feared the soldiers' return. For years, they had had drummed into them that an army constituted a permanent threat to their liberty and individual security; the mere sight of a soldier's uniform was enough to fill them with irrational fear.

But now Baudruche could understand the cause of the vast collective fear that had emptied and destroyed the villages. This cause, which none of them could put a name to, was the smell of war which preceded the soldier's retreat.

He considered this a very important and significant discovery, and he congratulated himself on having personally assumed the responsibility for the solitary man, the last refugee. What would have happened if he'd left it to Bicard? It could have been a frightful mess.

Baudruche waited until the man reached the bottom steps of the battlements, then followed him at a distance.

The man returned to the Hotel. Baudruche hesitated by the front door, then decided to abandon the investigation for the time being. He must do some thinking before he proceeded further. Besides, it was noon. No point going back to his office; he'd go home. "You can't think on an empty stomach." Perhaps the saying was exaggerated, but he didn't care. He had too much on his mind to waste time on self-analysis.

Baudruche was silent over lunch and Martha watched him closely. He spilled the wine, kept sighing with no apparent reason, and was about to put his elbow in his dirty plate when Martha stopped him. He was remembering the dialogue between the two men. The man from the Hotel was one of the few who understood the soldier's significance. In this respect— if in no other—he stood above the crowd, and that was why he was a solitary man, as was the Prefect, as was Labrique, poor old Pholio, and he himself. He therefore deserved respect, but for the same reason, he must be closely watched.

Her husband's absorption worried Martha. To be sure, he sometimes combined eating and thinking, but never before with this degree of concentration. Something must be going on in the City. Of course the newspapers would tell her nothing. Nor would Miss Bourrot. Miss Bourrot thought she was in on the secrets of the gods.

"Anything new in the City, Robert?"

"No, Martha. Just the usual."

Baudruche picked up his hat and left without another word. What else could he do if Martha was going to start yammering? It was impossible to think in his own house. At least in the streets there was some privacy.

One thing seemed certain: the soldier had no intention of entering the City, so there was no need to fear a panic. That took care of the soldier. But what about the man in the Hotel? He appeared to have lost no time learning the City's ways. He knew how important the machine was to the population, and he seemed to share Baudruche's opinion of both the machine and the population. Furthermore, he thought the enemy would come, but not from outside. From where, then? Inside, obviously. Was it firm knowledge or bluff? He had to find out. If he wasn't bluffing, the man must have inside information. But what was in it for him?

Perhaps it was personal ambition. The man must have nosed around and learned that Baudruche's men constituted the only power that mattered in the City. Everybody knew they would obey no one else as long as he was around. That was why the Prefect had been forced to promote him to the number two spot in the City. Baudruche tried to avoid thinking about that.

Baudruche mustered up his courage and headed for the Factory.

Today he was tired and let Leponte talk longer than usual.

This gave him time to think. When the technocrat had finally finished his exposé, Baudruche looked dazed and said:

"Forgive me, Mr. Leponte, but I didn't understand a word you said."

"But it was all very simple!"

"Perhaps, Mr. Leponte, but not for me. I haven't had your training."

"I'll start again. . . ."

"Don't bother, Mr. Leponte. Just write it down on a small piece of paper."

Seething, the Director picked up his pen with one hand, clasped his brow with the other and painfully wrote down what he had just said.

"There, Mr. Commissioner, if you would like to read it over. . . ."

Baudruche took the paper and deliberately held it upside down.

"The other way, Mr. Commissioner. . . ."

"I'm sorry. I can't see without my glasses."

He took out his glasses and adjusted them on his nose.

"Ah, that's better! Don't hold it against me, Leponte. An infirmity of old age. Just be patient. Another fifteen years and I'll be gone. The retirement knell will have sounded."

Baudruche examined the page with great care.

"You were right, Leponte. Your figures are much clearer than your letters. Your writing looks like chicken tracks. I don't mean it as criticism. It happens often with men of great intellect."

Leponte ground his teeth.

"I'm sure you're right, Mr. Commissioner, although most people seem to be able to make out my handwriting. Miss Niquel has no trouble at all."

"Ah, of course! How stupid of me. I'll take this to her and she can type it up for me."

Furious, Leponte watched him go. Once again he'd been unable to prevent Baudruche from closeting himself with his secretary.

Miss Niquel was pleased to see Baudruche. He might well mean an interesting change in jobs, away from the Factory.

"Do sit down and relax, Mr. Commissioner. I'll only be a minute."

She started to type and Baudruche watched her. She amused him, with her exaggerated expressions and elegant gestures. A charming marionette. It would be fun to pull the strings. . . .

Miss Niquel finished the report and brought it to him.

"I trust *you* didn't have an unpleasant encounter on your way to the Factory, Mr. Commissioner? I've been very uneasy myself since it happened."

"Since what happened?"

"Didn't the Director tell you? One of our workers was assaulted by a rat."

Baudruche started. "What are you talking about?"

"It's the truth, Mr. Commissioner. I swear it on my mother's grave. She didn't like rats either. Do you know, one day when she was working in the laundry . . ."

"The man, Miss Niquel, just tell me what happened to the man."

"Well, it was only a little while ago. About noon, a worker in the assembly shop was going to the café near the Factory. . . . You must know it . . . it's called the Social Progress Café. It says in big letters outside: 'Bring your own food.' Well, one of our workers was on his way there with his lunch in his lunch box when what should he see but a rat! A big, fat rat, bigger than any he'd ever seen. That rat went right up to the man, just the way I'm doing, and looked up at him—the way I'm looking at you—and told him he wanted what he had in his lunch-box."

Baudruche was in a turmoil. "What happened then?"

"The man had to give him his food, and I think the rat even went off with the lunch-box."

Baudruche leaped to his feet, pushed her aside and barged into the Director's office.

Leponte jumped. "What is going on, Mr. Commissioner?"

"I ask you that every day, Mr. Leponte, and you might do me the honor of giving me an answer."

"But I do answer you, Mr. Commissioner."

"Oh, sure. You throw meaningless figures in my face. But if something really serious happens, you keep quiet, don't you, Mr. Leponte?"

"I don't know what you mean, Mr. Commissioner."

"You don't think it's serious when a rat assaults a worker?"

"That was a minor incident of no importance, Mr. Commissioner. I wasn't going to bore you with such trifles."

"You call that a trifle?"

"But it's all been taken care of, Mr. Commissioner. The rat went away, the worker was compensated, and everybody is happy."

"I'm not. I want to see that worker."

"His name is Wiesel, a very good man. He works on the assembly line. But if I call him, it means the whole line stops and there'll be a drop in productivity. . . ."

"Your workers never go to the can?"

"Not during working hours. I make sure of that."

The worker walked in, looking uncomfortable.

"Sir . . . Mister . . ."

"Wiesel, don't you realize you are in the presence of the High Commissioner?"

Wiesel went up to Baudruche and held out his hand as if to make amends for his blunder. Baudruche shook it.

"Wiesel, you're mad! This is the High Commissioner!"

"I know he is, Mr. Director. I recognize Mr. Baudruche. I just wanted to ask after his and the missus' health."

"You will behave properly, unless you want to lose your job."

He couldn't lose his job. It would be impossible to find another one at age forty-four. It would mean eviction from his lodgings and, worst of all, loss of his machine. What would he do evenings?

Baudruche hadn't taken his eyes off him. It was painful to watch the change in his expression from friendliness to self-denial, and finally to fear. That lousy bastard Leponte! Baudruche thought to himself. He's got the poor man terrified. But maybe it'll be easier to make him talk now.

But Baudruche couldn't get anything out of him. All Wiesel would say was, "I don't know, Mr. Director," or "I don't remember, Mr. Commissioner."

Finally, Baudruche took him by the arm and said, "Come, let's have a chat down in the courtyard. It'll be easier to talk down there."

Once away from the Director, Wiesel regained his composure and explained calmly what had happened.

"The rat came up to me, just like I'm standing in front of you, Mr. Commissioner. He put his hand on the strap of my lunch-box like this, shook me like this [and he tried to shake Baudruche's two hundred pounds] and said: 'Give me that.' I asked, 'Why should I? It isn't yours.' 'I need it because I'm hungry.'

"I know what it's like to be hungry, but all the same, that's no way to ask. . . . But when I saw he was going to bite me, I gave him my lunch-box."

"You did wrong, Wiesel. You shouldn't give in to threats."

"No, I was right, Mr. Baudruche. We don't want violence. That rat was a proletarian, just like me. Make war on war. So I told our shop steward what I told you, he told the foreman who told the boss and he gave me the compensation. Look what they're paying me. That shows I was right."

Baudruche argued with him, but it was hopeless. Baudruche sent him back to the assembly line and left the Factory, dragging his feet. To see a man enslaved, virtually crushed by the machine, and then the inhumanity of those above him made Baudruche feel helpless.

40

Rats! That's all he needed. Of course everybody knew there were rats—in the City's sewers as well as in the distant villages —but no one had ever seen one expose himself to the light of day. No rat had ever dared assault an inhabitant of the City, and no one certainly had ever before given in to a rat's threats without attempting to defend himself.

Back in Leponte's office, the Director badgered Wiesel with questions. What had Baudruche said to him, what did he say to Baudruche?

"He kept saying I should have defended myself. He didn't give a shit about the compensation you gave me for the two red sausages and the quarter pound of cheese I lost."

"Well, I happen not to agree with the High Commissioner. You did the right thing, Wiesel. I don't want any trouble around the Factory. Besides," he dropped his voice, "we must always come to the aid of our fellows, right?"

He pressed his buzzer.

"Miss Niquel, give this man a bonus, for fraternal action and felicitous initiative. As you see, Wiesel, I always have my workers' welfare at heart."

Baudruche was dictating his report. It was slow going. There had been so many problems that day.

The usual comments on the state of the ramparts turned his mind back to that grayish column at the foot of the walls above the old moat. The ants. He hesitated. Damn. But it was better to make a fool of himself than be wrong. Aloud he said, "Miss Bourrot, take this down.

"The City's architect felt it his professional duty to call my attention to a column of ants climbing the walls."

And what was there to say about the man in the Hotel? That his behavior seemed neither disquieting nor abnormal? But didn't that reflect only what he had picked up at the Hotel? Wasn't there also what he had learned as he shadowed the man,

41

and most important of all, what had happened on the ramparts —the conversation with the soldier?

Baudruche didn't know what he should do. He felt at once too powerful and not powerful enough. Better keep quiet for now and gain time. But did he have the right to keep quiet? He worked for the Prefect and the Prefect trusted him and depended on him. On the other hand, he also worked for the City. He was its servant not only as Commissioner but as an inhabitant. There had always been Baudruches in the City, even before there was a Prefect. He thought of his father and his grandfather—the carpenter—who had helped build the Prefecture. They said: "Baudruches have always worked for the City, never against it."

He closed his eyes, stopped thinking and made up his mind.

"O.K., Miss Bourrot.

"I had just finished my visit to the Hotel when I saw the individual in question leaving by the main door. I immediately followed him. He headed for the ramparts, climbed to the top and joined a group of people watching the soldier who was still sitting near the main gate as he has since his arrival. The stranger hailed him; the soldier turned and waved. All the City inhabitants fled except for the man from the Hotel. Then I observed him as he talked with the soldier. They talked for quite a while. Unfortunately, I was not close enough to hear what they said. Had I come nearer, I might have been noticed and very possibly recognized. As a result, Mr. Prefect, I have nothing further to report on this subject today."

He had to say at least this much; there had been witnesses. But it was done. He let out a deep sigh of relief. Miss Bourrot looked up, not understanding what had caused the sigh. Baudruche continued his dictation, but more slowly as he struggled with Leponte's report.

"I paid my usual visit to the Factory Director. He termed the situation more than satisfactory due to the newly arrived engineer.

The Director asks that the engineer be granted a social promotion.

"Also, the Factory Director received a visit from a delegation of workers demanding an increase of 11 percent in wages, to be effective at the next announcement of an increase in productivity."

Baudruche added a few words on the condition of the population's spirit (calm, much too calm) and then passed to other subjects, the most important being the Public Library. Mr. Pholio had left an inventory which indicated a very large number of volumes—far larger than had been thought.

"I have directed that a competition for the post of Librarian be announced in the newspapers and on posters, and that qualified candidates apply at the earliest possible date.

"Where do we stand with the birds, Miss Bourrot?"

"The poor little things keep going to all the places where people used to throw them bread and there's nothing there. They hover about in great flocks, crying. They don't understand what's happened."

"Nor do I, Miss Bourrot. Take this down.

"The order forbidding the feeding of birds has been scrupulously carried out. However, it has been brought to my attention that the birds hover about, crying.

"Does that cover everything?"

"I think so, Mr. Commissioner."

Baudruche briefly described the incident of the rat to Miss Bourrot. She was appalled. As he dictated the report, he was careful to remain objective and keep to the facts, so that at the end, his anger would have a more telling effect.

"If the Prefect doesn't understand now! . . . Write that up and condense it a little, then rush it over to the newspaper. It's important; I want it to come out tonight."

Miss Bourrot left and Baudruche breathed again. It had been a hard day, but he wasn't complaining. He was going to do

43

battle and this gratified him. He loved a fight in a good cause and this one was that.

He turned on the lamp on his desk, settled himself comfortably in his chair and picked up the book from the table.

As he read Montesquieu on Rome, he compared it to his own City. And when he learned the causes of Rome's fall, they made him afraid:

Only two kinds of people were left in the city; the slaves, and those whose selfish interests kept them slaves.

He thought of Leponte and how the Factory's increasing productivity guaranteed him his job while it turned his workers into slaves.

Better the risk of an unfortunate war than peace through bribery.

He thought of Wiesel and the rat and was convinced that he, Baudruche, had been right and had behaved like a good servant of the City. After all, wasn't Montesquieu of the same mind?

Preoccupied, he walked home slowly. Never had he thought as much as he had that day. He stopped a newspaper vendor, bought a paper and examined it under a streetlamp to see if the story on the rat was on the front page where it was supposed to be. It wasn't. He leafed through the paper and finally found a parody of his story on page 7 under the heading: "Generous Act by One of Our Workers."

"Those bastards. . . ." Baudruche crumpled the newspaper, threw it in the gutter and continued home. Martha and Labrique were waiting for him. He spoke little during dinner.

The meal was barely over and the plates cleared when Labrique put his elbows on the table. "I gather that funny things are going on in the City, Baudruche. What's all this about a rat?"

"If you want the news, read the paper. That's what it's for."

4

BAUDRUCHE was in a hurry to leave the house the next morning. He was afraid things might get out of hand if he weren't there. He reached the ramparts early. Labrique hadn't arrived.

While he waited, he glanced at the bulletin board.

"Will you look at this!" he cried. A guard ran up.

"Who tore that off?" Baudruche asked, pointing to what remained of his poster about opening the gates.

"I don't know, Mr. High Commissioner. It must have happened before we got here. You'll have to ask the night shift. We just came on."

Ask the night shift? Who would have seen anything in the dark? "Forget it," he said, and motioned the guard back to his station. He looked at the bulletin board again and tried to decipher the slogans scrawled on what remained of the poster. "Don't worry; nobody's leaving." "United against Fascism," "Who wants to get killed?" and others more vitriolic.

"Poor buggers," he said in a low voice.

"Who? The rats?" It was Labrique.

Baudruche answered: "The hell with the rats!"

"Listen, my friend, you can't brush them aside. According to the newspaper, they are an ethnic group which feels its standing to be incompatible with its dignity."

"I don't want to hear any more."

"I'm trying to appeal to your conscience. . . ."

"My conscience! My conscience shits on you, Labrique!"

They started climbing the stairs. On top, Baudruche glanced beyond the ramparts. Yes, the soldier was still there, in the same position, his back to the City, eyes on the distant horizon. Baudruche thought about calling him. But what good would it do? The soldier would turn around and the people walking along the ramparts would bolt as they had the day before. There would be talk and Baudruche would be accused of plotting. . . .

Labrique grabbed him by the sleeve and pulled him to the same place as on the previous day. They leaned over the wall.

"So what's to see?"

"A second one."

"A second what?"

"A second column of ants. Keep your eyes on them, Baudruche. I can't do anything; it's outside my competence."

"But what do you expect me to do about them?"

"Stop them from climbing."

Baudruche shrugged. If this was Labrique's idea of a joke . . . The two moved slowly away along the sentry walk. From time to time, Labrique stopped to examine the walls, the turrets, the spy holes. Everything was solid. Not a sign of a crack in those well-laid stones.

"Come on, Labrique, let's go. They'll last a lot longer than you and me."

"Let's hope so," the architect said with a sigh. "But what's bothering you today? Why the hurry?"

46

"I want you to take a look at a big new construction project you'll be involved in."

"What is it? Where are we going?"

"To the barracks, my friend, to watch the demolition."

Labrique was startled. "What do you mean? They're tearing the barracks down? What are they going to put in its place?"

"Need you ask? Annexes to the Factory."

"It isn't big enough already?"

"It won't be big enough until it's swallowed up the whole City."

The architect took a few steps and stopped abruptly, eyes cast down, hands on hips.

"Damn it, no! I won't take on that job! I dreamed of building cathedrals. . . ."

Baudruche made a gesture of helplessness.

The Commissioner cut across the Public Gardens to the Hotel and headed for the Manager's office. Baidroume leaped from his chair.

"What's going on, Mr. Commissioner?"

"Nothing unusual. Is the handsome stranger in?"

"No, Mr. Commissioner, he has gone out."

"Give me his key. It's number twenty-three. You see, I have a good memory."

"Would you like me to go with you?"

"I don't need anybody."

Baudruche groaned as he climbed the stairs. His feet hurt. He'd probably walked too much that morning. He unlocked the door to number 23, closed it carefully behind him and slipped the key into his pocket.

He made the rounds of the room, opening closets and drawers, but found only the usual things, nothing that meant anything. But there had to be something unusual among the effects of a solitary man. . . . A suitcase stood in a corner of the bathroom. He picked it up, placed it on a table in the bedroom and tried to open it. It was locked.

He took a small kit out of his pocket, opened the suitcase—and was dumbfounded. It was stuffed with bank notes in large denominations, tied together with string.

Baudruche put on his glasses, took out one of the packets and tried to guess its value. It was too much to guess. Then he looked closer. The bills were certainly Central Bank issue, but there was something peculiar about them. He took one of the same denomination from his wallet. There was a tiny difference in the printing.

"Too bad," Baudruche murmured. "I'd rather he'd been an honest man."

Money wasn't the only thing in the suitcase. There was also a long flat case. A weapon, of course; that was to be expected. He opened the case and took out a long black tube with little metal pieces attached. What on earth was it? Baudruche looked it up and down and inside, then put it back in its case. An illustration he'd seen in a dictionary flashed through his mind: it was a flute.

So people still played these things?

Baudruche was closing the suitcase when the door opened. He jumped. A girl of sixteen or seventeen stood there, looking at him boldly.

He asked, "How did you get in? What are you doing here?"

"What are *you* doing here?"

The girl must be one of the more recent refugees not to recognize him.

"Don't you know who I am?"

She made a funny popping noise with her cheeks. "You're Baudruche to the Prefect, Robert to your wife, and Mr. High Commissioner to the people of the City. That's right, isn't it?"

Baudruche had to smile. He was both amused and abashed by the girl. He took her arm in a gesture of appeasement, but she slapped his hand.

"Hands off! Are you trying to make me on top of everything else?"

No, it had never even crossed his mind. Not that she wasn't pretty. Quite the contrary. She was spirited and as fresh as a daisy, but . . . Now if Miss Niquel were the one standing in front of him right now . . . But this girl, looking him straight in the eye, was something else again. Obviously she didn't fool around.

"O.K. Since you know my name, tell me yours."

"Posey."

"And what were you coming in here for?"

"To clean the room. It doesn't clean itself."

With that, she left. He heard her go down the hall, but she was soon back armed with cleaning rags, a feather duster and a broom.

"If you are done with your work, please move on and let me do mine."

He sat on the table and watched her in silence. Unconcerned, she took the suitcase and put it back in the bathroom.

"Unless you like dust, you'd better leave."

She took hold of the broom and swept the rug with vigorous strokes, sending up great clouds of dust. Baudruche asked, "You like this kind of dirty work?"

"It's cleaner than yours. I don't go poking into other people's suitcases."

Baudruche was silent. She had struck home. He got off the table and tried to think of something to say. He had to say something; the silence was crushing.

"How did you get in here? The door was locked."

"What are pass keys for?"

Baudruche had had enough. He opened the door and disappeared down the hall. The girl didn't so much as raise her head.

"Baudruche, get a hold of yourself!" he muttered as he went down the stairs. Clearly the girl must be removed, gently but firmly, as long as matters were pending with the owner of the suitcase—the counterfeiter. And he must act quickly, before she saw the man again and could tell him of Baudruche's visit. He opened the Manager's door and sat down.

"Who's that young girl named Posey?"

For a brief second, Mr. Baidroume was surprised, then he understood. "She's a cutie, isn't she?"

"I didn't ask you if she was cute. I can see that for myself. All I want is information. Understand?"

Yes: the Commissioner wanted particulars. "No two ways about it; she is a pearl. Lively and straightforward. Eighteen. Fit for a king."

"You're on the wrong track, Mr. Baidroume. Just tell me how long she's been working for you?"

"Eighteen months."

"Talkative?"

"A little, like all women; but it's not without its charm."

"Parents?"

"No, she's an orphan."

"Lovers?"

"None that I know of."

"Well, you'll have to let her go. Fire her; I'll find her another job—something far away."

So Mr. Baidroume had been right after all.

Baudruche drummed on the table with his fingers. "Call her in right away. Tell her what I just told you, then send her to my office. But do it nicely. Is that clear, Mr. Baidroume?"

"Absolutely, Mr. Commisioner."

Baudruche felt the door open behind him. He recognized the voice as it said, "My key isn't on my hook."

The Manager didn't lack presence of mind. He rose to his feet. "It must have been hung on the wrong hook by mistake. You go up and I'll have it brought to you right away."

Baudruche heard the stranger's footsteps recede down the hall toward the stairs; in another moment, he'd find Posey in his room. All was lost. Baudruche would be exposed, like a rank amateur. After all these years, to have lost his touch. . . .

"Mr. Baidroume, I've changed my mind. Don't do what I just told you."

Baidroume was nonplussed. Was the Commissioner trying to make a fool of him?

Baudruche took the key to number 23 from his pocket and handed it to the Manager.

"I want to be alone for a moment, Mr. Baidroume. I want to make a phone call."

Baidroume left, taking the key with him. Baudruche took the receiver off the hook and dialed.

"I want to speak to Bicard, if he's there. . . . Is that you, Bicard? Come to the Hotel right away, to the Manager's office. I'll explain later. I'm trying to straighten out one of your blunders."

Fifteen minutes later, Bicard was there.

"Would you recognize the man you let through the gates the other day—the one who lives here at the Hotel?"

"As well as you, Mr. Commissioner."

"Well, you won't be forgetting me if you pull any more of these half-assed tricks. Listen to me: I want you to wait by the door of the Hotel. If he goes out, follow him. Is that clear?"

"Yes, Mr. Commissioner."

"There's more. Let him go wherever he wants to in the City. But if he starts to leave the City, grab him. Understand?"

"Yes, Mr. Commissioner."

"O.K. Go stand by the door. And *bon appetit!* You'll be eating well tonight."

Bicard was about to leave when Baudruche caught his arm.

"I almost forgot. If he's carrying a suitcase or a large package, don't let him leave the Hotel."

How would the man react to Posey's story? No doubt he'd try to escape and alert his accomplices. There he was: the guilty man was passing the glass door, seemingly unconcerned, a smile on his lips. He was heading for the restaurant across from the Manager's office.

What if Baudruche were to leave now? Out of the question. He would be noticed going through the lobby. This time the man would be sure to recognize him.

The man was sitting at one of the nearer tables, and from the look of his appetite, Baudruche began to wonder if Posey had told him of his visit. The meal seemed endless. Baudruche was growing faint with hunger at the sight of all those people eating. At last, the man got up, passed the office and headed for the revolving door.

Baudruche saw Bicard follow the stranger; at last he was free to leave his cage. It was past two o'clock! His hunger had been feeding on his ill humor. He crossed the lobby and took a table off to one side, facing the last guests.

"Let me see the menu."

The staff rushed to his side and Baudruche ordered. Everything he wanted was gone; the Manager came to apologize. The chef was called up from the kitchen and read off a list of dishes not on the menu which he would be pleased to prepare. Baudruche shook his head at each suggestion; the Manager looked on with a glassy eye. Baudruche finally gave up in sheer exhaustion and left the satisfaction of his needs to the combined efforts of the chef and Mr. Baidroume. They succeeded, but Baudruche was careful not to let them know. He criticized the cooking, the wine, the poor service. . . . The game calmed his bad humor along with his appetite.

Baudruche was on the rampage in Leponte's office. A fine mess! Hadn't he warned him this would happen with his policies of appeasement? This time, at high noon, in the very same spot, not one but three workers had been assaulted by rats!

"But, Mr. Commissioner, you're looking only on the dark side. Everything went very pleasantly. The three men—Wiesel was one of them—were on their way to the Social Progress Café when the scene took place; this time the rat had four of five friends with him. They chatted amiably with our men, and our men gave them some of their food of their own free will. There's a fine spirit among our workers, Mr. Commissioner!"

"I'm afraid we don't see eye to eye on the meaning of the word 'spirit,' Mr. Leponte. Who were the two men with Wiesel?"

"Dupont, a good, quiet man, and Gonzales, a stubborn fanatic who almost wrecked the whole thing. He's free to look for another job beginning tonight."

"I want to see Gonzales."

"I'm not sure he's still here, Mr. Commissioner. He may have left already."

"You will find him for me. Now about the Factory: let's have the lesson for today. Then condense it and I'll have Miss Niquel type it up."

Leponte had been waiting for this moment. He rose to his feet and took a piece of paper from his desk.

"You don't need to bother, Mr. Commissioner. I was prepared for you this time. Here's the résumé, all ready for you. I know how precious your time is and I hate to see you waste it."

Baudruche bit his lips. The bastard had him this time! But he'd get back at him sooner or later. Now he had to see Gonzales. He walked to the door with a forced smile.

Evening was falling and the birds were gathering in the trees. They were screeching louder than ever; it was hard on the nerves.

"Just what I need, these damn swallows!"

He opened his door, his face so contorted that Miss Bourrot thought he was sick.

Before he could speak, Miss Bourrot announced, "You have a long message from the Prefect marked confidential."

"Which you've read, of course."

53

She blushed.

"Yes, Mr. Commissioner. I knew I shouldn't have . . ."

"It's quite all right. I have no secrets."

He took the message and read it through quickly. It was four pages long—and filled with advice, remonstrances, appeals to his wisdom, appeals to his conscience. It all came down to one thing: leave the rats alone!

He crumpled the pages and threw them in the wastebasket.

"He gives me a pain in the ass!"

Miss Bourrot lowered her head. She wished she hadn't heard.

Baudruche relaxed and began: " 'Mr. Prefect . . .' "

Suddenly Miss Bourrot sat up.

"Mr. Commissioner, I forgot . . . Bicard is outside and refuses to go until he's seen you."

Baudruche exploded.

"Am I to have no peace today!"

Bicard came in, wreathed in smiles.

"I've got it, Mr. Commissioner. I've got the lowdown."

"What is it?"

"The man went to the ramparts. Once there, he talked to the soldier, and the soldier answered."

"That's all?"

"Yes, Mr. Commissioner."

"He's done that before. I didn't need you to tell me."

"It's not my fault he didn't go someplace different. I didn't let him out of my sight. I didn't even stop for lunch."

"You think I had lunch? Get out of here. If you keep on like this, you'll end up at the Factory. Where were we, Miss Bourrot?

"Mr. Prefect, may I stress the seriousness of the new incident which occurred in the same place as yesterday. This is no longer a question of an isolated, spontaneous incident, but of a concerted action against three of our workers by a band of five or six rats who, employing violence, robbed them of their lunch-boxes.

"One of the three, a man named Gonzales, bravely tried to defend himself and his lunch box. Unfortunately, he was prevented by one Wiesel, the hapless victim of yesterday's incident, and a third man named Dupont, a bloodless individual with no will to fight. They both insisted that Gonzales give his lunch box to the rats and accept compensation.

"I feel no hesitation in blaming the outcome of the painful incident on Mr. Leponte's attitude, on the press censorship exerted by the Prefecture, and in general, on the pressure exerted over the past few years on the City's state of mind. In my opinion, it is of prime importance that we avoid any repetition of similar incidents, despite the humanitarian reasons that impelled you to write the confidential note I recently had the honor of receiving.

"No candidate has offered himself for the post of City Librarian.

"The birds are in a turmoil. They fly over the City in huge flocks and cry without letup. Their screeching should be stopped before it plays havoc with the City's nerves. Reason dictates that we rescind the prohibition against the feeding of the birds.

"Finish up with the weather report—no change, of course— and the sentry's report."

Baudruche was late getting home. He wasn't hungry. The Hotel lunch, the wine, the brandy . . . He wasn't over it yet. And there was something else: someone at the Factory about five feet five with nice eyes and dark brown hair.

"You're not eating anything, Robert. . . ."

5

BAUDRUCHE was as prompt as usual for his rendezvous with Labrique. When they reached the top of the steps, he tapped the architect on the shoulder.

"The Prefect doesn't seem very interested in your ants. He sent me a note."

"The worthy man does me honor."

"He asked me to remind you that you're paid by the City to concern yourself with architecture, not zoology."

"I expected no less. A reflection based on common sense, which couldn't be more wrong. What does he say about the rats?"

"He counsels patience, justice and understanding."

"A City goes to hell on that kind of advice. Don't you think we should get rid of him?"

"Shut up, Labrique. There are people coming."

They watched the soldier until they were alone again. Then Labrique led his friend to where they had seen the columns of ants the previous day. He leaned over the wall. "Do you see what I see?"

Baudruche put on his glasses: the gray area had grown considerably. He could make out several columns climbing slowly but surely, all at the same pace.

"Baudruche, we've got to stop them!"

The Commissioner looked helpless. "What do you want me to do? If I tell my men to go out there and get rid of your beasts, I'm not at all sure they'll obey me; and if they do, I'll get hell from the Prefect."

"My dear Commissioner, it might be worth it."

"It's clear you are not in my shoes, Hector."

"I made certain I never would be, Robert."

"You weren't man enough, Labrique."

No, he certainly wasn't man enough. Baudruche looked at his friend's tall, skinny body, his slight stoop, the graying hair. Labrique gave the impression of never wanting to get involved, of trying to get through life without ever bothering or being bothered by anyone. Had he been in Baudruche's shoes, he would have let everything go hang. Although Baudruche felt deep affection for Labrique, it was mingled with not a little contempt.

Baudruche knew he had his own faults but he, at least, was involved. He had never retreated from his responsibilities. Had he not had many solid qualities to compensate for his few minor faults, he would never have risen so high so fast. After all, wasn't he the number two man in the City, just under the Prefect? Of course luck had played its part. When he was young, the job of High Commissioner hadn't been all that important. But little by little, the seemingly permanent centers of power had been whittled down, some even disappearing altogether—like the army which, to the Prefect's great relief, had vanished years ago.

So many things had collapsed around him that Baudruche had reached his position by default. Since he was never afraid of taking risks, he had been put in charge, first of the police, then of the City's administration, and given a wide range of activities and responsibilities that no one else wanted. If the Prefect hadn't been there, he could have had the City.

But he stood up for the Prefect. Not for his person, but for the institution. Ever since he was born, the City had been governed by a Prefect. His portrait was everywhere: in the classroom, in his father's house, in all the public buildings. They prayed for him in church on Sunday. They swore by him. No, he could not imagine the City without a Prefect, any more than he could see himself in the Prefect's shoes.

Baudruche, a Prefect? He started to laugh at the thought of his portrait hanging in every corner of the City. No, Mr. High Commissioner was quite enough. From earliest youth, it had been his secret ambition. He never mentioned it for fear people would laugh. He'd been teased enough when he started up the ladder of success.

But everybody who had made fun of him was in his pocket now. They bowed low, and were corrected when they used the old familiarities. They were to address him as Mr. Commissioner without swallowing a single syllable. He'd been strict all right. Everybody was pretty much dependent on him, including Labrique—who would do well to take his job more seriously.

"Are you dreaming, old man?"

He jumped. It was Labrique, interrupting his reflections in a most unsuitable manner.

"What are you thinking about?"

"Me. My career. My job. It's a tough one, you know."

Labrique gave him a dig in the ribs.

"You bore me. You adore your job, and you know it."

Baudruche left him hurriedly. He was anxious to get back to his investigation of the counterfeit money.

The Commissioner walked to the Central Bank and saw its director.

59

"It's a very serious matter that brings me here, Mr. Blankman."

"Mr. Commissioner, I don't imagine you would do us the honor of a visit in order to make some change.

Baudruche took out his wallet, extracted the bill he'd taken from the suitcase and handed it to Mr. Blankman. The bank official examined it carefully, looked surprised, then reached for a magnifying glass.

"So?" Baudruche asked with impatience.

"I'm afraid to tell you. . . . I might be wrong. . . ."

He picked up the telephone.

"Will you please ask Mr. Waters to come to my office?"

Mr. Waters arrived and examined the bill in turn.

"What do you think, Mr. Waters?"

"I don't know, Mr. Blankman. I think we should ask Mr. Pressman."

"Who is Pressman?"

"Our head engraver."

Pressman went straight to Blankman's desk without acknowledging Baudruche's presence. He wiped his glasses on a corner of his gray smock and bent over the bill.

"What do you think?" Blankman and Waters asked in unison.

Pressman thought some time before answering. "It's one of them, all right. I didn't know they still existed. It's real."

"What do you mean, 'real'?" Baudruche asked heatedly.

Pressman removed his glasses to see him better.

"Mr. Commissioner! If you're the one who made this, may I offer my warmest congratulations."

"No jokes, please. What is this bill?"

"These men will explain it to you. They know what it's all about."

Blankman took the bill from Pressman and placed it in front of Baudruche: "Mr. High Commissioner, as Mr. Pressman just said, what we have here is a real bank note. . . ."

"What do you mean, a real bank note? What about ours?"

"Mr. Commissioner, we are forced to admit that ours are counterfeit. They are all we've been able to print for a long time. No one will ever notice unless a real bill like this one is placed in circulation."

Baudruche felt a quiver run down his spine. Blankman continued, "May I ask where this came from, and if there are any more like it?"

"I cannot answer the first question. To the second, yes, there are more."

"Many?"

"Thousands upon thousands. . . ."

"Mr. Commissioner, may I suggest that it is of utmost importance that these bank notes not circulate in the City."

"What would happen if they did?"

"There would be a large-scale panic."

"A panic? Over fake bank notes?"

"It is precisely because they are *not* fake that everybody would immediately reject ours, which are."

"But if worse came to worst, what's to prevent our withdrawing the ones in circulation and replacing them with more like the one you have there?"

Mr. Blankman shook his head sadly.

"Were we able to print real ones, we wouldn't be obliged to circulate fakes."

"Is that true? You can't make real ones anymore?"

Blankman looked at Pressman.

"That's so, isn't it, Pressman?"

Pressman shook his head slowly. "Can't be done, Mr. Director."

Blankman and Waters saw him to the door.

Baudruche hurried away with the word "panic" ringing in his ears. Although he was almost running, the way to the Hotel seemed endless.

Forgetting his aching feet, Baudruche dashed up the stairs,

knocked on the door and walked in. He had been rehearsing what he would say to the man all the way to the Hotel: a few brief, brutal words. But he never had the chance. The man spoke first.

"Come in, Mr. Commissioner. I suppose you are returning my bank note? I was very sorry to have missed your first visit. You should have told me you were coming."

"Change your tone, please. I don't like the way you are addressing me. Now, how did you find out about the bank note?"

"There was a string in the bottom of the suitcase, so I guessed somebody had been in the notes. And you aren't a thief, so I knew you took only one. I even knew why: because you were intrigued."

"And why was I intrigued?"

"Because of the way they looked."

"They're fakes."

"You know perfectly well they aren't."

"Be that as it may, they spell danger to the City, so I'm taking them. I'll give you a receipt. I'm an honest man."

"Can I live on a receipt the rest of my days?"

"The City's interests come before personal interests. It is essential to the City that these bank notes never get into circulation. I'm going to put them in a safe place."

The man disappeared into the bathroom, returned with the suitcase and placed it before the Commissioner. Baudruche was about to take possession.

"I have a key too, Mr. Commissioner. May I? Look. What do you see?"

"Some of them are gone."

"You were born for your job; you miss nothing. Yes, some are gone."

"What did you do with them? Did you put them in circulation?"

"No, Mr. Commissioner. I entrusted them to a dependable person in anticipation of your visit."

"Why?"

"You disappoint me, Mr. Commissioner. You're not so smart after all. Can't you guess? All right, I'll tell you. Either you are going to take my suitcase, in which event I will need to have some money tucked away for myself, or you are going to take me and my suitcase, in which event there are arrangements for the other bills to be put into circulation. Which do you plan?"

That was precisely what Baudruche had feared.

"Either way, the public interest is not served."

"I'm glad to hear you say that. That means you're becoming more reasonable. But you still don't know what to do, do you? Yet the solution is easy: get the hell out of here."

"And leave you free to distribute your bank notes and create a financial panic in the City? Not on your life. I'd rather kill you with my own hands."

"That would solve nothing. Besides, I have no desire to spend these particular bank notes. Quite the opposite, in fact."

"What do you mean?"

"I mean that if you give me enough to live comfortably, according to my tastes—which are modest—I will not spend these bills. After all, I have a sentimental attachment to them."

"Why, for God's sake?"

"Why not? These bills represent the entire heritage of all the branches of my family for generations. I've been accumulating them gradually."

Baudruche felt trapped. He had no reason to think the man was lying. So some of the money was locked up safely somewhere. Baudruche was being blackmailed, but could he afford to do anything about it?

"Where do you think I'm going to find the wherewithal to support you?"

"Mr. Commissioner, I think there's a misunderstanding. I

wasn't asking *you* for the money; I was asking the City."

"You are too kind. I hadn't expected that. You think the City has money to throw away on a lazy good-for . . ."

"You know how much the City wastes as well as I do. A little more, a little less . . ."

The man stopped and Baudruche tried to think again. He had to make the decision alone and take the consequences. What bothered him this time was that the solution involved his defeat—defeat by an unknown person, a nobody without a title, without any position in the City.

"You are asking me to do something quite irregular."

"And what do you call what you did in my room yesterday?"

This was too much. Baudruche faltered. His tone changed. "Please don't think I do everything my job requires with a light heart."

"Then why don't you resign?"

"Who would take my place?"

The answer popped out before he had time to think. He was absolutely sincere. Nobody was capable of taking his place. The man knew that.

"Protect yourself, and you'll be protecting the City."

"It isn't easy, you know; I'm afraid for the City. It has no rival, but somehow I believe it is weak."

"It is."

"Do you know why?"

"It has lost its soul."

Both were silent for a moment. The two enemies understood each other. Baudruche broke the silence.

"I'll do what I can for you. I have some influence with the Prefect in this kind of thing. When must you have your answer?"

"Right away."

"Why right away?"

"Because I have no money except for what's in that suitcase."

Baudruche took out his wallet.

The stranger said, "I'll give you a receipt, Mr. Commissioner."

Baudruche took the receipt and absentmindedly stuffed it in his pocket. Then he put his head in his hands.

"If, as I hope, everything goes well with the Prefect, I will have to ask two things: that these bills be put safely away under lock and key, and that you give me your word that you won't take advantage of your special situation to defy the laws of the City. Is that clear?"

"Yes, I promise. You keep your word and I'll keep mine."

"Tell me something: why did you come back to the City?"

"I was the last one. A man can't live alone."

"What are you going to do now?"

"I have no idea."

"I'll have to keep you under surveillance, but we can use the agent to send each other messages if you like."

Mr. Baidroume was waiting for Baudruche outside his office. Baudruche advised him that, from this day on, the City would assume all expenses entailed by the guest in room 23.

Then Baudruche walked off. He wasn't proud of himself. Yet he felt he had at least avoided the worst. What was hardest to bear was that he had been forced to give in to someone other than the Prefect.

Baudruche smelled an odor of agitation in the streets as he returned to his office after lunch. People were talking on their stoops. Some were excited, some disturbed, a few seemed sad. He couldn't make out what they were saying, for they stopped when he approached. But he knew something had happened.

He speeded up, taking the stairs of his office three at a time. Miss Bourrot was just returning the telephone to its cradle when he barged in.

"Thank God you're back!"

"What's happened?"

"It's all right now. It's all been straightened out."

"It's when things have been straightened out that it's most dangerous around here. Tell me what happened."

"There was an incident in front of the Factory at noon."

"The rats again."

"Yes, Mr. Commissioner."

"They assaulted more workers in front of the Social Progress Café?"

"Well, not exactly. They waited until about a hundred men had come out, then they swept forward from basement windows, doors and sewer holes—as if at a command—and surrounded the workers. It was just like yesterday and the day before, except that this time there were a hundred workers. As for the rats, there were more than you could count."

"How did the workers react?"

"Everybody was very calm. There was no fighting, only a halfhearted protest from a few of the workers and some of the people in the windows. But some applauded the rats and egged them on."

"I don't believe it!"

"It's true, Mr. Commissioner. At least, that's what Revere and Payne told me. They got there for the end of it."

"Are they still here?"

"I don't know, Mr. Commissioner. I'll find out."

She picked up the phone and located them at the canteen where they were discussing the event with their colleagues. They were in the office soon after and confirmed Miss Bourrot's account.

"Absolutely, Mr. Commissioner. There were even some attempts at fraternization."

Miss Bourrot let out a small scream.

"How horrible! Touch a rat . . .!"

"There are those who can't resist them, my dear girl!"

Miss Bourrot pursed her lips in disapproval.

"Some of the rats were whistling to the women in the windows and making signs to come down—even to old ones like you," Inspector Payne taunted her. "Some were even showing them their . . . I won't go on. I can see that this makes you uncomfortable."

Baudruche enjoyed the Inspector's tactics. He loved to see Miss Bourrot shocked. But he was still angry. "Couldn't either of you do anything?"

"What could we do against a mob like that? It wasn't the workers we were afraid of; it was the rats. We would have needed a brigade. We thought of blowing a whistle or telephoning, but it was too late. It all happened so fast."

"The Director didn't do anything?"

"It was all over by the time he arrived. When he was told what had happened, he got up on the wall and made a speech."

"What did he say?"

"He congratulated the men on their restraint. He told them they were right not to listen to the militants."

"Of course. He meant me."

"Then he told them they'd all get a bonus. What did he call the bonus, Revere?"

"A fraternization bonus."

"That's it."

"What about the rats?"

"They'd gone. They'd gotten what they wanted and scrammed. We could hear them whining as they shoved their way back into the sewers. It made us sick to watch them. And Revere and me don't get sick easy. We went and had a drink at the Social Progress. The bartender wouldn't let us pay. I guess he figured he could afford it. He was doing a big business; the place was jammed. What we should do, Mr. Commissioner, is all of us should go down there some noontime, but there ought to be a lot of us. I promise it'll be a good show."

"I wish I could, of course. But you must remember there's the Prefect, and the newspaper."

67

"We don't give a shit for the paper or the Prefect!"

"Careful! You don't know what you're saying!"

"What's the diff, Mr. Commissioner? It's all among ourselves, right?"

Revere and Payne left reluctantly. They had hoped for something more from Baudruche. A promise of something, a special mission, a little encouragement, or at least a conspiratorial wink. But nothing.

Baudruche felt drained. He dropped into his big chair, his eyes glued to the ceiling. He felt that he must act, that he had to fight. But fight against whom? Against what? Miss Bourrot watched him sadly. She would have liked to do something too. If she could come up with an idea or a word that would help the Commissioner . . .

Suddenly, Baudruche leaped to his feet, picked up his hat and strode out of the office, banging the door behind him.

He walked rapidly, hands deep in his pockets, eyes riveted to the sidewalk. He marched through the gates of the Factory, up to Leponte's office and opened the door without being announced.

"I didn't hear you knock, Mr. Commissioner."

For a moment, they looked at each other in silence. Baudruche's face was livid.

"From your expression, Mr. Commissioner, I gather that things aren't going to your liking. A personal disappointment of some kind, perhaps?"

"Would you call the recent incident in front of the Factory 'a personal disappointment'?"

"Mr. Commissioner, may I say that I am deeply sorry to see you so upset. It surprises me, although I should have expected it. I'd like to help you. . . ."

"That surprises me. . . ."

"Perhaps it is within my paltry means. You deplore what seems to you a tragedy; to me it is the first sign of an awaken-

68

ing collective conscience. Those men whose behavior offends you so are struggling against a sordid egotism with every means at their disposal. What's wrong with that?"

"Mr. Leponte: I didn't come here to listen to your drivel, nor to be read a lecture. I came for your report."

The Director answered with a wide smile. Baudruche's exasperation was beyond his wildest dreams.

"For my report? But of course, Mr. Commissioner. It's all there and waiting for you, as usual."

He handed him the sheet which Baudruche flung in the air. "That's not what I'm talking about!"

Leponte examined him from head to foot, saw that he was at his mercy and changed his tone. His voice became very dry.

"Mr. Commissioner, this is the only report you have any right to claim. I know you are alluding to a certain scene that took place near the Factory. But I would like to remind you that although I may be responsible for what happens inside the Factory, I am in no way responsible for what happens outside. I could remind you who is, but out of respect for you, I won't."

Baudruche decided to cut things short. The day was Leponte's. His would have to come later. He walked to the door. Leponte rushed after him.

"Mr. Commissioner, you're forgetting my report."

Baudruche plucked it from his hand and stuffed it in his pocket.

Leponte was suddenly very gentle. "Mr. Commissioner, it is madness to obstruct the people's will. Listen to what the people are saying. Read the editorial in today's paper. They are speaking with one voice. I may not have the honor of being able to address the Prefect, but I'm convinced that if . . ."

Baudruche left before he finished the sentence. Leponte whistled as he sat down at his desk. He called for Miss Niquel.

She entered, as sullen as he was expansive.

"You want to dictate?"

"No! Let's just have a little talk, the two of us." He dropped into his chair and opened his arms wide.

"Play with yourself; I don't feel like it. These rats are wrecking my nerves."

Baudruche knew his face reflected his defeat, so he avoided people as best he could. He bypassed the Public Gardens and Prefect Avenue, and took the street that paralleled the ramparts. It was almost deserted. But as he approached the main gate, he noticed the flock of birds in the sky. Instead of flying off as they did every night when darkness came, the birds flew in tighter and tighter circles toward the belfry of City Hall. Baudruche ran up the steps to the sentry walk for a better look.

The birds had converged in one immense circle and were wheeling around the belfry. The screeching which had made the last few days unbearable was deafening. Gradually, they slowed their flight and alighted, not on the branches of trees as they usually did, but on the belfry and its neighboring roofs.

Baudruche was joined by other curious onlookers. They stood, mouths agape, eyes glued on the City's center.

The birds had grown quiet, and the usual sounds of evening had reasserted themselves, when suddenly a vast lament welled up from around City Hall. And just as suddenly, it turned into a giant scream of anger that sounded as if it came from one enormous bird. There was another silence—of barely a second —and then all the wings spread wide, there was a great sound of flapping, and the birds swooped into the sky. Like a huge squadron, they moved into position, forming one head and two enormous, seemingly endless wings.

With a last cry, they turned away from City Hall and flew east, almost brushing Baudruche's head as he stood watching their shadow against the gray clouds. They stayed in tight formation, wings interlocked, then one lone bird broke away and seemed to lead them.

70

Baudruche and his companions spun around to follow their flight toward the horizon. There, they broke into smaller flocks and slowly floated down to earth. Baudruche guessed they were going to nest in the ruins of the villages.

His companions stood rooted to the spot, speechless. In some obscure way, they felt that something very serious had just taken place and that somehow they were responsible. They went down the stairs in tight little groups, clinging to each other with fear.

"Oh, maybe they feel a little guilty now, but for how long? Until tonight, when they're back in front of the pacifying machine? The fools!" Baudruche gave a last look at the vast plain; he could just make out the outline of a few charred remains. "Maybe the birds will put a little life back into those houses."

The man from the Hotel was talking to the soldier again.

"How are things out there?"

"On the last front? Not too bad. But it's pretty dull; nothing ever happens."

"That's not the way it is in here."

"Why? What's going on?"

"Oh, they're beginning to have trouble with rats."

"What's with the rodents?"

"Some of them are demanding food and in a tone that isn't exactly friendly."

"Do the people give it to them?"

"Unfortunately, yes."

"They're crazy. You feed dogs and cats—and birds, because they're nice and they sing. But not rats!"

"They're not allowed to feed the birds. Anyway they've all just left."

"Yes, I saw them going. It doesn't surprise me that things are like that in there. But what are you doing in the City?"

"I'm doing what you're doing: waiting."

"What are you waiting for?"

"War."

"War? My kind?"

"Yes, if you like, but in a slightly different form."

"I hope you have better luck."

"You're talking with your mouth full. What are you eating?"

"Ham and cheese."

"Where did you steal it?"

"I didn't steal it. Somebody gave it to me."

"Who?"

"The guys who came here to mow last night."

"To mow? Mow what?"

"You may not realize it, but last night there was a great big field of wheat here. And the sun was out! The place was full of people. They came on wagons drawn by cows and their big wooden shoes were full of hay. But they didn't stay long."

Wearily, Baudruche pushed open his office door, sank into his chair without even taking off his coat, threw his hat on the table and started his dictation.

He reported that more ants had reached the walls and were doggedly climbing the ramparts in serried ranks. He briefly mentioned the soldier and moved on to the great events of the day. He gave a step-by-step account of the crucial dilemma posed by the stranger and his bank notes and assured the Prefect that one of the Commissioner's best agents would keep the man under constant surveillance.

Then he turned to the rats, about whom the Prefect had sent another note demanding prudence, tact and understanding on Baudruche's part. Baudruche countered by asking for full freedom of action to prevent further disorders outside the Factory.

"I'm afraid that won't do much good," Baudruche said to Miss Bourrot, "but at least I tried. Oh, I almost forgot something. I want him to know about it because I think it's funny.

"As a result of the recent disorders, a delegation of workers presented the Director with a demand for a risk bonus and lunch compensation. It appears that this is not included in the fraternization bonus.

"It cannot be denied that the attitude of Mr. Leponte, the Factory Director, constitutes an encouragement to his workers' cowardice. The choice of a new and more energetic Director would be a first step to the reestablishment of order and honor.

"Well, that's it. Mention the flight of the birds and end it with the weather report—unchanged—and the sentry's report. It's probably the same—nothing seen, nothing heard."

Baudruche picked the sentry's report off the desk.

"Wait a minute. No, I'm wrong. Last night, they heard voices and the mooing of cows outside the City. We should all be sleeping out there; it's a lot more interesting than in here."

It was very late. Baudruche went home exhausted. Labrique was waiting for him, fresh and in high spirits.

"You're taking things too hard, old man. Are you getting anywhere?"

"Why don't you read the paper? That'll tell you."

"I did while I was waiting for you. Everything's just fine; the City is prospering. Only the rats aren't fine."

"What are you trying to tell me?"

"Why don't *you* read the paper? It would appear that they are undernourished, underdeveloped, underestimated, under—I don't know what else. . . ."

"I know what they're under. They're under the City's streets, that's where, and I wish they'd stay there."

"That's not what the religious editor says."

"What does he want?"

"Fraternization. And we're to be an example."

"Great!"

"Don't take it so hard. Nobody reads the religious column."

73

After dinner, Baudruche and Labrique sat opposite each other like two china dogs. Martha placed the deck of cards between them. To his great surprise, Baudruche won, which restored some of his good humor. As they were going to bed, he said to Martha:

"I'm going to need a woman who's passably good-looking, a little stupid, but discreet."

"A little like me, perhaps?"

"I said passably good-looking . . . and younger than you, my dear."

"I think I know exactly who you're looking for."

6

EMIL POULET had slept badly. Too many worries, too much responsibility, too much intellectual strain. He had to conceive, design and create—as he did every year—the cabinet for the machine. And he had to do this with a worthless team of designers, engineers, technical and artistic advisers who were no better than messenger boys. That's why he slept so badly.

"You'll crack up if you go on like this," his daughter had said the evening before.

Her father, then her mother, had slapped her.

"That will teach you to respect your father!"

"He gets enough of that from you." The girl had fled.

"You look tired this morning, my chick. Had a bad night?"

"I couldn't sleep. I'm at the end of my rope."

"Why don't you stay home and rest? I'll call the Factory."

"But what about the cabinet? Who'll design it? You, my dear?"

"I'm not capable."

"Nor are the others."

Emil slowly pulled his feet from under the covers, painfully slid them into his slippers, stood up, rubbed his back and scratched his head.

Elisa jumped out of bed. "I'll go fix your breakfast."

Sounds of clattering saucepans were already rising from the kitchen. Ten-year-old, flat-nosed, redheaded Sophie was lovingly preparing her own breakfast of braised cabbage mixed with bits of ham and sliced salami.

Her father took his seat at the table. "It's very difficult, my dear Elisa. We have to come up with an entirely new conception, yet one near enough to the old so that people won't be put off. It must be essentially functional but at the same time take into account the legitimate artistic demands of an increasingly sophisticated clientele."

"Daddy, why don't you recite the prospectus for us?"

"Sophie, be quiet when your father's talking."

"How can I follow a train of thought with that little fool around?"

Sophie hurried her breakfast. A few more cabbage leaves, two or three small scraps of ham, and she got up, grabbed her schoolbag and was gone.

She ran to the Public Gardens where she sat on her usual bench and took from her schoolbag a pack of cigarettes, a box of matches and a thick notebook. She struck a match, inhaled deeply, opened her notebook, *The Journal of a Disillusioned Woman,* and started to write.

Emil made ready to leave.

"I don't know why you had to give me such an idiot for a daughter!"

Elisa was finally alone; her loved ones were gone. It was the best part of the day. She wandered around the apartment, opened empty boxes in the closets and wondered what to put in them, laughed just to hear the sound of her voice, put the clock ahead to see if it would make time go faster, counted the butterflies on the tapestry and scratched her calves for no reason.

Then Elisa stretched out on the bed, fixed her eyes on the ceiling, opened her pajamas and scratched her navel in a fit of introspection.

"Elisa, you're happy; that's why you're bored."

It wasn't easy to be happy. There were the vague glimmerings of intellectual deprivation.

She was abruptly wrenched from her thoughts by the ring of the telephone.

"Is that you, Elisa?"

The voice belonged to Martha Baudruche, her best friend and benefactor—for wasn't she responsible for Emil's job?

"Can we have lunch," Elisa said quickly. She needed to share with Martha the intellectual problems she found so difficult to define. Perhaps Martha could help her. . . .

Baudruche met Labrique at the base of the ramparts.

"I had you last night, you four-flusher! You're not in my league when you don't cheat."

"But I did cheat last night. I cheated so I'd lose. If I hadn't, I would have won in spite of myself."

Without a word, the two men made for the same place as on the day before.

"Baudruche, look."

Labrique pointed to a grayish spot on the parapet. He walked up to it and brushed away the several dozen ants that had reached the top. He waited a moment and the same gray stain was back. Once again he swept the ants away.

Baudruche laughed. "That can go on forever!"

"This is no laughing matter, you fool! The day may come when you can't sweep them back into the moat."

"You're being a pessimist, like everybody who doesn't do anything."

77

"And you're an optimist, like everybody who acts without knowing if any good will come of it."

Baudruche got angry.

"It's easy to criticize when you don't do anything."

"I'm not criticizing you, my friend, only what you do. I hate useless effort. I'd rather you did less but knew where you were going."

He brushed the ants away one last time and leaned out over the parapet. The ants were climbing like a giant ivy.

"I can't assign a squadron of ant sweepers to the parapet. Everybody would laugh," Baudruche said.

"In a matter of days, a squadron won't be enough. But at least it would be something."

"I'll see what I can do. But I still don't see why it's really all that serious, Labrique."

The architect didn't reply but continued to observe the ants' endless advance.

On the table in his office, Baudruche found a flat case and two letters bearing the Prefect's letterhead. He opened the case and let out a snort: it was a decoration. He opened the first letter. It was written in the Prefect's own hand, four pages of eulogies and gratitude for the spirit of initiative Baudruche had demonstrated over the "delicate problem of the bank notes which posed such a grave threat to the City."

Baudruche slapped his thigh with delight. It was clear the Prefect had been frightened. He folded the letter and put it in a desk drawer.

Then he opened the other envelope and pulled out another four pages. These were typewritten. This time, it was about the rats. The Prefect was unalterably opposed to all forms of violence or even threats of violence that might be taken as provocation. "Don't show your strength, Mr. Commissioner, for fear you may have to use it." Still the Prefect gave him full powers to resolve the problem in the City's best interests, "knowing full well that, as in the past, Robert Baudruche would know, etc., etc., . . ."

Discouraged, Baudruche stretched out on his couch and tried to figure out where all this was leading him. Miss Bourrot entered, thinking the office empty.

"Forgive me, Mr. Commissioner! I didn't know you were in."

"I am, Miss Bourrot, but not for long. I'm thinking of offering my resignation."

Miss Bourrot froze. "But what will become of us all?" she asked, her voice quavering.

Baudruche was touched to the quick. He bounced off the couch, grabbed his hat, hurled it on the floor and launched into a tirade. Miss Bourrot tried to stop him, or at least make him lower his voice, but it only made him shout the louder. Miss Bourrot was used to the Commissioner's outbursts, but she'd never seen one like this. "He's going to wreck everything," she said to herself in terror.

But Baudruche wrecked nothing, his color returned to normal and he regained a semblance of calm. But his anger had turned to bitterness. It was as hard to take the Prefect's praise as it was his disastrous exhortations. The eulogies offended Baudruche's sense of justice. The compromise he had brought off was actually a defeat. He had agreed to the terms under duress, to avoid a calamity. He felt ashamed, and yet the Prefect was covering him with flowers and decorations. It made him sick.

On the other hand, in the face of a far more serious danger he had asked for a free hand and this had been refused. It pays to be a coward, Baudruche. Leponte is in for a cushy period. The Director's repulsive face flashed before him. He must finish the Prefect's letter. Perhaps it contained an answer to his suggestion that the evil little sneak be replaced. Yes, the answer was there, all right. The Prefect thanked Baudruche for calling his attention to Mr. Leponte's attitude and asked

Baudruche not to oppose any action that Leponte might take outside the Factory gates.

"I feel like a soldier sent off to war without a gun."

The idea of resigning came rushing back. No, if he left, the Prefect would replace him with another Leponte. That would be the end of everything, of the City, as it had been of the villages.

Instead, he would go home early to lunch.

Elisa had arrived before him. He could see her through the glass doors of the dining room. He beckoned to his wife.

"Is this idiot the girl you thought up for me?"

"She's what you asked for, Robert. You always think people are stupider than they really are. But if you don't want her . . ."

"I'll try to make the best of it. When do we eat?"

Elisa sat opposite the Commissioner and was the first to speak.

"Well, Mr. Commissioner, how's business?"

Great beginning. It would take all his devotion to the City to make him be pleasant to this fathead.

"What business?"

"The City's, of course. In other words, yours."

"They converge from time to time, but they're never quite the same, thank God! Mine is going well enough: my feet are better, and Martha is leaving me in peace for the moment. As for the City's, it couldn't be worse, my dear Elisa. It is my pleasure to inform you that, in the very near future, you will probably be devoured by rats."

"Mr. Commissioner, you must be joking!"

"I've never been more serious."

"You're pulling my leg. I've read the paper. Productivity is flourishing, we're on the threshold of a new golden age. I completely agree with the paper's position: these first contacts with the rats are most encouraging. We're entering a period of fraternity and cooperation. We're all brothers together, Mr. Commissioner!"

"Do you live with a family of rats?"

"Certainly not!" She shuddered. "I was talking only in general terms."

"Ah, of course. The altruistic ideas are for others. . . ."

He couldn't help it. For all his good intentions, five minutes of Elisa's company was all he could stand. He cast an inquisitive eye to his right and was delighted to see Martha's look of annoyance.

They were in the drawing room when he finally broached the subject.

"Elisa, you don't do anything with your life, do you?"

She stiffened.

"What about Sophie's education? You think that's nothing?"

"From the results, I can't see that you've done much." It was instinctive; he was at it again. "No, I'm talking about serious things, things that grab you body and soul."

"They belong to Emil, Mr. Commissioner!"

"Of course. But Emil aside, do you think you could give yourself to an important cause, to something in the public interest? In a word, would you consider serving the City for profit and glory? It might round out your life."

Elisa became thoughtful.

"Commissioner, you've touched on a tender spot. I sometimes feel, how shall I say it . . . a yawning abyss growing inside me; that abyss is my heart."

"You are becoming eloquent, Elisa."

"It's not for me, I assure you. It's Paul Géraldy."

She felt a pang of remorse. Were those two lines actually from the great Paul? She knew his work almost by heart. If the great Paul hadn't written these lines, he was certainly capable . . .

81

"So you have a yawning heart, Elisa! Well, I suspected it for a long time. I think I can fix it up. Stand up, please."

Transfixed, Elisa stood up.

"Turn your head. Smile. Arch your back. Stick out your breasts. Turn. The legs are okay. The body will do. I won't put you through a mental examination. No problem there; I know you only too well."

Baudruche blinked his eyes and bit his lips to keep from laughing.

Martha was less amused. "What have you in mind for Elisa, Robert?"

"I'm going to make her a heroine, my dear."

He saw the change on Elisa's face and knew he had won. He explained what he had in mind. All she had to do was to live in the Hotel for a brief time, without really having to leave her own home and family, in order to observe a certain man and serve occasionally as a sort of liaison. What mattered most was absolute discretion: no one was to know the nature of her mission. She would be well paid. How could she refuse?

"When do I begin?"

"Tomorrow. You can start packing."

"But what about Emil? What will he say?"

"If he gives you any trouble, I'll make it my business to convince him."

"I don't know if I can be ready in time. I must do some shopping. I have nothing to wear."

"Do it this afternoon," Baudruche said and took some bills out of his wallet.

"I don't know what's happening to me. But I'll do it. Perhaps my destiny is calling."

Martha left the two to their tête-à-tête and went in search of her copy of Baudelaire. She returned with the book open and held it under her husband's eyes, pointing to the passage Elisa had quoted. Baudruche stopped at the last two lines, looked at Elisa and quoted:

"Work out your destiny, soul in disarray
And flee the infinite you carry within!"

Elisa's admiration for Baudruche soared. He read Géraldy too!

She started to leave.

"Wait for me," Martha said. "I'll go with you."

Baudruche was about to go. His wife accompanied him to the door.

"My dear Martha, your Elisa is a very stupid woman but I'll try to use her. Funny; I forgot all about asking her for news of her cuckold of a husband."

Martha drew back.

"Robert, you must be joking! Elisa is a faithful wife!"

"Oh, Emil isn't a cuckold yet? Well, he will be soon enough. I've done my best to bring it about."

He closed the door after him, ecstatic over that arrow he'd been patiently sharpening for an hour.

But his enjoyment lasted only a moment. His foot was barely out the door when he heard a great clamor that seemed to come from the direction of the Factory. He stopped and listened. The noise stopped, then began again. Baudruche headed toward it.

The closer he came, the more it seemed as if the City had been struck by some kind of fever. People scurried from here to there in search of more news. Snatches of conversation reached his ears: "What do they want?" "What are they going to do?" "Somebody ought to do something."

He hurried his steps. The clamor grew louder and louder.

Baudruche caught sight of some of his men and beckoned them to follow. They knew little more than he. It was the rats, all right; they were demonstrating. Revere came running toward him out of breath. They had tried to call the Commissioner at home but he had just left. Revere had come to find him to tell him he must hurry.

"What's going on? A repeat of yesterday?"

"Much worse, Mr. Commissioner. This time there are thousands and thousands. They control all the areas around the Factory. We can't do anything. There are only four or five of us."

"What are the rats doing?"

"Nothing much yet. Shouting and demonstrating. They have big posters. But the people are yelling with them. The rats surrounded the Factory at noon when the workers left and now the workers can't get back in again."

Baudruche had reached the wide avenue that led to the Factory. A small group had gathered behind him and seemed to be pushing him forward like a shield. The timid applause he heard as he went by sounded strange to his ears. It wasn't that he was hated; rather, he was feared. For a moment, he hoped it meant the people thought he was ready to fight and were lending him encouragement and support. But more likely it was applause for the Prefect's man who had turned up to put things right and restore the calm so essential to their lives.

The crowd, a mixture of rats and people, stood aside to let him pass. The rats looked at him without surprise, as if they had been expecting him. A handful who had learned a smattering of the language, cried out: "Commissioner with us!" They saw that the workers and the people who lived in the neighborhood were applauding him, so they awkwardly tried to imitate their gestures. Others were arguing vehemently, but calmed down at Baudruche's approach. He noticed that a few of the rats had sticks or stones in their hands, but no one was using them.

The most agitated group was in front of the closed gates. With the help of his men, he forced his way through the mob. Leponte was anxiously discussing something with his engineers. He rushed into Baudruche's arms.

"Ah, you're here at last! I didn't think you'd ever come!"

Baudruche gave him a slight shove. The two rats who were holding the Director let him go.

"What's going on? I've never seen you in such a state."

84

"The rats are barring the Factory entrance. The workers can't get back in."

Baudruche motioned for the workers and rats to clear an access to the Factory. An endless line of rats, arms crossed, stood in front of the gate and along the wall as far as the eye could see. Everybody was silent, waiting. So much tension couldn't be contained for long. He turned and looked up.

Rats were watching the scene from the rooftops, their legs dangling over the sides. A few had slid down to the balconies and windowsills and were tapping on the windowpanes to be let in. Though the rats below were disciplined and silent, those above were screaming, shouting and haranguing. A window shattered and three rats dove through.

Baudruche placed his hand on the gate lock. A rat stopped him.

"One moment, Mr. Commissioner. Not yet."

"Why not?"

"We don't mean to interfere with the City's activities, but before we leave, we would like to have a dialogue with you."

A dozen large rats formed a silent circle around the two. Baudruche looked anxiously for his men: they were far away, lost in the crowd. He exchanged glances with a group of workers standing near him, but their eyes were either empty or fearful. Baudruche let go the handle of the gate.

"You want a dialogue? On what subject?"

"Us."

"But I don't know you and don't want to. You have no business here. Go away."

"Of course you know us, Mr. Commissioner, and we even know that you are sympathetic to our cause. I read about it in your paper. Let's have a little chat; I know you'll come to understand our point of view. Then order can be restored and we'll be on our way. Please come. What harm can it do?"

"I can't imagine what you want to tell me, but I'm ready to listen."

"Mr. Commissioner, we can't talk here. Let's go next door,

to the Social Progress, where we've set up our command post."

If only Baudruche could grasp that gray neck, hear the tiny squeak, then the cracking sound, and see the body collapse on the pavement. But it wasn't possible. He was surrounded by hundreds of thousands of rats. His men were too far off to be of any help. And besides, there was the Prefect and the paper and public opinion. So he followed the rat who, with an expansive sweep of the arm, made a path through the crowd.

The owner of the café was sitting at a table, chatting with a dozen rats. Baudruche's companion ordered them to leave; they obeyed without a murmur. He took a bottle and two glasses from behind the bar, sat down and motioned Baudruche to do the same.

"Mr. Commissioner, how well do you know the actual condition of our people?"

For the next hour, Baudruche was told what had been in the papers for days: that they were dying of hunger, their infant mortality rate was shocking. And they knew of the comfort in which the City's inhabitants lived. The rat had been made spokesman for his people in order to explain their situation calmly and amicably to the one man most likely to understand.

Then the rat took out of his pocket what he termed "a plan for constructive collaboration," and he and Baudruche argued each article at length. Baudruche gave in when there was nothing to do but give in or invite immediate violence. The rat said that he himself would be castigated for his moderation but that he was willing to take the risk in order to reach an understanding and avoid the use of force. So they signed.

The rat drank to the Prefect's health, opened the door and left, waving the treaty over his head. He was greeted with an acclamation. Baudruche followed, crushed and humiliated. An even noisier acclamation greeted him. Reporters and photographers surrounded him, flashbulbs went off, and a reporter approached Baudruche, pen in hand.

"Mr. Commissioner, may I have your impressions for the evening edition."

86

"You may go to hell."

The crowd would have crushed him but for a double line of rats, arms intertwined, who kept open a narrow path to the Factory. Baudruche stomped forward as the enormous crowd of rats and workers shouted in rhythm:

"Bau-druche! Bau-druche! Bau-druche!"

When he reached the gates, he saw that they were indeed open and that the workers were entering in tight formation. When the last man had gone in, the rats perched on the house-tops slid down the drainpipes or clambered down the walls, using cracks or rough patches as footholds. They joined the others in the street and together rushed into their sewer holes and disappeared. Few were empty-handed: their arms and shoulders were loaded with sacks, bags and cartons.

Finally the last rat was gone and the City returned to normal. Tired and bewildered, the inhabitants went back to their homes and carefully locked their doors.

Baudruche stood alone with his men on the front steps of the Factory. The area was completely deserted now.

"You can go home now. I don't need you anymore." His men left slowly, reluctant to leave their chief alone. Baudruche turned on his heels and entered the Factory courtyard. It was only then that his fear caught up with him. His legs turned to jelly, his knees shook. Why should he be trembling when the worst was over? It wasn't until he reached Leponte's door that the ridiculous spasm passed. He walked in.

"Well, Mr. Leponte, feeling better now?"

Leponte rushed to offer him a chair.

"Please sit down, Mr. Commissioner. You must be all in."

"All in? Whatever for? A small incident of no importance. You agree, don't you, Mr. Leponte?"

Leponte looked away, uneasy. At last, the Director spoke:

"I hope you won't hold it against me, Mr. Commissioner, but my report is not quite completed, owing to certain events beyond my control. . . ."

"Beyond your control? Are you quite sure, Mr. Leponte?"

87

"I will have to finish it in your presence. It won't take me a minute. Five minutes, no more."

Baudruche stretched out in the chair, head back, eyes on the ceiling, hands in his pockets as always.

The Director rose and handed him the paper without comment. Baudruche gave it a quick look.

"You wrote it yourself this time, Mr. Leponte! But I can't say your handwriting is improving. I even detect a certain trembling. . . ."

Downstairs, he ran into Miss Niquel in the deserted courtyard. She had been waiting for him.

"Mr. Commissioner, I can't stay here. I'm frightened."

"Then you should leave."

"Where can I go? I thought maybe you could help me. You look so kind."

"Don't you make fun of me."

"I'm telling the truth."

"Then I'll see what I can do."

Baudruche hadn't gone three steps when she caught up with him. She put her head on his shoulder.

"Please take me away."

"All right. Come along then."

As they walked, she recited the speech she had been rehearsing for so long. But Baudruche's mind was at the Factory among the rats.

The last refugee was climbing the stairs of the ramparts. He leaned over the side and called: "Hey, soldier!"

"Oh, it's you. What's new?"

"Things are getting hot in the City."

"Things were pretty hot here last night."

"What happened?"

"First, one old union group appeared, and then another showed up. They started to swear and curse, and it began to look bad."

"Did they fight?"

"No, they suddenly had this idea of building a house, and you can't fight and build at the same time. Once they got started building, you couldn't tell one union from the other. It was beautiful. It looked as if the house was building itself. By sun-up, the house was finished. Then they and the house disappeared. I have to tell you these things or you wouldn't know anything."

"I know every story you've told me. That's why I stay inside the City."

"Will you be back tomorrow?"

"I'll try to come every evening."

Baudruche climbed the stairs to his office, little Miss Niquel behind. He opened the door.

The crucial moment was at hand. Now she would know if she'd been right to give up the security of the Factory for this adventure. Baudruche stood there, hands on his hips, looking at her fixedly. She closed her eyes, and once again placed her head on Baudruche's shoulder. This time, she grasped his other shoulder with her right hand, near the neck.

"Help me. It's hard for a girl like me, alone in the City."

The Commissioner's arms enfolded her.

They were on the big leather sofa. She had rehearsed this scene, along with her earlier speech, many times. Every motion had been thought out, every word, even the expression in her eyes. But it was all for naught, for Baudruche was oblivious to all the nuances. He was on top of her, crushing her, pressing her tightly against him and shaking her in a frenzy.

He thought he was in front of the Factory gates, struggling with a rat—and winning. The body of the rat slid to the ground, inert. He heard a voice saying: "Ahhhh, Mr. Commissioner," and found himself in his office on top of little Miss Niquel.

She dressed herself, thinking what she'd accomplished for all that she'd be black and blue the next day. But he was

89

already back at his desk, thinking hard about the rats.

"O.K. Don't you worry. I'll take care of you."

Baudruche buzzed for Miss Bourrot. One glance at the actors and she was able to reconstruct the scene that had just taken place, a scene that had happened all too often in this office. She thought it unworthy of the Commissioner. He should be without weaknesses, without faults. When forced to, she admitted that there was a Mrs. Baudruche, and obviously he and she sometimes . . . But she erased such pictures from her mind as demeaning to her hero.

"Miss Bourrot, do we have an interesting job available in the City for a young girl who presents an unusual case?"

She thought for a moment. Actually, there was. Miss Teller on the first floor was about to retire. A wonderful job, secure, near the boss, not much to do—liaison with the press. But instead she said, "They need an assistant director in Lost and Found."

"All right, Miss Niquel, there you are! See how wise you were to come to me. Come back tomorrow morning and Miss Bourrot will make the necessary arrangements. Now go home, and sweet dreams."

Miss Bourrot watched her go with a satisfied smile. She'd do fine over there at the other end of the City among the single gloves and umbrellas.

"To work, Miss Bourrot!"

"Mr. Commissioner, a reporter has been waiting outside a long time."

"I have nothing to say to him."

"He's come with a letter from the Prefecture. The Prefect is very anxious that you see him."

A young man came in and sat down. Baudruche recognized him as the man with the pen who had accosted him on the steps of the Social Progress.

"You want to know what really took place this afternoon?"

"What we want are your impressions, Mr. High Commissioner. We can't go to press until we have them."

"Very well. This is how it happened. It is not a pretty story. . . ."

Once the reporter had gone, Baudruche called Miss Bourrot back in.

"Let's get to the report. Tell the Prefect the results of my discussion with the representative of the rats. Stress that I tried to save the City's money while reaching an accord that conformed to the Prefect's wishes: I managed to decrease the amount of food the rat considered a minimum for his people.

"Give the Prefect some of Leponte's message for today: it appears that the recent and happy modification realized by the refugee engineer rendered obsolete a basic part of the machine. But now a young engineer at the factory has discovered that by adding a new part to the one the refugee scrapped, production will increase not by eight point fourteen percent but by seventeen point three percent. So in spite of the loss of time caused by this latest improvement, the Director is eager to realize the new modification and has given orders that the part prematurely scrapped be put back into production.

"Cover the appointment of Elisa Poulet to keep watch over the stranger, and don't forget the weather and the sentries' report.

"Oh, and put in a paragraph for Labrique: the lead columns of ants have taken over the parapets, and there are new columns climbing the exterior walls."

Baudruche already had his hat on when he remembered:

"Please add that the soldier hasn't moved. That should be a comfort to the Prefect. That man worries him too."

Baudruche walked home slowly, his mind a blank. Labrique was waiting for him, the evening paper in his hand.

91

"You double-crossing son of a bitch! I just read your interview. I suppose you're proud of what you accomplished today?"

Baudruche grabbed the paper from him. The headline across the front page read: "Commissioner Baudruche declares: 'I am satisfied.'"

"Those dirty bastards!" and he tore the paper to shreds.

He spent the rest of the evening sulking and wouldn't play cards.

"Baudruche, aren't you going to tell me about the rats?"

"Do I ask you about your wife?"

7

BAUDRUCHE awoke slowly and painfully the next morning. But once he'd had his coffee, he was back on the rails, the steam pressure up, the engine ready to start.

"Tell me something, Martha: about that fool, Elisa. Do you really think she can be trusted?"

"I think so. You're too hard on her. She has many virtues. She's pretty; she has a good figure . . ."

"She's not my type."

"I'm glad of that, but it may not speak well for your taste."

"When a woman is that stupid, she can't be pretty. What did you two do yesterday?"

"We shopped for Elisa."

They had gone off as planned. An incredible moment for Elisa. She was off to the conquest of elegance, with Martha as her companion. Martha's personality no longer overwhelmed her; they could now talk as equals, since she had just received a confirmation—heretofore only vaguely guessed at—of her own importance.

She hid her bag under her arm. It was worn and she was ashamed of it. But now at least it was crammed with Baudruche's money. She had underestimated the Commissioner: he was generous, and he read Géraldy.

Yes, now she could see that it was possible to be Baudruche's wife, in spite of his appearance, especially since it made you wife of the High Commissioner—a title worth its weight in gold. Funny: Martha never made anything of it. She could have done anything she wanted around the City because there was hardly anybody who didn't want something from the City. Almost everybody had some tale of injustice: this one was overtaxed, that one had an idiot daughter he wanted placed in a ministry, yet another wanted a building easement. And everybody complained of his neighbor.

All she had to do was to listen with a condescending smile, ask for it in writing and promise she'd give it to the Commissioner. It was in the bag; she would have a devoted slave. Whether or not she gave the note to the Commissioner was of no importance. What mattered was that she promised. From time to time, true, she would have to place a burdensome old man in a nursing home, or slip some cretin into the Postal Service, or "recycle" some public servant who had been caught red-handed. But that's all it would take to make her the City's Good Fairy, its Golden Goddess.

But Martha would have none of it. She was content to tell the suppliant that she never meddled in the City's affairs, and suggest he go directly to the Commissioner whose honesty and integrity were known to all.

But she was still the Commissioner's wife and everybody sought to please her, which was all too evident in the shop they had just entered.

The entire staff came running, the owner in the lead. Someone found her a chair, though Elisa had to remain standing. The owner declared how happy and proud he was to serve

Madame Baudruche, and smiled less broadly when he found out it was for Elisa.

Elisa's eye had fallen on an enormous alligator bag with room enough for three coats and four dresses and garnished with the beast's claws and a marble closing as big as a fist. Martha dissuaded her, saying it was in questionable taste. Elisa gave in, as always, and the owner agreed with Martha because she was the Commissioner's wife, and Martha made her buy a simple black bag with a silver snap which looked like nothing and cost almost as much.

"Why didn't you say it was for yourself, Martha? Then we wouldn't have had to pay. . . ."

It was quite late by the time she reached home, her arms weighed down with boxes and bundles. She was dazzling, bursting with joy and reduced to very little cash.

Her husband's welcome was disappointing; it lacked response, admiration. He just said with a suspicious glare:

"Where did you get all that?"

She gave him a brief, vague account of what had happened. He exhausted her with stupid questions about the nature of her work, what is was exactly, how come she had all that money. She answered simply that she wasn't allowed to say more but if he was so determined to find out, he could go ask Commissioner Baudruche.

Before, she had always spoken his name with contempt; now he was all she could talk about. Emil watched the sudden metamorphosis of his wife with bewilderment. He tried to guess at the amount of money Baudruche had given her, but even more, the reason why.

Emil spent the night on the edge of the connubial bed to show his disapproval. But when morning came, he lunged at Elisa before she was fully awake. She fought him in a rage, wrenched his hands off her, and screamed, "Don't touch me! You disgust me!"

Finally, she was mistress of her terrain. She eyed the pathetic figure standing there, stooped, beaten, accepting his defeat without a word.

When Emil and Sophie finally left that morning, she didn't feel like her usual caper around the apartment. Instead, she decided to start dressing. She opened wide the doors of her closet and examined its contents with disgust. She disavowed the woman who had made do with such a pathetic display, who had spent twelve interminable years with that contemptible fool of an engineer with no talent or future and who had never given her anything except a daughter she didn't know what to do with. Her mind turned to Baudruche; he was even less handsome and less young, but at least he was somebody.

At the Commissioner's home, the master was engaged in interrogating his wife about every last detail of the previous day's shopping expedition.

"Why are you interested in such nonsense, dear Robert? This is very unlike you."

"Don't I have a right to know where the City's money is going?"

"See! I was right, wasn't I?" Labrique was pointing to the paving stones on the sentry walk. They were alive with swarming black patches.

"You're right, Labrique. It's worse than I thought, though it's still no great calamity. But I'll alert the Sanitation Department. It must lie within their jurisdiction."

"Remember, this is no ordinary situation. It's not normal for ants to take over the ramparts. And that isn't all: I want you to take a look at the Church. It's a different situation, but I don't like the looks of it either. I've been complaining about it for a long time, but the Prefecture refuses to do anything about it. It may already be too late."

Baudruche stopped at the Hotel to leave an envelope in number 23's box. Then a half hour later, he was in front of the Church. Labrique was right; it was not a pretty sight. It had been years since Baudruche had felt like visiting the old monument. But the Church had been there in the middle of the City for so long that he, along with everyone else, thought of it as eternal.

The immense edifice had been put together with so many disparate elements that he could no longer make out its original form. Now the rubble of different stones at its feet were like so many reproaches aimed at the City. "We're all a little guilty," Baudruche said to himself. "It was what it was, but still, it had its place in the City. The carcass must be saved." As he walked nearer, an old woman leaned out of a window.

"Don't get too close! It's dangerous!"

Baudruche kept on going until he reached a large Gothic window. A stone fell behind him with a thud. He put his head through the window; the glass had long since gone. The walls might have started to crumble, but the interior seemed to be holding up. He recognized the unlikely jumble of decorations on the inside walls and the funny, childish figures scattered around. Had they removed all that junk, they would have seen what was happening to the structure. But, as usual, nobody wanted to take on the responsibility. On one of the rare undecorated expanses, Baudruche noticed a long deep crack. That was serious.

He toured the whole building and everywhere there was the same decay. Suddenly he caught sight of a child leaning through one of the gaping windows. Baudruche said, "What are you doing there? Don't you know it's dangerous?"

"I don't care. It's fun watching."

"Watching what?"

"Look, over there," and the boy pointed toward the far end of the Church where two men in black were sitting on broken-down chairs, arguing and gesticulating.

"That's all they do, sir. They never stop."

97

Baudruche took out his distance glasses and looked again. The two puppets took shape: one was dressed in a long robe, the other in something not unlike the regulation dress worn by the City's inhabitants. He recognized the one in the long robe as someone he'd seen often in his youth. The man hadn't changed: the same indefinable smile, the same look of belonging to another world. Things didn't change much around this place!

He strained his ears to hear what they were saying. They were using an old-fashioned language which sounded absurd. It was incomprehensible. A second stone came loose, this one from an arch, and fell at his feet. Baudruche cupped his hands around his mouth and called out:

"You mustn't stay there! It's dangerous. Please leave!"

The two men continued their discussion, paying him no heed. Baudruche called louder. Still no reaction. He took the child by the hand and left.

Some people from the neighborhood had recognized him and now stood expectantly on the sidewalk across from the Church. He walked toward them.

The people who lived around the Church remained aloof from the rest of town, thinking themselves different if not actually superior. They had preserved some of the old ways—at least, the less inconvenient ones. When people from other parts of town wandered into the area, they were politely received but treated as strangers.

Baudruche spotted a man of about fifty and asked, "Why do those two men stay inside the Church? Don't they realize it's dangerous?"

"We don't know. They never come out, and when we speak to them, they don't answer."

"Are you sure they hear you?"

"We don't know that either."

"How do they get food?"

"We keep an eye on them, and when we see they're getting low, we throw them some more. One must have pity."

"Why don't you go up to them and explain that the Church is crumbling and they must leave?"

"We don't know if we have the right. I don't think we do."

Baudruche felt he was treading on delicate ground. The faces around him froze and, one by one, his audience moved away.

"Are we going back to them, sir?" the child asked him.

"You stay and wait for me."

Baudruche went through an opening that had once been a door and walked up to the two men.

"You must leave right away; you cannot stay here. It isn't safe."

But they continued their discussion without seeming to take in his presence. So he grabbed the arm of the man in the long black robe, shook it and pointed to the exit. The man rubbed at his sleeve as if it had been touched by a tainted hand, rose to his feet and addressed him angrily in his incomprehensible language while pointing to the same exit. There was a small avalanche of rubble behind them, followed by a cloud of dust. Baudruche shrugged his shoulders and left.

He had barely returned to his office when Miss Bourrot came in to announce that there was a young engineer who wanted to see him immediately.

"What does he want? Did he give you his name?"

"It's Poulet, I think. I don't know what he wants. He said it was personal. He doesn't look happy; he might be dangerous."

"Emil Poulet dangerous? You make me laugh. Show him in."

It was exactly the kind of visit Baudruche liked at the end of a morning's work. It would be good for his nerves.

Poulet entered.

"What the hell are you doing here at this hour?"

Poulet was disconcerted. He had been prepared to see the unmasked and humiliated Baudruche grow pale face to face

99

with his victim and ready to atone for his sins. Yet here instead was a calm and confident opponent.

"Did you hear my question? I asked why you weren't at the Factory during working hours? Have you Mr. Leponte's authorization? He will hear of this. O.K.; quickly, tell me what brings you here. It must be something very important."

Emil Poulet finally found his tongue.

"You know perfectly well . . ."

"If I knew perfectly well, you wouldn't have needed to go to the trouble of coming. Now be off with you."

Emil Poulet was seized with rage. He shouted:

"You want to know what I have to say? Well, it's that last night, my wife was much too elegant and much too beautiful, that's what!"

"So the idiot is complaining that his wife is too beautiful!"

"Right. And I'm here because she's married to me and not to you."

"I'm still in the dark. If you're going to be obscure as well as foolish . . ."

"You're making a mistake if you take me for a fool! If you think I don't know she's your mistress and that you bought her with money . . ."

The game was almost too easy.

"Why should I buy what I could have had for nothing? No, Mr. Poulet, I'm not sleeping with your wife, and for one simple reason: I don't want to. She's all yours. It's entirely possible that she's been unfaithful, but not with me."

"Well, whether she has or not, I don't want her working outside my house, for you or anybody else. I have my rights."

"Yes, Mr. Poulet, and it's my right to send you back where I found you, before I put you on the City's payroll. If I remember correctly, you were sitting on some cloud, doing a treatise on the social significance of the abstract line? Well, I'm sending you right back there. And I'll telephone your boss to that effect right away; he'll be delighted to see the last of you."

Baudruche got up, pressed his buzzer, and walked slowly up to Elisa's husband, who backed away, stammering:

"Maybe I didn't understand. Maybe I was wrong."

Baudruche cornered him by the leather couch and yanked his ear like a child. Miss Bourrot entered.

"Please remove this joker and see him to the street."

He dragged him to the door, but before he let him go, pity got the better of him.

"Send me a letter of apology and I'll reconsider your fate."

"Was he an anarchist?" Miss Bourrot asked when she returned.

"No, much worse than that. A technocrat!"

During the course of the afternoon, Baudruche paid a visit to the newspaper. Although he was well aware of the controls over its editorial policy, he was still smarting from the previous day's interview. All too often his words had been mutilated or soft-pedaled, but never before had he been quoted as saying the direct opposite of what he had said.

"To what do I owe the honor of this visit, Mr. Commissioner?" the Editor-in-Chief asked.

"Yesterday's edition, Mr. Newman."

"You weren't pleased?"

"Even less than usual."

"What didn't you like? The layout of the front page?"

"I didn't like what it said I said."

"But it was the text of your interview, Mr. Commissioner."

"It was not what I said to the young reporter you sent me, Mr. Newman."

"A boy with a brilliant future. I have no idea what you said to him. I know only the text of your interview as it was printed in the paper."

"I'd rather you printed the truth from time to time."

"I know only one truth: the one imposed on me. I have orders, Mr. Commissioner . . ."

"What was that story your man told me yesterday? Something about a series on the rats?"

"They're all ready, Mr. Commissioner. They start today. Would you like to see them?"

"Not especially. Just give me the general idea in a few words."

"We are to remind the people over and over again that rats are beings like us, like you and me, Mr. Commissioner, and that consequently they have their right to a place in the sun."

"We don't have any sun anymore, Mr. Newman."

"It was a figure of speech, Mr. Commissioner. Sun means civilization, culture, or perhaps—to be more precise—one's standing, one's status. We can't say it often enough, but thank God, our readers have already taken a big step in the right direction. The letters we receive daily reflect that. And, actually, Mr. Commissioner, do you feel so very different from a rat?"

"Absolutely, Mr. Newman. Don't you?"

"I, no. I have orders . . . Allow me to finish; it won't take long. In addition, we must impress on our people the need to make our underdeveloped neighbors forget the selfish policies of our forebears, and prevent them from succumbing to a discredited paternalism. An end to elitism! We must have cordial human relations! Believe me, the people will understand. Besides, that's what we're here for. I know I'm preaching to a convert, Mr. Commissioner, for you are already a partisan to these reforms."

"I am?"

"Of course. It was in your interview."

"While we're on the subject," Baudruche pulled a piece of paper from his pocket, "I wonder if you could do me a small favor. . . ."

"Your word is my command, Mr. Commissioner."

Newman read over the note Baudruche had given him.

"A denial? Out of the question, Mr. Commissioner. I have orders."

It was what he'd expected . . . with the Prefecture next door, dominating the whole City, including The Newspaper.

Years before, when he was young, newsboys went around calling out *"The Union," "The Independent," "The Conservative,"* and many others. Now there was only one: The Newspaper, which, by its very name, indicated it was the only one. It had eaten up all the others; they had floundered, then been digested, one after the other.

For a while, the victim's name still appeared—in smaller letters—under the victor's, not unlike the outline of the rabbit in the snake after it is swallowed. Then, little by little, the letters diminished in size until, one day, they disappeared altogether. The rabbits had been digested and The Newspaper gained a bigger circulation.

Things being what they were, he would have liked, if not exactly to control it, at least to prevent its spreading so many lies. But that was beyond hope: the paper had been created by the Prefect, belonged to the Prefect, and allowed no other master.

These bitter reflections occupied him all the way to the Factory gate. As he passed by the custodian's hut, he heard the usual greeting of "Good evening, Mr. Commissioner," but it sounded odd. He looked up and saw that it was a rat instead of old Smitty raising his cap in greeting. He looked inside the hut and saw another dozen rats sitting around.

"What are you doing here?"

"We are guarding the Factory, Mr. Commissioner. We are protecting the workers' security. The Director has given his approval."

Baudruche rushed into Leponte's office.

"What do you mean, letting the rats guard the gates?"

Leponte smiled at Baudruche, but his smile had changed. It had lost its mockery. At first Baudruche was surprised, then he understood: fear, which changes so many men, had left its mark on the Director. As long as the danger lasted, Baudruche was no longer his enemy but a potential protector who must be flattered in case of need. Mesmerized, Baudruche watched him ring for his new secretary and ask her to bring in refreshments.

A rather vulgar-looking girl with pale blonde hair came in, filled his glass and disappeared.

"Leponte, I still want to know what the hell those rats are doing here."

Mr. Leponte answered that he was actually quite pleased with the development. Admittedly, the day before, he had been afraid of violence against the workers and even the Factory. In the eyes of the Prefect and the City, he was responsible for both them and it. But the rats weren't enemies. Not at all. He didn't need the articles in the newspapers to convince him of that! Therefore he'd been delighted to receive the rat who had signed the agreement with Mr. Commissioner the day before. The rat repeated what he had said to the Commissioner, then offered to set up a guard at the Factory entrance. A most gracious act. . . . "They do have a way with them, don't they, Mr. Commissioner?"

Baudruche said that henceforth he would take charge of the situation, and he left with the daily report the new secretary put lingeringly in his hand. He had no time for her today.

As he came abreast of the guards' hut, the rats rose to their feet, abandoning the game of dominoes they'd been playing among the bread crumbs and puddles of wine.

"I would like to speak to your representative."

Nothing easier; he was only a stone's throw away, at the Social Progress. One of them offered to accompany him.

"No need. I know the way."

As he walked in, he recognized the representative sitting at a table reading the paper, the owner looking over his shoulder. Half a dozen rats in a far corner got up when they saw the Commissioner. The noise caught the representative's attention; he looked up and noticed Baudruche. He dismissed the other rats with a motion of the head. Turning to Baudruche, he was as amiable and deferential as on the previous day, but there was a new note of confidence and a certain crispness in his speech.

Yes, what the Director had told Baudruche was correct: all he had in mind was helping maintain order in the City, a modest attempt to supplement the Commissioner's efforts. Besides, he could tell Baudruche what he had not dared to tell the Director—who was a little nervous—that there was an element among his people—as in all groups, the Commissioner knew better than anyone—an extremist faction with little real influence so far, but capable (yesterday was an example which he deplored) of fomenting considerable disorder in the City.

"I will see to the order," Baudruche said.

"But you run the danger of enlarging the racial conflict, Mr. Commissioner! Whereas, together, we can achieve reconciliation and understanding." The rat pointed to the newspaper in his hand. "You keep order among your people, and I'll see to it that order is maintained among mine."

Screwing up his eyes, he added, "I'm sure the Prefect would approve if he were here."

But what about the occupation of the café? Wasn't that strictly illegal? No, there was no law against it; the owner was entirely in accord. He could have anybody he liked in his establishment, and he was very pleased to be able to offer his wares in such a sacred cause. The Commissioner mustn't worry; the problem would solve itself. Besides, he had just had a visit from a young reporter the Prefect had sent over.

"What did he want?"

"He wanted to do an interview with me which I was pleased to grant. It will appear in tonight's edition, a kind of sequel to yours of yesterday. I took the opportunity to mention a project —still in an embryonic stage—which could be very constructive to both sides. It involves, not an embassy—we're not that ambitious—but just a simple structure, something roomy in the center of town, given to us as a symbol of our new understanding. What do you think of the idea, Mr. Commissioner?"

Baudruche felt a shiver run down his back.

"I'm not sure. I need time to think."

"Take all the time you want. I don't need to tell you how much we would appreciate your approval—almost as much as the Prefect's, who of course will be the deciding factor."

"Which is as it should be," Baudruche said, barely containing himself. "I think we've covered the situation . . ." and he made ready to leave.

"Mr. Commissioner, I can't tell you how happy your visit has made me. . . ."

Baudruche clenched his fists in his pockets and left.

A few minutes earlier, the stranger had left the Hotel. A five minutes' walk and he was at the top of the ramparts. This time, the soldier spoke first.

"What's new in the City? What are the people up to?"

"They were beginning to get fed up with the rats, so they got rid of them."

"Good for them! How did they do it? Beat 'em up?"

"No, they fed them."

"That's no way to get rid of them. Tell me, what are you doing in the City? Are you all alone too?"

"Yes, but I think they're sending me company."

"I had company last night—just before dawn. I was cold. A horseman in a thick coat galloped toward me. When he got close, I saw he was a soldier too. He pulled out his sword. I said, 'Don't be an ass. I'm no Kraut.' He laughed, then cut his coat in two and gave me half. Funny things happen here at night. It's very interesting."

Elisa entered her room. Following the Commissioner's advice, she had asked for a room on the second floor. She'd been given number 26. She noticed with satisfaction that it was almost opposite number 23.

"Do you have everything you need, madam?" the maid asked her.

As if talking to herself, Elisa said, "No, I need a great many things."

"Can I bring them to you?"

"No, thank you."

Posey went out.

Elisa contemplated her almost empty suitcase: a couple of nightgowns, a toilet kit and her copy of Géraldy for her night table. Petulant, she opened wide her closet door. It looked immense! What it wouldn't hold. . . . She hung up her gray coat which swung in the void like a mockery. She slammed the door shut and made a tour of the room. She opened all the drawers, memorized the notice on the back of the door, tested the quality of the sheets. Then she went into the bathroom, turned on the faucets and took a bath.

She dried herself, put her clothes back on and sighed with pleasure at her reflection in the mirror. Then she walked downstairs and took a seat in the lobby to await the unknown.

Her task that first night was simple; the Commissioner had spelled it out meticulously. One, she was to identify the man in question. Baudruche told her to sit where she could see all the guests' pigeonholes and wait until a man claimed the key to number 23. Two, she was to establish contact with the guest in number 23. Baudruche made no suggestions here, allowing that it would be a simple matter for a pretty young woman.

She called a bellboy and asked him for a deck of cards. As she played successive hands of solitaire, she watched the guests come to claim their keys. Finally, a man took number 23 off its hook. Her heart leaped. He was young and slender. She lowered her eyes as he walked past. Suddenly all the cards landed on the floor. The man leaned down and picked them up.

"What were you playing?"

"Solitaire. What else is there when you're all alone?"

Seconds later, the man was sitting opposite her, shuffling the deck. She wanted to try a hand of poker.

To her great embarrassment, she lost all the money she had left. She showed the man her empty purse.

"I can't go on. I haven't a cent left."

He took her bag and filled it with the money she had lost. She was stunned.

"It doesn't belong to me. I cheated. The next time you play poker with a stranger, make sure you don't sit in front of a mirror."

She got up and fled. The man filled his pipe, lit it and took out of his pocket the note Baudruche had left him: "Pink dress, black and white gloves, black bag with silver clasp, stupid." How could he miss?

They dined tête-à-tête.

Later that evening, she took off her shoes, tiptoed over to room 23 and looked through the keyhole. The man was standing, blowing into a kind of black stick. She strained an ear but couldn't hear anything, went back to her room and closed the door.

Baudruche was already fast asleep and snoring. His day had been long; his report was short. He gave a progress report on the ants and passed on Labrique's warning about the condition of the Church.

The stone is disintegrating in spite of earlier attempts to repair it, windows are missing, walls are cracking. Only the large cross on the facade seems to have survived.

I noticed that the two men in black, whom you once feared as a threat to your authority, were still in the Church. It is quite clear that your worries on that score were groundless. No one takes them seriously anymore; few are even aware of their existence.

Then he turned to the Factory:

Even though calm has been restored around the Factory, the Director has decided to continue payment of the risk bonus to his workers lest the workers think that the recent agreements were concluded only as a pretext to avoid paying the bonus.

The production of the new part for the machine, as well as the one prematurely scrapped, are proceeding normally. The Director proposes that the young engineer responsible for this most recent contribution be named Chief of Technical Services. On the other hand, he would like you to consider recycling the refugee engineer responsible for the earlier mistake into another discipline as soon as feasible. He was tested and the results indicate that he is a technocrat rather than a technician. For my part, I do not see where we can use him in the City.

The weather report indicates no change so long as the cloud cover remains over the City.

The sentry heard nothing last night, except for the sound of horses' hooves. No enemy has appeared on the horizon.

8

FOR ONCE, Baudruche did not join Labrique at the foot of the ramparts. He was fed up with the architect and his ants. It wasn't his job to fight a lot of insects. The rats were worth bothering about: they were aggressive, intelligent, clever and brave. A battle worthy of a man. But ants . . . They let themselves be crushed underfoot; they had only one defense, to keep coming back in ever-increasing numbers to replace their dead. Labrique could stamp on them if he liked. At least it might keep his mind off his wife.

Esther was a strange female. No one quite knew why Labrique had married her. A red-headed giraffe totally deficient in the breasts and buttock department. But she seemed to satisfy Labrique: he adored the cheating, meddling, good-for-nothing parasite. . . .

He tried to joke about it with Martha, but it bothered him that his best friend was a cuckold. Not that he didn't deserve it. He shouldn't have chosen such a woman. But it was humiliating to have a cuckold for a best friend. He had a juicy dossier on

Esther in his archives. He was often tempted to take it home and place it on Labrique's plate to see what it would do to his appetite. But he knew he couldn't.

Well, he could do something to get Labrique off his back about the ants. He could go to the Department of Sanitation. He did.

An impeccable old man named Javel dusted off a chair for Baudruche.

"I suppose you've heard about the ants on the ramparts, Mr. Javel?"

"Yes, Mr. Commissioner. Isn't it exciting? I went to have a look myself. What activity! What courage! They are extraordinary beasts!"

"I'd rather they were somewhere else—far away. . . . There are too many of them. I want you to get rid of them as fast as possible."

Mr. Javel looked pained.

"I can't do that, Mr. Commissioner. Anything to do with animals is outside my jurisdiction. My department is charged with overseeing the removal and destruction of household refuse, unclogging sinks, checking the cleanliness of school toilets. . . . This problem should fall within the scope of the Department of Civilian Defense."

There was little in common between the Department of Civilian Defense and the Department of Sanitation. Where the latter was modest and informal, the former was a vast, concrete mass. Sanitation needed only one director, Civilian Defense had five. They worked at a steady clip, in an aura of deep mystery. Nothing had come of their work in spite of years of research, but when it did, it would justify all the effort and expense.

To get into their headquarters required credentials and a pass signed by Baudruche and the Prefect or by one of the five directors who worked in relays to supervise the researchers who also worked in relays.

Baudruche was not happy about the two directors who were on duty this morning. He chose the older and more knowledgeable of the two.

"Mr. Paytard, can you rid the City of these ants?"

"Those poor strays on the ramparts? A mere day's work—once we have the powder ready."

That's what it always came down to: the powder. The great project, the City's salvation, the unstoppable defense against any and all attack. The newspaper was always full of it, especially when the population had been gripped by some irrational fear. The ramparts and Baudruche's men were nothing compared to the powder to which they'd given the name, "the powder of deterrence." Once it was perfected, its very existence would prevent anyone from even thinking of attacking the City.

"Mr. Commissioner, what can you be thinking? Ants! *De minimis non curat* . . ."

"Excuse me?" Baudruche said, unfamiliar with the language of Virgil.

"I said that we hope someday to be dealing with an enemy more nearly our equal."

"I know of no others, Mr. Commissioner, and if there were any, I would ignore them. Unfortunately, our powder is not quite ready. The results are very encouraging, but it needs more work, and we shall need a new appropriation. . . ."

That's what it always came to in this department: more money. The Prefect had been pouring the City's money into it for years without bothering to count the cost, and it always needed more. Meanwhile the Church was crumbling away, there weren't enough schools, they were cutting the old people's pensions, they were taxing everything that was taxable and much that wasn't, borrowing money they knew they could never repay, just to nourish this vast mass of concrete. Had it all been for nothing?

As he led Baudruche to the door, the Director whispered to him anxiously:

"Mr. Commissioner, you have influence with the Prefect: tell him we must have more money."

"I suppose your powder would roll right off the rats?" Baudruche snapped on his way out.

Elisa woke up late and lazed in bed. It was so lovely to be alone. No smell of male flesh to turn the stomach.

A woman is clean; a woman is appetizing, she thought as she stroked her arm. A woman is worthy of love.

She rang for the maid. There was a knock.

"Did you sleep well, madam?"

Nobody ever talked to her like that back home. She was the one who got up, did the work, served. . . . And whom did she serve? A man. It was so wonderful to be in the middle of the City, free, with no duties, and impulse the only master. But impulse to do what? To get dressed? If only she had something different to wear today, one of the dresses she had tried on the day before. . . .

"I'd like to see the blue dress in the window." They had recognized her right away as the Commissioner's wife's companion.

"How much is it?"

She had opened her bag. She didn't have it.

"Put it aside for me; I'll be back."

That wouldn't be necessary. They would put it in a box right away. She could pay for it the next time she passed by. Wasn't she a friend of Mrs. Baudruche's?

"You have Mrs. Poulet's bill?"

"Yes, Mr. High Commissioner; we'll have it for you right away."

Baudruche took out his pen and checked the addition.

"It seems to be correct. But what's this seventeen percent for service. Shouldn't it be fifteen percent?"

It was a mistake; they would fix it up immediately; it would never happen again. But why was the High Commissioner occupying himself with something unworthy of him?

Baudruche took several bills from his wallet. "I want you to give me all of Mrs. Poulet's bills. I'll take care of them."

Aha! So that's what it was! The Commissioner was keeping his mistress in the Hotel. What a trump for Baidroume! But he must use it skillfully.

"Why didn't you tell me you were interested in Mrs. Poulet! Forget the bill. I don't want questions of money to come between us."

"Mr. Baidroume, give me that bill and mark it 'Paid in cash by the High Commissioner.' "

Baidroume watched Baudruche go with a smile of pity. The Commissioner could go on playing his little game—and an expensive one too—but he wouldn't fool anybody, and certainly not him.

Baudruche was no sooner home than Elisa appeared at his door. She was in a hurry; she didn't want to be late for lunch at the Hotel. She just wanted to report that things were going marvelously. They'd had dinner together the night before. Wasn't she doing well?

"You must do better, Elisa. That man could be very dangerous. You must move in on him. What else has our man been doing?"

"He went out this morning, but I have no idea where."

"You must find out, Elisa. Is that all you have to report?"

The door opened again, without a knock. It was Labrique; he thought he was at home everywhere.

"Oh, excuse me, I thought you were alone. I'll be on my way."

"No, stay. I have no secrets."

He was eager to be rid of Elisa. "Have you anything else on your mind?"

She took a deep breath; it couldn't be put off. "Yes."

"What is it?"

She said very low, "I need money. It's all gone."

115

Impossible. He'd given her a large amount only two days before.

Softly and with a slight tremor—as if she were in the confessional—she whispered:

"I tell you, I need it."

The Commissioner showed her into the hall.

She made one last attempt. "Can't you give me just a teeny little bit?"

He was inflexible. Maybe, in a few days, if she really had something to report.

When she'd gone, Labrique slapped Baudruche on the shoulder.

"Aha, you old goat! Aren't you ashamed, hiding things from your best friend. How long have you been carrying on with little Elisa?"

Baudruche tried to defend himself, but in vain. Labrique was neither deaf nor blind: the stunning transformation in Mrs. Poulet's wardrobe and her manner with his friend had not escaped him.

"So she's a little costly? At your age, old man, that can be fatal."

Baudruche gave in and told him everything: the necessity of appeasing the Prefect by putting a fake secret agent on the stranger's tail, how he had chosen Elisa because Martha thought her discreet, and how the City was paying expenses. But the more he said, the louder Labrique laughed.

"You think anybody will believe you? But I didn't come here to pry. I came to find out why you weren't at the ramparts this morning."

"It's none of your business."

"I want you to go there with me now."

"Am I to have no lunch?"

"Of course you are. Did Martha set a place for me?"

"Don't you ever have any food at your house, you leech?"

An hour later, Labrique was marching down the sidewalk, his

116

hands behind his back and Baudruche at his side. Did Baudruche want to hear something funny? He'd just received a letter from the Prefect asking him to take on a big job, a building. . . .

"For the Factory?"

"Much better than that. It's for the rats! Yes, my friend, I am to build them a house, a palace, in the middle of the City. They love us, and they want to be closer to us. What do you think of that?"

"I was expecting it. Well, at least you have something to keep you busy for a while."

"I'll be busy a long time. It's a big assignment and requires a lot of thought. The Prefect says money's no object. He says it's going to give us cultural prestige. In that case, I can't fail him."

"You will accept?"

"With enthusiasm. Because I know no one will understand the problem better than I, and I don't have a ghost of an idea as yet. It's funny; the more I think about it the less I can figure it out. I don't know what's the matter with me."

"For once, I advise you not to hurry."

They had arrived at the foot of the ramparts.

"On the other hand, I think I've hit on a good idea for up here. Could you lend me about fifty of your men for a day?"

"I think so. Want them to bring brooms?"

"Wait. Take a look."

There were large stains all over the stones of the sentry walk. Baudruche put on his glasses: they were ants, obviously crushed under someone's heel.

"Yes, I did that this morning. But there's something much more interesting over here. Come and look."

Labrique leaned over the ramparts, swept the outside wall with his hand and came up with a gelatinous, reddish pulp.

"Do you know what this is, Baudruche?"

"No, but it looks disgusting."

"You eat it every day. It's jam."

"Jam? Whatever for?"

"I said, lean over."

About a yard below, Baudruche made out a long, colored band that stretched about fifty feet in either direction. It looked black toward the bottom. The ants had gotten stuck in it. Their invasion had been put to rout by a layer of jam!

"What do you say, Baudruche?"

"I say that, for an intellectual, you're not so stupid."

"And do you know that I did it all by myself with one bucket of jam. Tomorrow, if I can have your men, we can smear the whole length of the ramparts. That's all it will take. But the idea had to come from somewhere, right?"

"Oh, I agree completely, but I know what the Prefect's office will say."

"What will they say?"

"That it's not rational. So long, Labrique, see you tomorrow. I'm off to the Factory."

"Damn Labrique!" Baudruche said to himself as he turned into Prefect Avenue. Why hadn't he, Baudruche, had the idea? He felt a slight pang: another defeat. Head bowed and eyes downcast, he spotted a large piece of paper on the ground; it looked like a newspaper. He picked it up; it was a newspaper, but not the City's.

It was a poor thing, crudely reproduced, but the name was startling: *The Liberated Rat*. In the top left-hand corner was a childish drawing of a rat energetically breaking its chains. Underneath ran the rubric: "We shall win because we are stronger." Baudruche scanned the text. It was a collection of violent articles attacking those inhabitants of the City who harbored "evil thoughts," Baudruche's men, and on and on. Here and there, a column was interrupted by a cartoon. One of them showed a large, heavyset man, hat low over the eyes, hands in pockets; he was stamping on the rats.

"If it were only true," he said to himself.

But he took it back when he read the caption: "Big Baudruche must be crushed!"

"Very interesting," he said, as he folded the sheet and put it in his pocket.

At the Factory entrance, the rat on duty raised his cap in salute.

"Good evening, Mr. High Commissioner."

Baudruche answered with a flick of his brim.

Leponte seemed gayer than usual. His eyes sparkled and he was pink in the face.

"You look positively euphoric, Mr. Leponte."

"It must be the warmth and joy occasioned by a small intimate party here at the Factory—a farewell party for engineer Fouquet: he's the one who thought up the first modification on the machine. He's been recycled as a Director in Civilian Defense in the Technical Studies Section. You must have known about it, Mr. Commissioner?"

"Of course, of course. But aren't there five already?"

"Now they'll be six, and so there'll be more work. It's simple arithmetic, Mr. Commissioner. We scientists live with precision, and precision is the poetry of matter."

Elisa was on her way out. She was very pleased with the Hotel. They were being extremely solicitous, and the Manager himself had come to ask after her desires as she sat down at the table.

She was also pleased because her neighbor from across the hall had sat down at her table without waiting for an invitation. But when a leg went out in search of hers, she locked her legs firmly under her chair.

After lunch, Elisa went from store to store, while her luncheon companion took his usual walk to the ramparts. At the sound of his voice, the soldier looked up.

"Why do those two men come and look at the walls every day?"

"They're worried because ants are climbing up the walls and threaten to get into the City."

"There's nothing to it: burn them or drown them."

"To do that, the people would have to go outside the gates, and they don't want to do that."

"So what are they going to do?"

"They've been working on a powder of deterrence."

"What's that?"

"I don't know. Nor do they, I'm afraid. What makes it even worse is they don't know what its effect will be. Meanwhile, one of the men has come up with a scheme: he's spread jam all along the walls.

"Not a bad idea."

"But the rest of the people are going to say it isn't rational."

Baudruche was pacing back and forth, hands in pockets, as he dictated his report to Miss Bourrot.

". . . since the walls were laced with a ribbon of jam, thanks to Mr. Labrique's efforts."

Miss Bourrot looked up.

"Did I hear you correctly? You said 'jam'?"

"When I say jam, I mean jam. Continue.

"It is therefore my belief that it would be a waste of time to try to find another remedy against the insects' advance. In the best of circumstances, it would involve greater risks and be more complicated.

"I must now draw your attention to an incident we would overlook only at our peril. I chanced to pick up a newspaper entitled *The Liberated Rat*, obviously published by our neighbors. I enclose a photocopy so that you can learn the nature of its articles. They attack our institutions and our goodwill toward the rats to the point of calling your sincerity into question. I believe that a perusal of this paper will inevitably bring you to reconsider the agreement I was forced to sign with our neighbors. . . ."

Baudruche looked at Miss Bourrot while she finished the dictation. He found her particularly irritating this evening. It was probably a sign of merit that she had stuck by him so long, but by the same token, wasn't Baudruche also to be commended for putting up with her looks and character for twenty years? And what did she have to offer? Intelligence, devotion, discretion, sure, but what he needed was youth, vitality, spontaneity. . . .

"Miss Bourrot, what's all the commotion downstairs?"

"Miss Teller is leaving; she is retiring."

"Who is replacing her?"

"Miss Weller, of course. She's been her assistant for fourteen years."

"How old is she?"

"I don't really know, Mr. Commissioner. Fifty, maybe."

"That's ridiculous, Miss Bourrot! What we need is some youth in this department or it will atrophy. Why did you put Miss Niquel in a job where her dynamism and talent were wasted? That job would be much more suitable to an older woman. I want Miss Niquel brought back here starting tomorrow morning, and Miss Weller transferred to the calm of the Lost and Found Department. Is that clear, Miss Bourrot?"

She left the room without replying.

9

‛‛WHY DID you make me get up so early?" Baudruche asked Labrique.

"It's good for you; you need it. Shall we go up?"

"I can't wait!"

Baudruche was in an ugly mood. He climbed with effort, moaning at every step.

Labrique rushed past him. "Baudruche, look!"

"I'm coming, I'm coming. What's so unusual this morning?"

"Lean over and look."

The ribbon of jam stretched as far as the eye could see.

"Well, you told me you were going to do it."

"But that's not the whole of it. Put on your glasses."

Baudruche saw that immediately below the ribbon of jam the face of the wall was smooth and clean: the ants had completely disappeared.

"They've gotten the message, Baudruche! They won't come back!"

As Baudruche followed the architect, he felt a great relief at having that worry behind him.

"Where did you find all that jam, Labrique?"

"Your men and I cleaned out every store in the City. Here are the receipts; I'd like to be reimbursed, if you don't mind."

An hour later, Elisa was awakened by the sound of shrill cries, running feet and a series of blows outside her room. She jumped out of bed, slipped into her dressing gown and opened the door. Posey was standing in the hallway with a broom in her hand.

"What's going on, Posey?"

"Nothing, madam. Just a rat."

She stopped down and picked up an enormous gray beast by its tail. It was dead.

"Ugh! How horrible!"

"It's not horrible anymore, madam, now that it's dead. It's when they're alive that they're horrible."

"Did you kill it yourself?"

"I wasn't going to call the hangman."

"How did you do it?"

"With my broom. See, it's a big male."

Posey dangled the dead rat in Elisa's face. Elisa backed away, terrified. Suddenly she felt two arms grasp her from behind.

The occupant of room 23 said, "Posey's right. There's nothing to be scared of."

Posey walked off, her broom in one hand, the rat in the other.

"Come, pull yourself together. You must get used to rats, for I'm afraid we're going to be seeing a lot of them from now on."

The occupant of 23 pushed the occupant of 26 into room 26.

Elisa stretched out on the bed; the man leaned against the wall and looked at her without speaking. She turned and hid her face in the pillow. She couldn't get the sight of the dead rat out of her mind. She had never seen a rat before except in pictures. She had no idea they were so ugly. She glanced at the man out of the corner of her eye. He was smiling at her. All

124

of a sudden, she let out a scream. She thought a rat was biting her in the crotch.

The man came over to her. "What's the matter?"

She buried her head deeper into her pillow. The man sat down beside her and grasped her shoulder. She thought she was about to go through the sex scene that preceded her departure from home. She fought back.

"I don't want to! Leave me alone!"

She flailed the air even though he had let go of her. She was kicking and punching first the rat, then Emil. The man got up and left, closing the door behind him. Her body shook with uncontrollable spasms, then she began to cry. There was a knock on the door and Posey entered.

"Madam, you mustn't get into a state over such a small thing. It's the first rat I've ever seen in the Hotel. I come from the country, you know, and you should have seen them there!"

Elisa barely listened, but Posey's voice calmed her. The maid put her tray on the bed and begged her to eat.

"You know, if you don't kill the first one, the next day there'll be two, the day after three, then a hundred, and in the end, they'll be the masters. We should hang them by their tails outside the Hotel. That would put an end to it."

Posey left when she saw that Elisa was back to normal. Alone again, Elisa took a deep breath. It had been a close call. It was when a woman was scared that she was most vulnerable. Thank God, Emil's face had come to her rescue. Besides, she didn't feel like it. She knew she'd have to do it with the Commissioner eventually—especially since she needed money so desperately. Maybe she should get it over with now? She had a perfect excuse.

Her breakfast finished, she picked up the receiver and called Baudruche's number. She told the Commissioner she had to see him, that very morning. She described in detail the drama that had taken place in the hall. To her surprise, Baudruche became very excited: he was on his way; he'd be right over.

125

Before he hung up she slipped in a breathless, "I can't wait to see you."

Baudruche hurried to the Hotel, oblivious to his aching feet. He dashed past the doorman and Mr. Baidroume and took the stairs three at a time. He knocked on the door of number 26 and opened it without waiting for an answer. Elisa was in the midst of dressing. She jumped with surprise.

"Are you here already? You frightened me."

"You're frightening me. Where is it?"

"Where is what?"

"The dead rat."

"I have no idea," Elisa said, irritated by Baudruche's stubborn interest in the rat. "You'll have to ask Posey, the maid."

"What? Posey again?"

"Why? Do you know her?"

"It's my business to know everybody. Ring for her."

The room was stifling. He took off his coat and sank into a chair. Posey was soon there.

"Are you here again? What brings you this time, Mr. Commissioner?"

"That was a brave piece of work you did this morning."

Posey looked confused.

"What do you mean? I did what I'm supposed to—bring the trays, do the rooms . . ."

"Don't play innocent. You killed a rat."

"So what?"

Baudruche knew the consequences for the City if the news of the rat's death got around, how it would be exploited, the excesses it would set in motion, the blackmail aimed at the Prefect, the latter's concessions, while he—Baudruche—would be forced either to take his side and deal harshly with Posey or rebel openly against the Prefect—which is what he dreaded most.

"Who's seen the dead rat? Who knows about this?"

126

"Well, there's me, of course, and madam there, then the gentleman across the hall. . . ."

"Number twenty-three?"

"I see you remember the number. . . ."

So Posey and the stranger were crossing his path again? It must be a put-up job.

"Where did you put the dead rat?"

"In the garbage can. Where did you want me to put it?"

Hoping he wouldn't be seen, Baudruche took the back stairs down to the alley where the garbage cans were kept. With Posey's help, he carefully examined their contents.

"You're absolutely sure you put him in here?"

"I'm not a fool."

"What happened to him then?"

"Somebody must have taken him for his fur . . . or maybe the other rats carried him off." Posey burst out laughing.

He felt like slapping the insolent girl for making a joke of what he feared most: that the rat had been removed by its friends.

"Go back to work and don't you dare mention any of this or you'll be sorry!"

"Why should I? I have more interesting things to talk about."

Baudruche returned to Elisa's room. He didn't try to hide his distress. He warned her of disastrous consequences if the incident wasn't hushed up. She must say nothing.

He was sure of Elisa, fairly sure of Posey, but number 23 was a question mark. He would get to him in due course. But first he must get his hands on the dead rat.

Elisa tried to change the direction of his thought.

"You see how smart you were to come to me or you wouldn't have known about it."

True enough; for once, Elisa had been useful.

Elisa continued, "I was thinking of something else. . . ."

"What?"

The sharpness of his response unnerved her. She realized she had chosen an inopportune moment.

Baudruche fixed her with his eyes. "Put something on, Elisa. You'll catch cold."

Reluctantly, she slipped into her blue dressing gown, understanding less and less of what was going on.

Baudruche's thoughts took a sharp turn. "Ah, yes, you wanted to talk to me. Is it what you mentioned the last time? Yes, I'm very pleased with what you've done. Here."

He took some bills from his wallet and handed them to her. Better than nothing, but not as much as she'd hoped for. She mentioned her considerable expenses, but Baudruche only smiled. He'd give her more the next time if he was pleased with her work.

That was her opening. She sat down on the rug at his feet, placed her head in his lap and hugged his legs.

"Maybe I could do something else for you. . . ."

The Commissioner lifted her chin with his hand.

"Elisa, you must be dreaming."

Abashed, she sat back on her heels, put her face in her hands and broke into sobs. Then she told him everything: what she'd understood—he could laugh if he liked—but that's what she thought he wanted. Between sobs, she confessed to her string of debts on Prefect Avenue.

Baudruche sighed. God but she was stupid! Worse than he'd thought. He lectured to her, scolded her as if she were a child, but her tears tempered his harshness. Finally, he got to his feet, picked up his hat and coat and opened the door. Then he turned and said, "Listen: if you find that dead rat, I'll pay all your debts."

He closed the door, leaving her sad and perplexed. She had bungled it, and it could have been so simple. . . .

The Commissioner knocked on number 23, first making certain that no one was watching. Thank God the man was there.

The interview was quickly over. Baudruche was pleasant, the

stranger understanding. He found the whole thing amusing and promised he would divulge nothing of what had happened. He was particularly happy to be at home for the Commissioner because he had run out of money. The City was expensive, and while Elisa had been doing the shops for ladies on Prefect Avenue, he'd been patronizing the stores for men. Baudruche parted with the last of his money.

As he left the Hotel, Mr. Baidroume gave him a conspiratorial wink: the Commissioner had been collecting his dividends.

Upstairs, the stranger was about to leave his room when he had a sudden thought. He went back, locked the bottom drawer of his bureau and put the key in his pocket. Not that the rat would run away. . . . But there did seem to be a certain amount of snooping in this Hotel. . . .

Not unusually, Baudruche had dozed off in his chair after lunch. He shook himself awake and left in a hurry, for he had a great deal to do. He walked with a light step, already tasting the pleasure of his coming interview with the representative of the rats at the Social Progress.

The guard at the door made way for him. Baudruche looked up: the café sign was gone. In its place was a brand-new inscription indicating that it was now an embassy—the official headquarters of a foreign government. Inside, files and cartons had replaced the bottles on the bar; on the old marble-topped tables, rats were trying to type on ancient dusty machines. Baudruche was ushered into the back room which had been converted into an office for the head of the delegation.

The delegate expressed great joy at the Commissioner's visit and thanked him for approving the Rathouse, as he had just read in the newspaper.

Baudruche sat down without replying, took out the newspaper he had picked up off the sidewalk and threw it on the rat's desk.

"Do you recognize this?"

The delegate unfolded the paper slowly.

"Yes, Mr. High Commissioner, unfortunately I do. And I'm truly sorry that it fell into your hands."

It was, he explained, the organ of a small party of extremists. "I'm sure I don't need to tell you that the great majority of our people, including myself, will have nothing to do with these fanatics." As he came to the caricature of Baudruche, he added, "I'm particularly upset on your account."

"I don't give a damn for myself. But I'd like to know how long you think this is going to go on."

The delegate was afraid that, inevitably, the paper would gain in influence because it had no competition. What they needed was a real newspaper, their own!

"Something more like yours," and he took the day's edition of the City paper from his pocket. "Another paper, but our own which, like yours, would help maintain the excellent climate that exists between us, and which in large part we owe to you, Mr. Commissioner."

Baudruche tried to protest but the delegate wouldn't allow it.

"Obviously, we will need money. I was just discussing this with your journalist, Mr. Canard, who understands the problem of underdeveloped nations better than anyone. He is going to write an article on the subject and is certain that the Prefect won't be deaf to our appeals. Besides, it's in the City's interest, since the paper will serve your point of view as well as our own."

Baudruche was seething. Would he never be able to do anything? Would the newspaper, the Prefecture and the Prefect always stand in his way? It would go on this way until the people came to their senses and rose up in arms, until Baudruche no longer felt he had to keep taking it and would finally—no, he mustn't think of that—until the day when the Prefect's eyes were opened. . . .

Suddenly there was a roaring in the distance, punctuated by explosions, screams and the sound of running feet. Baudruche rushed to the door and pushed aside a group of rats who were standing on the sill and laughing uproariously. He looked out. Smoke was billowing from the direction of the Factory.

He raced down the steps. Voices were screaming "Fire!" "Fire!" and groups of workers were fleeing in disorder. He ran faster. Flames were leaping from the windows of the Factory's main building. The whine of a siren announced the arrival of the first fire engines. He followed them into the Factory courtyard and toward the flaming workshop.

Near the door, Leponte was standing with a group of engineers, his arms stretched to the sky.

"What's this, Mr. Leponte? Arson?"

"No, Mr. Commissioner, just a small technical incident. But we should move away. The building could explode."

Baudruche made Leponte stay until the firemen had the fire under control. Then they went to the Director's office.

"Your 'small technical incident' looked pretty serious to me. What happened?"

"We were starting tests on the machine with the latest improvements when it began to heat up to a degree none of us—not even I, Mr. Commissioner—could have foreseen. The lubricating oil caught fire, the flames reached the walls and you know the rest. It's a catastrophe."

"Let's not exaggerate, Mr. Leponte. The fire is out, the City has not gone up in flames. Or at least not yet."

"But it has nothing to do with the City, Mr. Commissioner. It's our productivity!"

Leponte got up and went over to the enormous graph covering one entire wall of the office. He shook his head sadly. Then he returned to his desk, dropped into his chair and buried his head in his hands.

"It's Waterloo!"

"Well then, Mr. Leponte, I think there's nothing left for you but to resign and hand over your job to someone more competent."

Leponte sat bolt upright.

"Resign? Never, Mr. Commissioner. I'll put the situation to rights. The productivity curve will rise again. Reassure the Prefect, I beg you. Tell him that it was just a small technical incident totally beyond my control. It was all the fault of the lubricating oil."

While Baudruche was heading back to his office to write his daily report, the last refugee was going to the ramparts for his evening chat with the man below.

The soldier raised his head.

"What's new in the City?"

"What drama! They killed a rat."

"So they're finally getting around to it."

"No, it's a 'she' who did it. A girl."

"She had guts."

"Right. I'm beginning to wonder if the women don't have more guts than the men in here."

"But what's the drama?"

"They're afraid the rats may find out about it."

"Maybe that'll make the rats think twice."

"Yes, but they don't want them to get angry."

"That's a lot of crap!"

"What are you doing, soldier?"

"I'm looking for lice, and I'm going to kill them, not make friends with them."

"Where did you get them?"

"Here, last night. It wasn't their fault, but they were a crummy lot."

"Who were?"

"The soldiers who passed by here last night. It was raining buckets, see, and they were soaked and muddy. I ate with them and one of them asked me:

132

" 'D'you think they'll hold out?'

" 'Who?'

" 'Those guys,' he said, pointing to the City.

" 'I don't think so,' I told him.

"They all started to laugh. I said:

" 'I'm not kidding. It's very serious.'

"Somebody blew a whistle, they went off to get their guns, then started marching again, still bitching about the mud. At the same time, they started to sing, if you could call it singing."

"What did they sing? The 'Marseillaise'?"

"No. 'Madelon.' "

"It's the same thing. What happened then?"

"They marched straight ahead, but I think they got sucked up in the mud."

"They didn't leave you anything?"

"No, they could see I had everything I needed."

"You don't really need anything?"

"Now that you mention it, yes. I'd like some paper."

"Paper? What for?"

"Guess."

"Here, catch."

"What's this? There's printing on it."

"It's the prospectus for their machine."

"Come, come, let's get on with it, Miss Bourrot. Are you dreaming or what? Continue.

"Having completed the manufacture of both the new part and the old one which was prematurely scrapped, it was decided to subject these parts to tests. Due to an excess of speed, the machine became superheated which caused it to catch fire.

"As a result of this incident which, according to Mr. Leponte, was 'entirely unforseen in that it failed to conform to production norms,' the Director has decided to scrap the recently manu-factured new part and return to the original part which means that the earlier model can still be presented to our clientele as an improved model with only the slightest change in the prospectus.

"Obviously, we must waste no time in recycling the young engineer responsible for the most recent modification. His overlong tenure at the Factory is sufficient explanation of his inability to adapt to new techniques.

"The weather report indicates no change.

"The sentry heard the sound of many footsteps at the base of the walls, some singing. They saw nothing.

"That is all, Miss Bourrot. When you finish it, you can go. Oh, tell Miss Niquel I want her to come up. I have something I want to dictate to her. She can do it faster than you."

Little Miss Niquel went to work with dispatch, just as she had on the floor below. And she was very knowledgeable about the City.

She made so bold as to say that there was a lot of talk about the Commissioner's great generosity to someone named Elisa Poulet.

Good God, how stupid of him! Of course everybody thought Elisa was his mistress! Had he been so preoccupied with the City's affairs that it had never occurred to him? He looked straight at Miss Niquel:

"So?"

She didn't know what to say and looked at him unhappily. Hadn't he gotten the point? It was the normal thing. . . . He opened his drawer, counted out a few bills, hesitated a moment, then took out the whole lot.

"Here, you go out and buy yourself some clothes too."

She flung her arms around his neck.

"Thank you, my Commissioner. You're much more generous than Leponte!"

Nothing could have caused him greater pleasure.

Elisa was careful not to go downstairs for dinner until she knew her neighbor was there. Then she took a table in an opposite corner of the room. He had told her at lunch that he

134

had no money of his own. What did she want with a man without money?

As soon as he had finished his meal, the man left. It was ten o'clock. He seldom came home before midnight. She stood up. There was no one in the lobby. She took the key to number 23 and crept up the stairs like a thief. The hall was deserted. She went up to room 23, her heart thumping in her breast. With any luck, there must be something in that room worth money to the Commissioner; she needed it so badly.

The door opened without a sound. She walked in. There was a little light from the lamp on the bedside table. Someone was asleep in the bed. It was Posey! Elisa closed the door carefully and ran down the stairs. Still no one in the lobby. She hung the key to 23 on its hook and took her own.

Back in her room, she fell on her bed, buried her head in the pillow and punched it with her fists. All men were pigs, all of them, all of them! That's all they ever thought about.

10

"ISN'T IT CHILLY this morning, Labrique?"

"Not surprising. The warm days are over. There's not a soul on the ramparts. They've gone, just like the ants—thanks to me."

"I know, I know. You act as if it were some great exploit. It didn't cost you much, you know."

"It cost me a great deal. You'd be amazed how expensive jam is. I wish the Prefect would hurry up and pay me back. And while we're on that subject, I just had a letter from the Prefecture. They telephoned yesterday and asked how I was getting on with the Rathouse project. I told them I hadn't thought it through yet. So they wrote giving me an extension. A very nice letter. They must really need me! They said that the building would redound to my glory, that it would always bear my name. . . . Do I give a shit? Fortunately, I have no children, but in another twenty years, there may still be a few decent people around who'll look at the damn thing and say: 'So that bastard Labrique built it for them.' No thanks. I'd rather resign."

Baudruche thought for a moment.

"It's quite possible they'll ask you to do that very thing, then offer the job to somebody else. The results will be the same."

"Maybe so. But at least they won't be able to attach my name to it."

Baudruche felt as if he'd been kicked in the groin. Labrique's name wouldn't be attached to anything connected with the City's enemies, but what about his name? Not to a building but to something far worse: the most cowardly policies the City had ever practiced—policies of abdication and surrender. If later on, when nothing remained of the City, another Montesquieu came along to write of its granduer and decadence, who would figure in it? Baudruche. And what would they say about him? That he'd been a son-of-a-bitch. Oh, they'd use nobler, more refined words; in elegant language, a son-of-a-bitch is a traitor.

"I see no solution," he said firmly, his back to the parapet.

"To the Rathouse? No, I don't either," Labrique replied.

"No, I mean for me."

"Are you by any chance beginning to reflect, Baudruche? It's none too soon, you know."

Baudruche turned his back and was silent. He looked at the soldier sitting motionless as always, his eyes on the horizon. Not everybody had the luck to be a soldier. Those men did their job without asking questions, just so long as nobody asked them to step out of their role. They didn't have to keep asking themselves if they shouldn't have done this instead of that. . . .

He was soon back at his office, hat brim turned down and ready for battle. Miss Bourrot had better watch it; he was in no mood for her.

"Mr. Commissioner . . ."

"What do you want?"

Miss Bourrot had something for him: a note from the Prefect. Baudruche opened the envelope. It was as he feared: a retreat on all fronts. The rats were to have their newspaper . . . a remarkable idea. . . . An ideal outlet for the City's propaganda. The Prefect's own ideas disseminated among their ex-enemies through their own efforts! Baudruche was to drop by the chief delegate's, or have him come to his office to make the final arrangements—always keeping in mind the City's interests, of course, but with no haggling over details.

Another dirty job. Why didn't the Prefect do it himself? No, he would let the rats walk all over him. They were that clever, the scum! Baudruche would try to keep the damage to a minimum; it was all he could do. He was about to pick up his coat and leave. Then he decided it would be better to face the rat after lunch. Eating helped him to think.

"Elisa is stopping by after lunch," Martha said.

"Has she anything important to report?"

"I don't think so."

"Then what does she want?"

Martha would have liked to know too. She was beginning to think that her husband had been showing undue interest in Elisa. Besides, this story of the man who needed watching was pretty suspect. Weren't there professionally trained people for that? Why did Robert have to take a woman away from her own home? And why this one? He'd known her twelve years, and for twelve years he'd treated her as if she were a fool. Now suddenly . . . It must be a case of September love.

The Commissioner left soon after Elisa arrived—but not before Martha could see how uncomfortable Elisa seemed in her husband's presence.

As soon as the two women were alone, Martha started to talk about her husband: how nervous and upset he seemed. . . . Then, surprisingly, she asked Elisa what she thought of the Commissioner.

"Martha, you know that I never see him except on your account, because he's your husband."

139

Martha couldn't think of what to say. Elisa advised Martha to stop worrying about her husband.

"But it's normal that I should worry about Robert, Elisa. Don't you ever worry about Emil?"

Elisa shrugged and her mouth turned down.

Martha persisted. "Are things not going well between you and Emil, Elisa?"

Elisa examined her fingers.

"It's nothing, really. We just don't get along anymore."

"What about Sophie? What will become of her? Do you still see her?"

Elisa looked at her lacquered nails.

"I don't really have the time, with all I'm doing for the Commissioner." She laughed dryly. "She probably spends all her time arguing with her father."

Martha hesitated for a moment then made a suggestion: Why didn't Elisa let her look after Sophie while she was involved in this investigation? Martha could make her feel at home; she had all the time in the world. And the Commissioner adored children, even if he wouldn't admit it.

Elisa reexamined her fingernails. Well, why not? If it didn't put them out too much. So far as she was concerned, she had nothing against it.

There was nothing more to say. Martha saw Elisa to the door, trying to appear as friendly as before.

Elisa thought as she walked, but reflection made her suffer. Something had irritated her during the visit.

Why did Martha have all the things she lacked? Elisa was certainly no stupider; she was prettier and probably ten years younger. Martha must be forty at least. But if Martha wanted her daughter, let her have her. What did it matter where she was. . . .

Posey was smiling as she walked back from the ramparts with her empty basket. The man in 23 was right: it had been great fun and the soldier was comical. He reminded her of the ones who sometimes passed through her village when she was small. Whenever a troup stopped in her parents' village, her father or mother sent her off with a basket of food and wine. They were impressed with soldiers in those days. The soldiers often accompanied her and her basket home so that they could thank her parents. Sometimes they even carried her on their shoulders. That made her very proud.

She was sad when the soldiers left. Especially one tall one with curly black hair. When would a new lot come? Her parents didn't know. "The soldiers will come back if you're a good girl. . . ."

Well, she hadn't been that for a long time. And only one of them had returned. The man in 23 told her about him one morning when she was barely awake and crawling out of his bed to go to work. She'd been eager to see the soldier. And her lover was pleased that she still remembered soldiers. So, he sent her to the ramparts with two sets of orders and a full basket.

She sat down in a turret, her basket next to her, legs dangling over the side. She made crumbs of the bread and threw them in the air, calling out, "Here, birdies, here birdies. . . ."

It didn't take them long. A big flock came winging over from one of the nearer villages and swooped down to pick up the crumbs as they fell into the moat.

The soldier got up and walked to below where she was sitting. He said:

"What are you doing up there?"

"I'm feeding bread to the birds. It's so the rats won't get it."

"Funny. My grandmother used to say 'It's so the Prussians won't get it.' "

"It's the same thing. Only, there are more rats."

"Who told you that?"

"The man who sent me here."

"To feed the birds?"

"And soldiers. Here; catch!"

Posey took a long rope from her basket, tied it to the handle and slowly lowered it into the soldier's outstretched hands.

"What's left is for you."

"It's high time. I was beginning to get hungry. All I have to eat is what I pick up from the people who pass by here at night."

"I guess that isn't much. Well, do you have any messages for the man who sent me?"

"Tell him, thanks. Though he's only doing what he's supposed to. It's up to civilians to feed soldiers."

Posey leaned out as far as she dared and motioned the soldier to come closer. She cupped her hands over her mouth and asked with some embarrassment:

"Listen: you haven't seen a tall dark soldier with curly hair—very good looking? I'd like to know where he is."

"He's gone for good. I'm the only soldier left."

Posey cried as she walked down the rampart stairs, but the main street was long and she was laughing by the time she reached the Hotel.

Baudruche was not laughing. He was at the ex-Social Progress, trying to win an argument with the delegate—who was now "Mr. President."

"I was elected yesterday by popular vote, Mr. Commissioner —with ninety-six point eight percent of the votes cast. Naturally, I'd like to have been elected unanimously, but we have an opposition too, as do all real republics. Those votes belonged to the small party of extremists I told you about earlier, the same ones who publish that infamous newspaper you had the misfortune to find on the sidewalk. There are black sheep in every group, Mr. Commissioner. . . ."

But, he went on, thanks to the Prefect, and obviously the Commissioner, everything was going to be put to rights. Yes, he'd been given his subsidy, and he expected to put out the first copy of the newspaper in the very near future. There was just one small hitch.

"What is it?" Baudruche asked nervously.

They had no printing presses, no equipment. . . . How could the President fight that miserable rag—*The Liberated Rat*—if the means at his disposal were inferior to theirs? A mimeographed sheet would be unworthy of their republic and could hardly compete with *The Liberated Rat*. They must go into battle with better equipment.

"You, Mr. Commissioner, can make this possible."

"By doing what?"

"Without going to any trouble at all. You have presses lying idle—the ones on which *"The Independent"* was printed before your newspaper swallowed it up. It's such a small thing that I don't suppose you even need to ask the Prefect. A simple authorization from you will do the trick, Mr. Commissioner."

Baudruche gnashed his teeth at the veiled threat of the Prefect's intercession.

The President continued: They would not accept this capital outlay for nothing. They were a proud people. Poor, but honest. They would be responsible for the maintenance of the building and the machines, and in addition would pay an interest rate of one and one half percent of the building's value, this last to be determined jointly.

Baudruche was reduced to minor defensive tactics.

"Do you have the money to pay us?"

"Where would we find money? We are rich only in hope, Mr. Commissioner. We will pay you out of our recent federal loan."

"What is your collateral?"

The President appeared stunned by the question.

"The collateral? Why, the loan you are about to make to us. It's all been agreed on. Now you see how productive our collaboration is for both of us. Had the Prefect refused us this loan, you would have refused payment out of our own funds (don't laugh, Mr. Commissioner, it's perfectly understandable). In that case, I would have been unwilling to use your printing presses because I couldn't pay you back, I wouldn't be able to print our newspaper, *The Liberated Rat* would increase its circulation, thereby strengthening the extremist opposition which would finally take over and we'd be back in the old days of hatred and violence. There's nothing like mutual aid, is there, Mr. Commissioner?

"While we're on the subject of aid, we have a serious problem. Like you, Mr. Commissioner, I am deeply shocked by the provocations in our extremists' newspaper. But you must try to understand these people: poverty is a poor counselor, Mr. Commissioner, and too many of our people suffer from poverty. Your donations of food provide a mere drop of water in our sea of distress. We can only relieve the want among the people who live in the immediate vicinity of the Factory. The rest feel frustrated and are growing restive. And that is why a copy of *The Liberated Rat* turns up in your path.

"The time has come to extend your alimentary aid to our entire population. Only then can we build a just and lasting peace based on mutual aid and generosity. . . . You don't appear to be convinced, Mr. Commissioner? I'm so very sorry our Mr. Canard isn't here. He's more eloquent than I am on the subject of oppressed people. But in any event the food deliveries can be increased by easy stages. We are a patient people, Mr. Commissioner!"

That was about it. The President reminded Baudruche of the urgency for getting the Rathouse under way: their need for living space was growing desperate, for it was hard to expand without inconveniencing their neighbors. . . . It would be wise to speed things up in order to avoid unnecessary friction.

As he made for the door, Baudruche said to himself: "The

144

next time, he'll ask for my watch and my wallet and tell me it's in my interest to hand them over."

On the doorstep, the President startled Baudruche by giving him a hug and saying in ringing tones:

"Mr. Commissioner, together we are preparing for our mutual future."

There was a blinding explosion of flashbulbs and Mr.Canard emerged from the crowd. The President addressed him under his breath:

"I'll be all yours in a moment, dear friend."

Two or three hundred people had gathered around the ex-café. Shouts of "Hurray for Baudruche!" went up, and a woman thrust a bouquet into Baudruche's hands.

The daily visit to the Factory, which he used to find so irritating, had become a pleasant interlude of light banter compared to his larger torments. Besides, the recent difficulties with the machine and the fire at the Factory had put Baudruche in the driver's seat. He could have forced Leponte to resign or even had him dismissed, but what was the point? Another Leponte would have taken his place, since only Lepontes were left in the City. Of course, the best solution would have been the complete destruction of the Factory. That would have brought peace for a while. But the firemen had botched that one. . . .

At that moment, the stranger from the Hotel was scaling the ramparts.

"What's new down there, soldier?"

"You know damn well there's nothing new down here; nothing moves until night. Though I did have a visitor today: a girl, but she stayed up on the ramparts where you are."

"She brought you something to eat?"

"If you know everything, why do you bother me with all these questions?"

"I can't help knowing about her because I'm the one who sent her."

"Why don't you tell her to come keep me company? That would help pass the time."

"I can't. I need her inside."

"Maybe she has a sister?"

The man laughed:

"I don't know. It's not likely, but I'll ask her. What happened last night? They say they heard footsteps and singing."

"It was pretty much like the night before. There was still this fog. Then I saw soldiers marching past. It was pouring and there was deep mud all around. They were trying to stay in line, but at a given moment, they stopped and piled up arms. It was then I saw they were wearing greenish uniforms. They were Krauts. They asked me if I wanted to eat with them. I couldn't refuse, but their grub was terrible! I told them:

" 'This is worse than yesterday's.'

"They asked me who'd given me food the night before. I told them. They looked interested.

" 'They're the ones we're looking for. We're supposed to join up with them.'

"A sergeant started to shout and they left with their guns.

"They started singing—'Lili Marlene.' It isn't as good as 'Madelon,' but it's not a bad song. They disappeared just like the others did."

"Did they leave you anything?"

"Yes. An Iron Cross."

Baudruche was dictating his report. Among other things, he had to answer the Prefect's note of concern about the last refugee and his vast wealth.

"Mr. Prefect:

"There is no need whatever to worry about the man in question. The information I have would indicate that he is mentally retarded. He has confined himself to aimless walks around the City and seems uninterested in anything but himself. The only danger is that he may place his bank notes in circulation, but he has kept his word as we have kept ours. You have seen from the receipts affixed to my reports that I have been very careful to make sure he lacks for nothing.

"As for the Factory, Mr. Leponte desires you to know that, in view of the recent raise in wages, bonuses, new compensation, and the losses occasioned by the conflagration and by the two successive improvements, he will be forced to increase substantially the price of the machine. He does not anticipate any difficulty, since the old model will be presented as a modernized, functionalized and personalized machine, and its cabinet will be quite different from last year's.

"That is all, Miss Bourrot. Add the usual weather report and the report of the sentries. . . . What do they say today? They heard the sound of many footsteps at the base of the walls, singing. . . . Isn't that what they reported yesterday? They must be drunk. Type it up, and see that it gets to the Prefect right away. After that, why don't you go out and kick up your heels?"

"Who is that brat, Martha? You had a daughter and didn't tell me?"

"I think even you would have noticed, Robert. No, it's Elisa's daughter. I thought she'd be better off here than at her house."

"It's made clear to me every day that I'm no longer master of the City, but I did think I was still master in my own house. What am I supposed to do with her?"

"Nothing, my dear. All I ask is that you don't drive her crazy."

"She'll manage that all by herself. It runs in the family."

The door opened. It was Labrique. Martha had already told him that they had taken in Sophie Poulet.

"I didn't know you'd been carrying on with Elisa for such a long time. The girl is the spitting image of you."

147

11

‘‘S O T H E Y give you no peace, Labrique?"

"I had another call from the Prefecture this morning. They're digging their spurs into my ass."

"I had a brief confidential note from the Prefect myself; he wants me to keep an eye on you. He thinks you're looking for ways to thwart his policies. I answered that I could vouch for your good faith as if it were my own."

"That isn't saying much."

"This is serious, Labrique. When the Prefect gets angry, he can be mean. Send them something, a plan, a drawing, anything."

"I don't have an idea in my head. But I'll come up with something someday."

"By then, I may not be able to help you. It'll be too late. I didn't want to have to tell you, but the Prefect said he's going to fire you if you don't change your attitude."

"He won't have the pleasure, Baudruche. See, I've already taken care of it. Make sure it gets to him, will you, and also convey my total indifference and contempt. May he go to hell. . . ."

"What is this?"

"My resignation."

"Listen; think it over. Try to come up with something."

"It's useless; save your breath. So long as they were giving me merely ridiculous jobs to do, I did them. But now they're asking me to cross the frontier and work for the enemy. And I'm refusing. I may not be much of a hero, but show me a bigger one around here."

"Me."

"You? What's so damn heroic about what you're doing? It seems to me you're aiding the enemy. I saw the newspaper last night with that big picture of you hugging their President. And that caption: 'Commissioner Baudruche says "We are preparing for our mutual future." ' "

"I didn't say that; he did. And I'll bet it was that Canard who attributed it to me."

"O.K., then; get them to correct it in today's paper."

"You know that's impossible."

"And you know damn well that the moment the inhabitants of the City read that, they decide: if Baudruche can do it, we can too. Do you know what you mean to them—loyalty, honor, patriotism—all those words you don't even know the meaning of anymore."

Baudruche blushed. "You're going a little far, Labrique. You have no right to say that."

"Who will if I don't? You are encouraging the great mass of people to be even weaker and more susceptible then they are already, thanks to the machine—that daily dose of opium you and your crowd provide. When this business with the rats first started, opinion was pretty well divided. There were people who thought the rats should be resisted and pushed back down their sewer holes. But when they saw that you did nothing, they decided they didn't have to either. The others, the majority, wanted only peace, peace at any price and were afraid you were going to involve them in another war. Now that they see you bleating for peace and hugging the rats, they're delighted. Put yourself in their place. You used to be unpopular in the City. It is my sad duty to inform you that you are no longer. . . ."

Baudruche was silent, his eyes on the old paving stones. He knew there was some truth in what Labrique was saying. But if Baudruche had not been there, things might have been far worse. He rebelled.

"You'll never make me believe that an honest, intelligent and patriotic man in my position isn't more useful to the City than a no-good, stupid, cowardly . . ."

"On the contrary. The man you have just described is useful only when he acts out his honesty, intelligence and patriotism."

"What do you want me to do?"

"I'm not the High Commissioner. You ought to know. I think I've said enough."

Labrique looked at his friend and Baudruche looked at the ground. They remained in this position for a long time, silent, not moving. Then Labrique tapped Baudruche on the shoulder.

"I'm off. I'm through with the ramparts."

"I know; that's always the way. You leave me to face the burden that's gradually crushing me. Yet I do everything in my power . . ."

Labrique stopped and said with a dry laugh, "What about my jam? I haven't been paid for the jam."

"The Prefecture informed me that they were very sorry but they couldn't find any appropriation that provided for such an expense."

Labrique walked away, shouting over his shoulder: "They're all crooks . . . nothing but a bunch of crooks!"

Baudruche sat in his turret for a long time. Little by little, everybody who had shared his ideas had changed them or disappeared. Now, his oldest, dearest friend was deserting him. Baudruche looked at the vast City at his feet and felt as if it were gathering up its forces and pushing him to the very edge of the ramparts. One small shove and he'd fall in the moat. He moved away; it made him dizzy to know there was nothing behind him, nothing to give him support.

"Miss Bourrot, will you please ask Mr. Leponte to send Emil Poulet over right away."

Baudruche opened his mail, glanced at the notes from the Prefecture, and returned to his reflections as he waited for Elisa's husband. Labrique was right: he too had noticed how the population's attitude toward him had changed. The hostile, suspicious looks of old were gone; now he was met with timid smiles, heads nodded in his direction, an occasional hat lifted. Naïvely, he had thought it was due to a change in the people's feelings, but Labrique had understood it right away. The people were friendlier because they thought Baudruche had changed. Like a fool, he'd been pleased and gratified. Now he felt shame.

But at least he had an idea for Labrique's successor—not for the ramparts, of course, but for the Rathouse.

Emil did not cut a proud figure as he entered. He was frightened. This office held bad memories for him. The last time, he had feared the worst: brutal punishment or the loss of his job. Not that it would have meant a financial loss; the Factory paid its artists poorly. Only the mechanics were well paid—those soulless materialists.

No, it wasn't the money but the fact that at last he'd found a means of self-fulfillment through contact with the masses. That was why, once he'd calmed down, he decided to write the letter of apology to Baudruche. To his relief, he had heard nothing more—except a few snide remarks about his wife from his colleagues. What then could the Commissioner want from him today?

"Emil Poulet, you are an artist! No, no, don't try to contradict me. I know something about these things. I used to paint a little myself. I saw your design for the latest machine at the Factory. It's a triumph! You get better every year. It makes me wonder if this job is worthy of your talents. You're capable of greatness. Which gave me an idea. You must have some ideas about architecture?"

Ideas? The Commissioner must be joking. He explained that he'd long since moved beyond that materialistic art. Not that he despised it. One must never despise something which can render the essence of life sublime. But he spat on architecture as it had been practiced heretofore. Had he concerned himself with architecture, he would have thrown everything to the winds and started from scratch.

"What you've just said is very interesting. It was an inspiration on my part to have you come. You are exactly the man I need, Poulet. Now, this is what I have in mind. . . ."

Yes, Emil Poulet was interested in the Rathouse project, but only on condition that he had a completely free hand, and that he be given a team of technicians to realize his concepts.

Well, that's exactly what the Commissioner intended to do. He expected no opposition from the Prefect. Poulet could go to work right away, as soon as his year's work at the Factory was completed.

"I'll telephone him immediately to say that you've been transferred to the City's Department of Architecture. Success is around the corner, my friend; the future is yours. You may well end up as chief architect of the City."

They concluded the session with a sense of mutual gratification. Baudruche had his misfit—the dreamer and megalomaniac he needed. He knew Emil had tried everything: irresponsible art, instinctive art, and art art. No wall he built could possibly stand up. As for Emil, he had found his second chance. He wouldn't let this one get away! He could see the Rathouse already: a vast, streamlined, unsubstantial, almost diaphanous monument soaring into the sky—where the old market had stood.

153

With a single stroke, he had turned all forgiveness. More than that: he had erased Elisa's adventure from his mind. Men like Baudruche and he were above considerations of the flesh. He'd forgive Elisa everything if she'd come back. He would forget his old-fashioned, bourgeois prejudices.

An hour later, he was packing up his effects at the Factory and saying farewell to his colleagues as he sang the Commissioner's praises. But on the way to his new post at the Department of Architecture, a thought struck him. Was this offer Baudruche's way of making up for the moral wrong the Commissioner had done him? He couldn't be sure, but even if it were, Baudruche was a man who knew about life. If, after a while, they established a real bond (as he sincerely hoped), he might ask Baudruche to intervene with Elisa not to abandon him entirely. Then he would be completely happy. He had picked up a girl the night before and taken her home. But even with the lights out, he couldn't put Elisa in her place. She didn't rumple his hair the way Elisa did; she didn't have Elisa's way of murmuring, "My Poulet . . . my big Poulet . . ."

Elisa woke up refreshed from a good night's sleep. She rang for breakfast and ate it in bed; she could think more comfortably there. She absolutely had to get herself out of this disastrous situation. She had the superficialities: her bed and board. What she lacked were the essentials: everything else. These had to be gotten from men, obviously. She telephoned Baudruche. She asked, implored, wheedled, but nicely, timidly. The Commissioner was very kind but, quoting figures, reminded her that she had an allowance many women would have considered ample. She grew more insistent, raised her voice. . . . The Commissioner hung up.

Couldn't she find money somewhere in this Hotel? She ticked off the guests but everybody who had shown the slightest interest in her was either too old or too ugly, or even worse, already attached. Moreover, to go after another man meant giving up her bird-in-the-hand. If she appeared to lose interest in the tenant of room 23, the Commissioner would cut her off without a cent. Everyone was against her. And Emil . . . Emil was guiltiest of all, for all her troubles stemmed from him. You don't take a wife when you can't give her what she needs. As she thought of him, an idea suddenly crossed her mind. What a fool she'd been. . . .

Elisa fumbled in her bag for the key, finally found it and opened the door to the house. At this hour, Emil would be at work. She stopped in the front hall; Rutabaga, their servant, was singing in the kitchen. She crept along the hall and tiptoed up the stairs, her heart beating inside her breast. Why was she behaving this way? It was so stupid; after all, wasn't it her home? She opened the door to their room, went to the closet and took out a small metal box where they kept the housekeeping money. Wasn't it hers as much as his? And besides, there was so little left.

She was about to put the empty box back in the closet when she had another idea: the little jewel case. Why should she leave him the gold cuff links she had foolishly bought him years ago and which had cost her her eyeteeth? The money she could get for them would come in handy at Linon Taffeta's.

Baudruche was sitting across from the President. The Prefect insisted he do the negotiating himself. Other men might give in too easily.

The rat should be happy with all he'd delivered: the key to *The Independent*'s printing press, and the Prefect's agreement to all the conditions. . . .

The President answered with a smile. "I was quite certain the Prefect would accept. What I was asking for was so reasonable and modest, and the conditions were so advantageous, that you couldn't help but agree. The Prefect knows now that he's dealing with a generous and sincere people. I hope he remembers in the future. But where are we with our house? What is the architect up to?"

"He has resigned, for reasons of health."

The President frowned. Baudruche added quickly:

"I replaced him immediately with one of our most brilliant men—a dynamic, talented young man who's very enthusiastic about this assignment. He's starting this very night."

"I hope his health is better than his predecessor's. As I said before, I don't like to disturb our neighbors and we must have more space."

Once again, an appreciative audience greeted Baudruche as he emerged from the former Social Progress Café.

The President whispered in his ear, "I envy you. You don't have to deal with ingrates."

"Good evening, soldier. What happened last night? They say they heard the sound of carriages, footsteps, singing, laughter and God knows what else."

"It was quite a night all right. I was here, like always, except that I was sitting in a café by the side of a boulevard with trees, and carriages passing back and forth, and lots of people milling around.

"I was beginning to feel a little bored when suddenly an open carriage stopped in front of me. Inside was an old gentleman— spats, a straw boater, everything. Next to him was a young woman—you should have seen her!—and was she done up! She said to him:

" 'Oh, look, Edward: a soldier; Let's take him with us. As a favor to me. . . .'

" 'Emily, you know I can never refuse you anything.'

" 'Do I ever refuse you anything?'

"She raised her arm and beckoned to me.

"I jumped into the carriage. They had me sit facing them and we set off.

"She was very gay and funny. He was a cold fish, but nice all the same.

"They took me to dinner with them in a fancy restaurant. When I saw how dressed up everybody was, I felt uncomfortable in my dirty old uniform. The old man said:

" 'Don't let it bother you. You can go anywhere in a soldier's uniform.'

"At the end of dinner, she squeezed my leg and said to her gentleman:

" 'Edward, I'm tired tonight. I want to go home.'

"He left very politely. We went to her place. You should have seen that apartment! She led me into her room and I could see her talking to an old lady in the distance. The old lady asked her:

" 'Who is that?'

" 'A soldier, Mother.'

" 'Not again!'

"When she came back, she asked me:

" 'Why didn't you wear your red pants?'

" 'I can only wear the ones they give me.'

"She made me leave very early the next morning.

" 'Be careful nobody sees you.'

"That's all that happened. And here I am."

"Did she leave you anything?"

"Yes."

"What?"

"Syphilis."

It was later than usual when the last refugee left the ramparts. Baudruche was already dictating.

"It is therefore with considerable regret that I report the resignation of a man who has always rendered great service to the City, indeed one of its greatest servants.

"As a consequence, I have entrusted this most important assign-

157

ment—the building of the Rathouse—to a man of unquestioned talents with an undeniable future who will know how to give the edifice in question the symbolic elements it requires. It will hardly surprise you to learn that that man is Emil Poulet, the artist who has designed the cabinet for the machine with such singular success all these years. . . ."

Night was falling over the City on the heels of a grayish sunset. Little by little, lights began to glimmer, giving a rosy hue to the black clouds that hung obstinately over the City. People walking near the Factory heard strange songs and strident shouts of joy filtering through the closed shutters of the ex-Social Progress. A little nervous, they gave it a wide berth.

Labrique left the conjugal roof with a sigh of relief. He'd had enough. Esther Labrique refused to understand why her husband went off to dinner four times a week to a house where *she* wasn't welcome.

"Why do you do it? What do they take themselves for?"

"They take themselves for what they are, and you for what you are."

He had given in and answered her this time. Usually, he said little, but he had to say something from time to time. Five minutes after her husband's departure, Esther left too.

Labrique was attached to his habits and the familiar feel of his home, even though it included his wife's bilious presence. That's what kept him from deserting hearth and spouse for calmer refuge. Esther had proved to be more a quarreling machine than a wife. But without her, he would have been too happy at home; he would have felt guilty. Besides, she made him appreciate the Baudruches' house.

Emil Poulet hurried home to his deserted house. This time he gave little thought to Elisa's absence; his mind was on his new project and the drawings he had whipped up before the bewildered gaze of the technicians. In their opinion, the building wouldn't stand up on paper, let alone on the ground. Poulet thought they were just trying to prevent him from introducing new ideas into their moribund department. He'd get the better of them! He'd appeal to the Commissioner, and if it came to that, Baudruche would call the Prefect. . . . He drank to his success and fell asleep at the dining room table.

The soldier was lighting his fire; the two men in black in the Church interrupted their discussion long enough to nibble a few crumbs; the City—or most of it—was fixed before the machine; and Elisa was pushing open the door to the restaurant.

She sat down at a table in a far corner, already weary of the man she had been hired to get to know. She made a face; he was heading straight for her table and sat down without waiting for an invitation. He waited for her to speak; she said nothing. He tried a few words; she barely answered. As soon as dinner was over, he got up, said good night and left. She smiled; she had succeeded in boring him.

She stayed on in the restaurant, smoking one cigarette after another. Maybe she'd gone too far. She thought of the frosty expression on the Commissioner's face and it frightened her. Must she always be under his power? She rose from the table, went up to her room, opened the door, turned on the light and let out a scream: a rat was lying on her bed, his eyes staring at her.

Screaming at the top of her lungs, she ran into the hall. She felt an arm encircle her waist, a hand cover her mouth. The hand moved down and felt for her breast. She was being dragged across the hall. . . .

"Let go of me!" she said with a cry of despair.

She summoned all her strength, broke free, and instinctively ran toward the light that shone through the open door of her room. The man followed. She stumbled on her bed and fell across it, her arms outstretched. She looked up and saw the rat's face close to hers, the eyes still fixed on her. She let out another scream and sat up. This time she didn't resist as she was carried off.

It all went so fast that she was barely aware of what was happening to her. All she felt was two hands undressing her and caressing her body. The two arms picked her up and placed her in the middle of a bed that wasn't hers. She drew herself into a tight ball, her teeth chattering uncontrollably. She tried to move, to say something, but couldn't. If only she could make herself smaller, disappear. A bright light forced her eyes open; she was in room 23 and the man standing above her was laughing. She closed her eyes and buried her face in the pillow.

After a long silence, the man said, "Did you hear anything?"

She turned her head and saw that the man was now sitting and holding the strange instrument she had seen through the keyhole the other day. He seemed to be waiting for her to answer. He raised the instrument to his lips and blew into it as his fingers ran up and down the stick. He asked again, "Did you hear anything?"

She shook her head and buried it in the pillow once again.

The man said, "It doesn't surprise me."

The light went out. A moment later, the blanket was raised, letting in cold air that made her shiver. A warm body, naked like hers, pressed against her. The same arms embraced her. His warmth penetrated her and she grew calm. Her teeth stopped chattering, her nerves relaxed. The man's body began to rub against hers.

Her spirits returned. It was too late now to think, the die was cast, and besides, it was more agreeable than she had thought possible. She didn't just accept it; she desired it, wanted it again and again. She didn't recognize herself—or her gestures. Her nose buried in the hair of the man on top of her, she smelled an odor she had never smelled before. She filled her lungs with it. Something unknown was ebbing and flowing inside her. She felt hot; she felt cold. She had lost her footing, she was sinking. She tried desperately to hold on, digging her nails into his back.

160

12

TWO LIGHT knocks on the door woke Elisa the next morning. A voice from the bathroom said, "Come in." The door opened and Posey entered, carrying a tray with two breakfasts.

Elisa tried to hide under the covers but it was too late. Posey placed the tray on a table, saying, "I remembered the sieve for the hot milk, madam."

If Elisa felt humiliated to be following in the footsteps of the chambermaid, Posey was completely at ease. She picked up the four shoes scattered on the rug, looked at Elisa and said with a laugh, "This morning, you're in my place, madam, so tomorrow you take mine and shine the shoes." She closed the door behind her before Elisa could think of an answer.

The man came out of the bathroom in his dressing gown, a bathrobe over his arm. He threw it on the bed.

"Here, put this on. Isn't that Posey something!"

Barefoot and swimming in the oversized robe, Elisa sat down opposite the man. She took a piece of toast.

"Butter or jam, my darling?"

Butter. She watched him eat with rapture. His eyes which she found so beautiful now reminded her of the other pair that had terrified her the night before. She was dying to know but afraid to ask. . . .

"Were you afraid last night?" the man asked.

Posey was polishing the shoes in a closet. She didn't like to admit it but she felt sad. Still, she knew she had to expect these things. Men like him didn't stay lovers to girls like her for very long. But at least she'd had the fun of being in on the game. Without her and the second floor passkey, he wouldn't have been able to get into 26 and put the rat's body in the bed. Ugh. It had begun to smell awful in that drawer.

In room 23, Elisa had finished a large breakfast. The man pointed to her clothes scattered over the floor.

"Pick up your clothes and go get dressed."

"Yes, my darling."

But she was afraid to go into her room. She didn't want to have to look at that horrible corpse in her bed.

The man rang for the maid. "Posey, wrap up the rat in room 26 and put him in the bathroom. And don't forget to change the sheets."

The man took the strange instrument out of its case and put it to his lips. This time Elisa heard.

"I thought you would."

She had never heard the sound before. She looked at the man's back and her eyes followed the lines of his body under his clothes. She remembered the feelings he had stirred inside her the night before. Could it happen again? She got up and silently sat down behind him. She embraced him, her hands doing what his had done the night before.

He freed himself and pushed her gently but firmly toward the door.

"What are you going to do?"

162

"I'm going for a walk. But it wouldn't interest you."

"Yes it would. Please take me."

"I can't. You couldn't keep up with me."

She remained stationary by the door.

"Why did you want that rat left in my room?"

"Telephone Baudruche. He'll see that it's taken away."

He pushed her into the hall and closed the door. Elisa returned to her empty room.

Baudruche met Labrique's successor at the foot of the ramparts.

"What are you doing here, Mr. Edge?"

"I'm here to inspect the ramparts, like my predecessor."

"You do one side and I'll do the other. That way we can do the job in half the time."

Baudruche climbed the stairs ahead of him. He had little appetite for the morning ritual without Labrique.

When they reached the top of the stairs, Baudruche motioned Edge to take the right, he would do the left. He walked with slow, deliberate steps. He was disturbed. Elisa's stupidity was not to be believed. That she should have learned absolutely nothing from the last refugee was beyond comprehension. Should he take her off the assignment? But who could take her place? There was nobody on his staff. They all talked too much. And if there was a less stupid woman available, who was free to leave home and who could be trusted, he didn't know her. So he was stuck with Elisa. Still, how he wished he knew what was going on in the stranger's head!

He made quick work of the ramparts. He was in a hurry to get back to his office and find out if Inspector Payne had gotten anywhere with a certain investigation. Ah, wouldn't it be beautiful if it worked! He had thought of everything, including the power of attorney he had forced out of Labrique under the pretext that it would speed up his retirement pension. "Dear God, please let it happen," he said as he headed for his office.

Passersby were startled by the look of joy on his face. Things must be going well in the City. . . .

"Payne, how did it go?"

"Just fine, Mr. Commissioner. I was right. A little out of the ordinary, but there's no doubt about it. I saw it all through my binoculars from a roof next door. Delightful spectacle!"

"When did it happen?"

"About eleven this morning."

"All right. Get back to your roof and if it happens again, just wave your arm. Revere will be watching from the terrace here."

"O.K., I'll be off. But it's not a very pleasant job, you know."

"Maybe you'd rather work at the Factory?"

Baudruche kept looking through the window at Revere who had flattened himself against a chimney on the terrace. Suddenly, Baudruche saw him lower his binoculars and disappear. That must be it. He leaped from his chair, grabbed his hat and struggled into his coat.

Revere was waiting for his chief at the foot of the stairs. Baudruche grasped his arm.

"We've got to hurry if we're to get there in time."

"From what Payne says, we don't need to hurry. They're taking their time."

"All the same, I don't want to miss this one."

Baudruche and Revere waited in the courtyard of Labrique's house, their backs against the wall, eyes glued on Payne who was on a roof across the street. Suddenly, Payne raised his arm. That meant they were to go up. Baudruche took the duplicate key from his pocket, opened the front door and they silently climbed the stairs.

They tiptoed down the hall until they were outside Esther's room. Through the closed door they could hear muffled cries,

164

sighs and other inarticulate sounds. As Baudruche flung the door open, he just had time to see a big hairy body roll on top of Esther. At the sight of Baudruche and Revere, the architect's wife let out a scream. The brown body jumped from the bed, ran for the window and disappeared. Baudruche rushed to the window in time to see the rat clamber down the drainpipe to the sidewalk and into the nearest sewer.

"That son of a bitch!"

Baudruche turned around. For once, the fates were with him. He gave the poor bewildered woman a look of triumph.

"Cover yourself, Esther. You're not a pretty sight."

What had possessed Labrique to marry a body like that one? Was it one of his decadent intellectual ideas?

"Dear Esther, forgive me for interrupting your revels," Baudruche took the power of attorney from his pocket, "but I am here at the request of Mr. Hector Labrique, Chief Architect of the City, now retired, born at . . ."

"Stop! I get it," Esther said as she draped herself in the bedspread.

"You don't want me to read the rest? Well, thank you, Esther. That saves me precious time."

Revere hadn't moved since he came into the room. He was leaning against the back of a chair, watching. Finally, his eyes on Esther, he said:

"You really are disgusting!"

Mrs. Labrique bridled. "Mr. Commissioner, you're a witness: one of your men insulted me!"

"Really? I didn't hear anything. My mind must have been on something else. But it would surprise me; Mr. Revere is well known for his courtesy and good breeding—which are not commonplace in our profession, believe me. I chose him to accompany me out of consideration for you. Had I brought his colleague Payne, dear Esther, he would have called you the whore of all time."

"Are you going to insult me too!"

"I didn't say anything. I was only quoting what Inspector Payne might have said. . . . It's not for me to judge. That will be up to the courts. Good-bye, dear Esther. You haven't paid us a visit for a long time. We'd be delighted to see you. . . ."

Baudruche motioned Revere to go. Before leaving, he glanced around the room. The remains of a meal were scattered on a table—a dirty glass, a half-empty bottle of red wine, a few gnawed bones. Esther's lover had had a little feast.

He closed the door behind him. Payne came down off his roof and the three men walked away together. Revere was still stunned, but not Payne.

"I used to see a lot of that in the villages. The rats will do anything."

Baudruche paid them little attention, for he was tasting the sweetness of his triumph. But as they approached the Hotel, he remembered that Elisa had called that morning when he was too busy to talk with her. "She shall have the benefit of my good humor," he said to himself as he climbed the Hotel steps.

He could hear her singing in her room. As he opened the door, he saw that her face was transfigured, her eyes languid, her bearing soft and yielding.

"You look very happy, Elisa."

"I don't know what's the matter with me, Mr. Commissioner, but I've been so happy ever since last night!"

At last! This time she must have really brought it off. That would end Emil Poulet's smug pretensions.

"Elisa, I hope you didn't ask me to come just to hear how happy you were."

She answered "yes" because it was all she had in her head. But Baudruche was so pleased with his two little triumphs that he took out his wallet and counted out a few bills. She took them absentmindedly.

"Oh, that's right. I'm out of money. It completely slipped my mind."

"It's more serious than I thought," Baudruche said to himself. He was about to go when Elisa clapped her hands: she had just remembered why she'd called the Commissioner.

"I wanted to tell you there's a rat in my bathroom."

"What did you say?"

"I said 'a rat.' Don't look at me like that. I thought you'd be grateful."

"Where did it come from?"

She laughed. "My bed!"

Baudruche was nonplussed: was this striking transformation in Elisa the work of a rat and not of the last refugee? Were the rats about to find their way into all the beds in the City?

"Do you know what you are saying?"

"Yes, but I can see it doesn't please you."

"You were capable of permitting it in your room, in your bed, without throwing up . . ."

Elisa clapped her hands again and giggled.

"I had nothing to do with it; it was your man in twenty-three. He put the rat in my room, with Posey's help."

Baudruche felt he was going mad. The man in room 23, the last refugee for whom he had harbored such esteem, and that girl Posey who attracted him for all her familiar ways, those two were party to this abomination! It was hard to believe. But Elisa was much too stupid to dream up such a thing. He stood up.

"I don't believe you. I have to see for myself. If it's there, it'll be the man's tough luck. I'll make him pay for both of you. That makes two rats killed in this Hotel."

He opened the door to the bathroom, turned on the light, but saw nothing. That displeased him even more, for it began to look as if Elisa were pulling his leg.

"I find this joke in very bad taste. I would like you to apologize immediately."

Utterly confused, Elisa got to her feet.

"I don't believe it! He can't have gotten out. I haven't been out of my room."

She went into the bathroom and called out:

- "He's there, right on the chair. I forgot to tell you he was wrapped up."

Of course! What a dope he was not to realize it was the rat Posey had killed in the hall outside. He went into the bathroom and came out with the package under his arm.

"My compliments, Elisa. That was a splendid piece of work. Do you happen to know where the corpse has been these last few days? Has anybody else seen it?"

She knew nothing; she hadn't given it a thought. No, wait a minute: her lover had told her that he'd kept it in a drawer of his bureau. The Commissioner looked very pleased, and as he was leaving, he remembered his promise. He put the package down on a chair and took out his wallet again. Once he'd gone, Elisa looked at the money wide-eyed. So much money and so much happiness in twenty-four hours! She opened her closet and stood deep in thought.

Which dress would he like best?

Baudruche ran down the stairs and into the street. He was in a hurry to get rid of the compromising parcel; the smell was beginning to seep through the several layers of newspaper. The moment he reached his home, he went down to the cellar and threw the package into the furnace.

"Too bad I can't do that with all of them!"

He climbed the stairs, a smile on his lips. A good job well done. He couldn't wait to share his news with Martha: two misfortunes involving two people he heartily disliked! Martha was delighted at the sight of him rubbing his hands in anticipation.

"Am I right in thinking that something good has happened?"

"Two things, Martha. First, Labrique is a cuckold."

Martha sighed. "It doesn't surprise me. I've suspected it for a long time."

"I was certain of it, but I had no clear proof. Now I have. Do you know who the happy beneficiary is?"

"No, and I don't care. Such things don't interest me."

"Well, I'm going to tell you anyway. It's a rat."

Martha screamed, "I don't believe it!"

"I saw it with my own eyes and I can tell you it wasn't a pretty sight. . . . What a couple!"

Now Martha wanted to know everything down to the last detail. She interrupted him only to say an occasional, "I don't believe it," "It can't be," and finally, "So Esther has come to this!"

"You may think it's funny, Robert, but I don't. What's your other news?"

"Same general idea. Emil Poulet is a cuckold."

That was unexpected. Martha frowned, then to Baudruche's great surprise, she suddenly brightened. So her husband wasn't the other man!

"Who is the guilty party this time?"

"The man in the Hotel, the last refugee. I knew he'd do something good for the City."

"Aren't you ashamed, Robert? I bet you were in there pulling strings the whole time."

He didn't deny it; he was proud of it. He had killed two birds with one stone, making common cause of the City's interest and his private grudges.

"You know, Martha, if he hadn't succeeded, I'd almost decided to do the job myself."

Baudruche was disappointed in Martha: he had expected her to sail into him, but instead she sat there with a wide smile on her face. Women were incomprehensible! Then it suddenly dawned on him: What a fool he was! Of course, like everybody else, she had imagined . . .

They had just started to eat when the door flew open. Labrique walked in, his arms raised to the skies.

"This time, Esther has really gone mad."

Martha kept her nose in her plate and said nothing. Her husband remarked innocently, "That's nothing new, old boy."

"Never like this. When I got home, the whole house was

169

turned upside down. She'd broken everything. Things I really cared about. . . . But I guess I was lucky: it was either them or me. She told me some story about a writ of adultery that I'd been coward enough to dream up, when actually I'd abandoned her years ago, that I'd never understood her . . . and the usual crap. But what's all this about a writ of adultery?"

"She didn't make it up, Labrique. I have the proof. It's here in my pocket."

"You're joking."

"I am not. You signed over power of attorney to me yesterday. I took care of the matter right away. I'll read it to you. . . . But you don't know the best part! Do you know who her new lover is?"

"I don't give a damn."

"It's a rat, my friend. It is my privilege to inform you . . ."

Labrique was silent.

Baudruche continued: "I hope you make good use of that piece of paper. It could cause a nice little scandal. It might wake up public opinion. . . ."

Labrique refused. He wanted no trouble, no publicity. He wanted peace. Baudruche tried to reason with him, threatened, pleaded, but to no avail.

"Are you going to spoil the whole thing? It could be very important for the City. I went to a lot of trouble to bring this off. . . ."

"Look, Baudruche. Put yourself in my place."

"I'd love to. I'd make myself useful."

"And I don't like the way you got that power of attorney out of me. That was cheating."

"You taught me how."

"Not about that kind of thing."

He ate little and left. He must start reorganizing his life.

When he'd gone, Baudruche looked at Martha. "Nobody wants to help me. I don't understand Labrique. The one time he could be useful to me . . ."

"I think Labrique is absolutely right, Robert."

This made Baudruche furious. Only a woman would react that way. They were all mad, all of them. . . .

Certainly, Elisa gave that impression as she sat down in the restaurant. She had taken a table near the entrance so that her lover couldn't help seeing her. He had barely put a toe in the room when she waved her arm and called out, "Yoohoo!" She had already presumed to order both their meals.

Elisa spent the meal displaying herself, her lover and her happiness to the restaurant's appreciative clientele and personnel. The good news spread through the Hotel, from Baidroume to the assistant dishwasher. There was no longer any doubt about it: the Commissioner had indeed been betrayed by his mistress.

Passing from ear to ear, the news spread to the nearby shops and fanned out to the boutiques on Prefect Avenue. Everybody was of the same mind—cooks, maids, valets, shopkeepers: the man in 26 had made up for their impotence and mediocrity, and they rejoiced that Elisa had consented in his effort.

As soon as lunch was finished, Elisa led him outside. She wanted to show him off, outside the Hotel as well as in. They walked up Prefect Avenue to Linon Taffeta's and bought two dresses and three pairs of shoes. Her lover paid the bill. When they left the shop, she begged him to buy her a bouquet of violets from a street vendor. To her dismay, he left her as soon as the flowers were in her hands. He was in a hurry; he had better things to do than go from store to store. She watched him go with a heavy heart. What was the good of being happy if he was going to leave her like that!

As Baudruche approached the ex-Social Progress, he noticed a moving van parked in front of the building next door. A team of rats was hurriedly transferring furniture and objects through the doors and windows of the ground-floor apartment into the van. Baudruche asked what was going on. The people standing around told him that an elderly couple named Seculat was turning over their apartment to the embassy next door. "It may not be much fun for them, but the others need room too. That's what the newspaper says. . . ." Baudruche interrogated the Seculats. Yes, it was all right with them. They'd been given to understand, at first gently, then in no uncertain terms, that it would be to their best interest to move . . . they'd find it quieter elsewhere.

Baudruche offered to have his men empty the van and put everything back in place. They looked frightened and wouldn't reply. He even promised to see that their house was guarded, but they said no. They were very grateful to the Commissioner, but things were all right as they were.

The President greeted him at the door of the former café.

"Isn't it a splendid example of social solidarity, Mr. Commissioner! Imagine: the Seculats anticipated our needs! They offered to give up their apartment so that we could have more room. We tried to argue with them, but they insisted. So, to show our gratitude and not be in their debt, we offered to help them move."

Baudruche shoved the President into his office. He was anxious to express his thoughts.

"I warn you that I will not tolerate the City's inhabitants being moved out of their homes so that you can take them over."

The President raised his hands.

"Mr. High Commissioner, it disturbs me as much as you. We want to make ourselves as small as possible, not to be noticed. It's no one's fault. I'm sure that everybody—and you in particular, Mr. Commissioner—is doing everything in his power, but where is our building? Nothing has happened. We've received nothing but promises."

"We're doing all we can."

"I'm sure you are, but we can't wait forever. We suffocate

here, and obviously if another windfall comes our way, we can't be criticized for taking advantage of it."

Baudruche swallowed hard.

"Are you sure of your new architect's competence, Mr. Commissioner?"

"I'll answer for him."

"Then there's nothing more to say. By the way, our new newspaper is about to appear, thanks to your kindness and understanding. There's just one small detail: we lack qualified typesetters. Mr. Canard tells me that it shouldn't be difficult to find a good supply among the City's inhabitants. I would guess that those employed by the defunct *Independent* have not been able to find suitable jobs. Why not reassemble the group and give them work worthy of their skills? What do you say, Mr. Commissioner?"

"They'll have to be paid."

"Of course."

"Do you have the money?"

"You know perfectly well we don't, Mr. Commissioner. We're as poor as Job on his dung heap. But what is your Ministry of Cultural Propaganda for? It must cost you a pretty penny: why not turn it to some use? I know the Prefect will understand. Don't you concern yourself with such trifles."

Brimming over with charm, the President accompanied him to the door.

"We inaugurate our new quarters tomorrow, Mr. Commissioner. Mr. Canard has agreed to be on hand, and if you would do us the honor, we would be very proud. . . ."

"I won't have time," Baudruche said and hurried off.

The President caught up with him and whispered, "I forgot to tell you the name of our new paper, Mr. Commissioner. We're going to call it *The Rodent*."

Baudruche hurried to the Factory where he found Leponte deep in calculations:

"We have to get help from the Prefect, Mr. Commissioner. Our productivity's rise was three point twenty-five percent, as stipulated in the plan. But now we have to increase sales by the same amount. There's only one way: by advertising. I beg you to ask the Prefect to put the screws on the Ministry of Industrial Expansion so that we can get some money. We must shake the population out of its apathy. They've got to understand that they cannot forgo buying the new model. It's a question of both patriotism and personal status. The campaign's got to be a success or I won't answer for the consequences."

Baudruche shrugged his shoulders and left.

Elisa was just beginning to doze when the telephone rang. It was Martha.

Martha wanted to see her right away. She reproached Elisa for abandoning Sophie and since it was a school holiday . . . Elisa yawned and got up. Why wouldn't people leave her to her happiness?

Elisa arrived at the Bauduches' home, looking more elegant and more beautiful than ever. Love and clothes . . . that's what she was made for. The two women pecked each other on the cheek. They gossiped, and Martha commented on the strange things that were going on. "For instance, Elisa—and don't breathe a word of it to anybody—you know Esther, the architect's wife? . . . She was caught with a rat. . . ."

"I don't believe it, Martha! Can you really do it with a rat?"

They were in the middle of an animated discussion when Sophie walked in.

Martha changed the subject. "Elisa, why don't you take the child for a walk. She needs fresh air, shut up all day in school. . . ."

The idea had little appeal for Elisa. She was worried about being seen with a ten-year-old which would add years to her age at the very moment when she had managed to slough them off. But she gave in, vowing that the walk would be short and the conversation carefully controlled. Then, what was her luck but to run into the very man she most dreaded meeting!

"You didn't tell me you had a daughter?"

"Oh, I had her when I was very young—barely eighteen [a net gain of two years], and besides, I didn't think you'd be interested."

On the contrary, her lover was very interested. He walked along at Sophie's side and encouraged her to talk. Then he insisted she go to the Hotel with him, over Elisa's protests. He asked them up to his room. It made Elisa uncomfortable to see her daughter in room 23.

"Sophie, do you know what this is?"

"No, sir."

"Then listen."

He put the flute to his lips and Sophie heard a strange, piercing yet agreeable sound. The stranger put the instrument back in its case. So children could still hear what most men and many women couldn't any longer? He looked at his watch and got up.

"I must go."

His eyes rested on Sophie. Why not, since children seemed to understand?

"Come, Sophie. Let's go for a walk."

They went out, leaving Elisa alone in room 23. She felt quite at home here and why not? Didn't she have some rights to it? So she opened closets, drawers, cupboards, feeling ever so lightly in the pockets. Everything was neat and tidy. Then she found a large suitcase in the bathroom. She couldn't get it open so she shook it. It sounded like paper inside. Too bad it was locked. It was probably letters. Disappointed, she left.

They jabbered all the way to the ramparts, and climbed the stairs hand in hand.

"Hey, soldier, anything new?"

"Yes, that girl came again with her basket."

"Speaking of girls, I've brought one with me to look at you."

175

"Why? Because I'm so handsome?"

"Don't get excited: she's just a child; that's why I wanted her to come. It's important that she know what a soldier looks like. Otherwise how will she find out? All the grown-ups have forgotten."

The last refugee lifted Sophie up and sat her down on the ledge of the spy hole.

"Did anything happen last night?"

"Yes, but it would interest the girl more than you. What's your name, child?"

"Sophie."

"Well then, listen, Sophie: A girl came by and threw bread to the birds. Then, last night, seven little boys passed by, and the littlest one threw crumbs over his shoulder and the birds ate those too."

Sophie was intrigued. The soldier continued:

"After that, a large cat wearing big boots came. The cat said to me:

" 'What are you doing here? Don't you know this land belongs to the Marquis of Carrabas?'

" 'No, I didn't know. But if I don't have the right to stay, I'll go.'

"Then the cat noticed I was wearing a uniform and said:

" 'Why didn't you tell me you were a soldier? My master, the Marquis, will be delighted to know you're here. But what's that city over there? It doesn't belong to my master.'

" 'It's a beautiful city but it's full of rats.'

" 'The inhabitants allow it? How horrible! I'd better go.'

"And he left very fast—because he had on seven-league boots."

"I don't believe you."

"You'd better, because I'm telling it. After that, a beautiful carriage came and stopped in front of me. A ravishing young girl stepped down and she also asked me what city this was and

176

if she could go in with her carriage. When she learned the City was full of rats, she screamed with horror.

" 'Goodness gracious, I'm scared enough of mice!'

"She got back into her carriage and its four white horses galloped off. But she'd climbed in so fast she dropped one of her slippers."

"That's all make-believe. You're lying to me."

"I am not lying. And to prove it, here, catch!"

Sophie stretched out her hands and caught a small glass slipper on the wing. The man and the soldier laughed, but not Sophie.

She was silent all the way back to her mother.

It was late when Baudruche got around to his evening chore. In his report, he said a few words about his visit to the President, and the rat's new demands. He added a paragraph on Leponte's requests which he presented without comment. This done, he rubbed his hands in anticipation. He held a very nice card and he was going to play it for all it was worth.

Having been asked by your Chief Architect to conduct an investigation of his spouse's behavior, I paid a carefully timed visit to the couple's home, accompanied by a member of my staff whose discretion I knew to be unassailable. By using a key which the husband had entrusted to me for this purpose, I was able to confirm *de visu* that the Labrique spouse was in bed, not with an inhabitant of the City, but with a rat.

I therefore saw it as my duty to convey to Mr. Labrique the proof of adultery. Unfortunately the betrayed spouse intends to produce the above proof before the proper tribunal.

I don't need to tell you, Mr. Prefect, that the exhibition of such a document before a court of law will raise serious problems, whose ramifications neither of us can foresee.

There are two alternatives: either the judge, responding to your desires, will refuse to hear the case, since it involves a rat and not an inhabitant of the City, and Mr. Labrique will shout from the rooftops that the courts had refused to consider a rat as our equal, *or* the judge will pursue the matter, and Mr. Labrique will be in a position to advertise the danger that threatens the City's husbands.

I feel quite certain, Mr. Prefect, that should it come to this, a large part of the population is not ready to accept sexual relations between rats and the City's inhabitants.

I am unable to resolve this singular problem, but I know that as always you, Mr. Prefect, will have the right solution.

Well, he'd done it. It was better than nothing, but he could have done a hundred times better if that bastard Labrique had left him free to act. Now he was reduced to bluff and lies in the hope that the Prefect would be thrown off balance by the strangeness of the case.

"Finish it off, Miss Bourrot. What's in the sentry's report? They heard nothing? They must be sobering up."

Miss Bourrot went out. There was a knock on the door. It was little Miss Niquel.

"I haven't the time, my dear girl," Baudruche said, wearily dropping his arms on the table.

It was very late. What was the City trying to do to him . . . kill him outright? He picked up the late edition of the newspaper. There was a large picture at the bottom of the front page with the caption: "At the population's service: A team of rats helps an elderly couple move."

Elisa was holding forth to her lover. They had been given a table in the middle of the restaurant so that they would be in full view.

Elisa talked with increasing animation. She had so much to tell him! Actually, she'd never been allowed really to express herself.

To escape the inexhaustible flow, the man took occasional refuge in his thoughts.

178

"Tell me something: how come Sophie lives with the Baudruches?"

This caught her short but she recovered.

"How shall I say it, my love? It's not easy, you know. . . . Her father is a brute."

She whispered to him and he listened politely, then turned the conversation back to the Baudruches, and to the Commissioner in particular.

"If the Commissioner is so interested in me, tell him to come and talk to me. I have nothing to hide. Will you take him a secret message? It's extremely important."

He asked for paper and an envelope, and wrote: "I need more money. Your secret agent is costing me a lot." He licked the envelope and handed it to Elisa. She slipped it inside her corsage, first looking around to see if anyone were watching. They went upstairs, Elisa's arm around his waist.

13

BAUDRUCHE took the sentry walk slowly, occasionally glancing out over the plain. A thin mist still hovered over the ground; there was a smell of autumn. Overhead, the sky was gloomy with dirty gray clouds. But in the far distance, it was light.

He wished he could get out of these daily rounds. With Labrique it had been relaxation, but his successor was a torment.

"My dear Baudruche . . ."

"Would it be too much to ask you to call me Mr. High Commissioner?"

"Forgive me, Mr. High Commissioner, I was on the point of remarking that dear old Labrique . . ."

"Could you bring yourself to say Mr. Labrique? He's not decrepit yet, as far as I know."

"No, but he's retired which is the same thing. I was about to say that Mr. Labrique had done a wretched job with these walls—smearing them with all that jam. Where was his sense of hygiene? It's disgusting to have jam all over the walls."

"You prefer ants?"

"Mr. High Commissioner, our parents' time is behind us. We have at our disposal far more efficient methods of defense than old wives' remedies."

"What are you leading us to, Mr. Edge? I haven't much time."

"Simply this: I went to the Department of Civilian Defense to seek information. They were categorical: this insect invasion was within their jurisdiction, not mine. Should they return, I am to alert them. They will then take care of the matter."

Baudruche finally got away. The new architect watched him go with a sigh. Poor old Baudruche . . . everything was beyond him now. And there were too many like him too highly placed. Edge glanced at the exterior of the walls. It had been a terrible job: it had taken an army of men and tons of soap, but the walls were clean now. He looked at their smooth, white surface with satisfaction. To be sure, there were a few gray patches here and there, but nothing of importance.

Baudruche went to see Mr. Paytard at Civilian Defense, but a new director was on duty. Mr. Fisher was delighted to see Baudruche; he had so much to tell him, so much to explain.

Unfortunately, the Commissioner was pressed for time. He wanted just one piece of information: How was the powder of deterrence coming? Not quite ready yet?

Fisher looked at him with disbelief. Who ever had told him that? The other directors? Those old fossils! He had to laugh. Why, he'd seen the lab tests with his own eyes. The powder exploded all right, and how! Now they were just waiting for the right occasion. Yes, Mr. Edge had told him about the possibility of a new invastion of ants. He was hoping for the invasion. . . . Let them come! One match and "Wham!" they'd be gone.

Baudruche told his informant to put off any further tests and do nothing about the walls until he received authorization from either the Prefect or himself.

He marched back to his office in a rage. Although he understood little of this kind of science, he sensed they were treading on dangerous ground.

When he arrived at his office, Miss Bourrot handed him a confidential note from the Prefect. He tore it open and read it through. The Prefect gave him a free hand in the Labrique affair, was fully confident that Baudruche would arrange everything in everybody's best interest, including the rats. So, the Prefect had played his hand brilliantly, even to the ending with its veiled suggestion that if there was no other solution, it might be possible to produce an incident or to discover a heretofore unknown fact that would forever remove the ex-architect from further conjugal misfortunes.

Baudruche knew what that meant. In this City, they could always get you on something. Everybody was guilty of something. And there were so many ways of protracting court proceedings, while the accused was put away—with plenty of time to think.

Baudruche was beaten. All he could do was make the best of it.

"Miss Bourrot, call Mr. Labrique and ask him to come to my office right away."

Fifteen minutes later, nonchalant as ever and hat on the back of his head, Labrique walked in.

"Before you speak, I want to know if I'm here on private or official business."

"Both."

"In that case, I'll listen to the private business."

"Don't be a dope; this is serious. You've landed me in the soup with your damn writ of adultery."

Labrique dropped into a chair and burst out laughing.

"That's beautiful! There I was living in peace—if not

exactly ecstasy—giving no thought to what my worthy spouse was up to. The Commissioner comes up with a forged document which he wants to use for purposes I disapprove of, Esther goes on the rampage, I'm forced to leave the premises and find a semblance of peace elsewhere, and now I find that I'm responsible for your difficulties. You deserve whatever happens!"

"It had nothing to do with me. I'm worried for you. You may be in for serious trouble."

"I'm armed, and this time I know who to go after."

"Listen, I can help you out."

"No, please, don't do anything. I prefer not."

"You prefer going to prison?"

"Why should I go to prison?"

"Because you're a cuckold."

"Well, in that case, I guess I won't be lonely. We'll be a mob."

"Don't forget you're a special case. What would you think of an easy, quiet job with nothing to do?"

"That would suit me very well."

"With your full architect's salary, a comfortable house provided by the City . . ."

"In a pinch, I'd say yes."

"Okay, Labrique, you're the new City Librarian. I'll fix it up with the Prefect."

As soon as he had the keys to the Public Library and his new house, Labrique went into high gear. He had no time to lose if he was to salvage the last of his personal possessions. He ran to the offices of a moving company and promised them a handsome bonus if they would move him immediately.

"What's the hurry, sir? Is your house on fire?" the man in charge asked.

"No, much worse than that. My wife is in it."

Esther was indeed home, and when she caught sight of the moving van, her anger overflowed like a pot of boiling milk.

184

How could he abandon her, a helpless woman who had given him her youth? What would become of her in an empty house? She called the moving men to witness and challenged them on every item in the house. Everything was hers: the big chair from the architect's grandfather was from her Aunt Emma, the clock from his grandmother was from her cousin Victoria. It had been a wedding present. . . . The moving men, obedient to whoever paid the bill, took the things from her clinging hands without pity. Was she to be left with nothing?

Fuming, she watched the loaded moving van drive off. She had been too nice: she should have smashed everything. Weeping with anger, she treated herself to a brief temper tantrum on the mattress which now rested on the floor. Her husband had taken the bed but left her the mattress and pillows so that she wouldn't bruise her bottom the next time the rat came to call. . . .

It was late, so Labrique left the men to unload the van into his new house. He was hungry and emotionally exhausted. He went to the restaurant in the Hotel and took a table in a corner, a good vantage point from which to watch Elisa as she clung amorously to the guest in room 23. Poor old Baudruche: he was unlucky with his women as well.

As he got up from the table, Labrique felt the urge to try his second key on the door to the Library. He toured the vast room which he had used so often in the old days. Now he was no longer just a reader but its boss. He spent the entire afternoon inspecting the shelves. Everything was in order, every book in its proper place. Pholio had done his job well, but he could hardly help the mail that had accumulated since his death. Boxes of recently published books were piled high in the corners. From the stack of mail, Labrique picked out a letter at random. It carried the Prefect's letterhead. On opening it, he saw that it contained a long list of books to be withdrawn from circulation. He put it down without reading it. Next to the mail, he noticed a large register with "Loans" written on the cover. He opened it and the last entry caught his eye: "Baudruche, Robert." He found a postcard on which was printed: "You are requested to return the following book to the Public Library at once . . ." and filled it out.

Emil Poulet walked at the Commissioner's side, a large roll of paper tucked under his arm. They were going to see the President. He had been told what to do and say, which turned out to be exactly what he would have done and said by himself. After all, he was only being asked to tell the truth.

The Commissioner had given Poulet clear instructions: the rat must be lulled to sleep; he must be convinced that they were working their tails off for him, must be shown projects, plans, papers, piles of papers and given lots of hope, assurances and promises—as much as he could take.

Perhaps that way they would gain a little time. For, after lunch, Baudruche had received some very bad news: several more apartments near the Seculats had been appropriated by the rats. The Department of Relocation reported that a number of people had come asking for help. For want of anything better, they had been put in temporary barracks.

When Baudruche arrived at the former café, it was immediately clear that the situation was even worse than he'd expected. The two small streets that fanned out from the ex-Social Progress were thronged with people—both inhabitants and rats—who were dashing about and talking in excited groups. One rat offered to sell him a marked-down rug. Another rat pressed him to buy one of the five watches on his wrist.

Baudruche had great difficulty preventing Poulet from buying some suspect earrings and a pair of worn shoes. Then he lost him in the crowd. Baudruche sauntered along, looking into the houses along the sidewalk. They were full of activity: the rats were in the process of removing everything, passing furniture through the windows, emptying dressers, opening closets, taking down chandeliers.

Rats haggled over the furniture and objects that cluttered the sidewalks. A rat approached Baudruche and flipped open an album of obscene pictures under his nose. Baudruche looked at him closely and bought them. A little farther on, he came upon a group looking down at something. Among them stood Emil Poulet. Peering over their shoulders, Baudruche saw a rat shuffling three cards which he then spread out on an open umbrella.

"Which is the red? Which is the red?"

Emil Poulet handed him a bill and turned over a black card.

Baudruche grabbed the rat by the collar. "What's going on here. Are you gambling on City streets?"

The group broke up; they had recognized Baudruche.

"You come with me, Poulet." Baudruche led him toward the former café, his grip still firm on the rat's collar.

The President rushed out of his office.

"What's happened, Mr. High Commissioner? Has one of our people been disrespectful?"

"I caught him gambling on a public thoroughfare. It's strictly forbidden in this City."

"My compliments, Mr. High Commissioner. You are a great help to us."

The President bowed before the Commissioner and invited him and Emil Poulet into his office. The guilty rat was propelled with a swift kick in the pants.

"So, you've been gambling in the streets, have you? Aren't you ashamed to be displaying such vices before the City's inhabitants! What will they take us for?"

The rat rolled his eyes in terror. "President, I swear I didn't do nothing."

"Are you casting doubt on the High Commissioner's word?"

Emil Poulet stood up. "I can bear witness. I'm the one who gave him the money."

Baudruche would have happily killed the stupid fool. With a forced smile he said, "I forgot to introduce Mr. Poulet, the architect in charge of your project."

The President rose to his feet.

"I am delighted to meet you, Mr. Poulet, but I wish it had been under different circumstances." He looked grieved and turned to the Commissioner. "How could such a distinguished person, an official of the City, indulge himself in a disreputable game which is condoned neither by morality nor law?"

The President stepped forward, seized the rat by the collar, opened the door with his free hand and kicked him into what had been the restaurant.

The President wore an expression of desolation on his return.

"What a pity! For once I had my hands on one of the miserable wretches who dishonor our people, but what could I do? Mr. Poulet was an accomplice. And there's nothing more dangerous than a bad example at the top. You must know that, Mr. High Commissioner?"

Oh, yes, Baudruche knew everything. Everything, including Poulet's incredible stupidity and the President's superb footwork. He took the little album of photographs and threw it on the table.

"Look at what your nationals are selling in full daylight, under your very windows!"

The President seized the album and quickly leafed through it. "This is revolting. Who sold you this?"

Baudruche got up, walked to the window and pointed to the guilty party on the opposite sidewalk.

"See that man? The one in the yellow jacket?"

"Just a minute, please."

The President rushed out and Baudruche heard him bark out a few quick orders. An instant later, he was back, kicking and shoving the rat in the yellow jacket.

"Move, you scum . . . Do you recognize this gentleman?" he said pointing to the Commissioner.

"I've never seen him in my life."

"Yes, but he has seen you, and that's enough for me. Empty your pockets."

The rat threw an impressive quantity of pornographic photographs on the table. Emil Poulet's eyes popped at the display.

There was something for every taste . . . a challenge to the most assiduous practitioner.

The President went pale with rage. "You sell this swill in the streets! Aren't you ashamed to be displaying such vices before the City's inhabitants? What will they take us for?"

Emil Poulet picked up a handful of photographs.

"What makes it even worse is that our own people posed for these. Mr. Commissioner, these are inhabitants of the City!"

A smile of satisfaction crossed the President's face. He had not dared say it out of respect for the High Commissioner, but Mr. Poulet had taken the words right out of his mouth. They themselves had nothing to do with the production of these things. Their morals were too strict in such matters. He left the Commissioner absolutely free to pursue his own investigation. When it was completed, he would see that the purveyor was punished, and in no uncertain terms. He ejected the rat in the yellow jacket as he had the gambler.

"May we get down to serious business now, Mr. Commissioner? First, to the good news. By tomorrow afternoon, the first number of *The Rodent* will be on the stands. I know what this paper owes to the Prefect and you, Mr. Commissioner. We are forever in your debt. You and the Prefect will receive the first copies as they come off the press."

"You are too kind. I'm deeply touched."

"Not at all, Mr. Commissioner. It is only fitting. May we now pass on to a subject of equal importance: our building. Where are we at?"

Emil got up and unrolled his plans. There were dozens. Lines curved and crossed in every direction, sweeping this way and that and ending nowhere. The paper was never large enough. He leaned over the table, explaining, describing, boasting. Baudruche watched him out of the corner of his eye. Was he being sincere? He began to wonder. He was doing better than Baudruche had hoped—he was playing his role almost too well.

"I like it very much!" the President exclaimed.

189

Baudruche smiled. "Didn't I tell you?"

"But what about the time factor?"

Emil dropped into a chair and sighed.

"There's the rub. I am badly staffed. Except for a minority who understand my ideas, I am surrounded by incompetents who quibble and argue over every line. In a word, Mr. President, they clip my wings. Under these circumstances, I find it impossible to realize my potential. . . ."

Baudruche broke in with vigor:

"Why didn't you tell me?"

"Mr. Commissioner, you already have so much on your mind. Besides—and I don't mean to question your capacities —it would be difficult to discuss these matters with you. Your knowledge of architecture is perforce limited."

"Listen, I trust you. Get rid of the incompetents."

What Emil Poulet knew only too well was that these "incompetents" had great influence over the competents. If he dismissed them, they would never forgive him and would attack his projects with ever greater violence. That was no solution.

But fate was smiling on him: the President said with a diffident smile, "Mr. Poulet, I have a proposition to make. Why go on trying to work in the City where the atmosphere is so hostile when you could carry on your work here among our people, as our guest? You would receive respect and consideration from all of us. Choose the truly devoted and faithful from among your colleagues, bring them with you and they will be welcome as well."

Emil Poulet's face brightened, but Baudruche's darkened.

"I'm not sure if the Prefect will look with favor on one of the City's inhabitants—and one of our most illustrious to boot —deserting his post to work for foreigners."

"Foreigners! That's a cruel word, Mr. High Commissioner. It might have described us awhile back, but not today! The frontiers are open, Mr. High Commissioner; we are forging bonds. I look forward to the day when our two peoples will

190

merge, united by the same ideal of fraternity, and pass freely from sewer to City and City to sewer without feeling in any way like foreigners or émigrés. Isn't that what you hope for too, Mr. High Commissioner?"

"Of course, of course. . . . But it will take a little time. We still have to overcome certain prejudices. . . ."

"Not among our people, not here, Mr. High Commissioner. And if the City's inhabitants still harbor a few antiquated ideas, why not start breaking them down today? Mr. Poulet, you could be in the vanguard. . . ."

Emil was about to open his mouth but Baudruche broke in.

"We mustn't forget that Mr. Poulet isn't alone: he has a wife and child and a home he loves."

Emil jumped at this.

"Mr. Commissioner, you know better than anybody that unfortunately this is no longer the case. My wife has left me, temporarily I hope, but she has indeed left me. As for my daughter, you were good enough to take her under your wing, so I have no worries on that score."

The President gave a satisfied smile.

"You see, Mr. High Commissioner, there are no obstacles, unless of course Mr. Poulet wishes to refuse my offer, which is within his rights."

Emil leaped to his feet.

"I accept, Mr. President, and with the greatest enthusiasm. It will be an experience, a thrilling new slice of life. I'll go pack right now."

"Why bother, Mr. Poulet? Time is precious. Everything you need is right here," and he tapped the plans. "We'll do your packing for you, and your team will join you tomorrow— unless the Commissioner wishes it otherwise."

Baudruche was helpless. If he could just have fifteen minutes to warn Poulet . . .

"Yours is a very tempting proposition, Mr. President, but it must be considered from every angle. I see no reason why

191

Mr. Poulet can't wait until tomorrow to give his answer."

"But why wait, Mr. Commissioner? Such decisions are born of enthusiasm, as Mr. Poulet has just demonstrated."

Baudruche had to admit defeat. There was a shaking of hands, slapping of shoulders and a buzz of congratulations. There was nothing left but to leave. As if by chance, Canard was standing by the entrance.

Baudruche directed his steps toward the Factory.

"What's new, Mr. Leponte?"

"This time, nothing but good news, Mr. Commissioner. The Prefect used his full influence. Did you see the City walls this morning? And did you read the paper? We are all over it! A revolutionary model! No one wasted a minute: orders are pouring in. But we can meet them, even if we have to work overtime."

"Good. That's fine. Anything else?"

"Oh, indeed yes, Mr. Commissioner: an event—what am I saying?—two events! As I was rejoicing over our success, Miss Foyle came in to announce a visitor. It was a rat. He was sent by our neighbors' newspaper, whose first edition as you know is to appear tomorrow. He came to offer me his newspaper's advertising services. I didn't have to be asked twice, you may be sure. I signed on the dotted line: the same conditions as with our own paper, and in addition, exclusive rights. What do you think of that, Mr. Commissioner?"

"I think you've lost your mind."

"Think of the possibilities! And that isn't all: a half hour later, I had another visitor. Another rat, and—hold your hat, Mr. Commissioner!—from another paper. Yes, those people we considered underdeveloped have, or will have by tomorrow, two daily papers, whereas we have but the one. That should teach us humility! And this second paper is no fly-by-night: it has a guaranteed readership. It's called *The Liberated Rat*."

"I know it well," Baudruche said.

"Same circulation, same conditions as the first. In five minutes, it was in the bag and the check signed. Mr. Commissioner, this means we double our sales!"

"Did you also promise to empty the City's treasury?"

"Advertising always pays off! As our neighbors become acquainted with our machine, our civilization and our culture will expand—thanks to technology."

"How do you expect the rats to pay for your machines?"

"Why, we'll lend them the money, Mr. Commissioner!"

This gaggle of fools would sink the ship. Baudruche didn't know where to turn. He got to his feet.

"Mr. Leponte, your stupidity is beyond belief."

"Mr. Commissioner," he said as he handed Baudruche an envelope, "a tree is known by its fruits. Read my report and draw your own conclusions. The figures speak for themselves. But before I forget, you might be interested in a small detail that struck me about those two representatives. If they hadn't come one right after the other, I would have sworn I was dealing with the same individual: same face, same accent, same size, same clothes—twins! Amazing, the unity among those people!"

Miss Foyle accompanied the Commissioner to the bottom of the stairs. She was radiant.

"You look very happy, my girl."

"And why not, Mr. Commissioner? Everything is going so well. Business is booming. We'll get bigger bonuses."

Bonuses! . . . in a business that was always in the red! The stupidity was contagious.

The rats saluted as he walked past. At least they weren't fools.

The last refugee leaned out over the ramparts.

"Hey, soldier!"

"Finally. I was getting bored."

"Didn't anyone visit you today?"

"Yes, the same girl as yesterday. She feeds me like the birds. If I go on eating like that without doing anything, I'll be fat as a pig. Well, how are things in the City?"

"I'm afraid they may try to test their powder of deterrence

193

on the walls one of these days. It appears it's just about ready."

"What is the powder of deterrence?"

"Nobody knows—even those making it."

"Too bad it's ready, because with that kind of thing, if it isn't ready, you still have hope. . . ."

"That's right, and when it's ready, all you have is fear. What happened last night?"

"I was sleeping peacefully next to my fire when these two guys arrived. You'd think this was the only meeting place around. They sat down on either side of me. That's when I noticed that one guy was wearing a blue suit and a hat with feathers. He didn't look very friendly. The other one was in a red coat with white trousers. He looked much more relaxed, though his accent was terrible. I got an earful of it when they started talking. He said:

" 'General, your language was a little uncouth at Waterloo. You shouldn't say "shit" to a British officer.'

"The other man answered:

" 'I'm sorry.'

"I didn't have a clue what they were talking about. When dawn came, they disappeared and I was alone again. Say, the enemy doesn't seem to be coming. I'm beginning to wonder what I'm doing here."

"The enemy is inside the City."

The soldier rose to his feet.

"Just say the word and I'll come."

"What could you do? There are so many of them, and there isn't another soldier in the City."

"All you have to do is make them. You make soldiers by recruiting civilians."

"If the civilians are still capable of being soldiers. See you tomorrow."

Baudruche avoided the busier streets so that people wouldn't see how worried he was. The detour took him past Esther

Labrique's house. He could hear noises coming from inside; looking in the lighted windows, he saw a platform, tables and lots of chairs which were being hurriedly set up in rows. What was that blasted female up to now? Above the door he noticed a large banner: "Women's League: Main Office. President: Esther Labrique." Then he caught sight of another notice to the right of the door: "Lecture on Racism and Police Provocation by Esther Labrique."

What was that damned woman up to?

Baudruche spent a restless night. The next morning, he tried to shake off his weariness by unburdening himself to Martha. He told her about the powder of deterrence—the Prefect's "gadget"; he told her about the ants, even though they were so small and quiet they seemed unworthy of anyone's concern; about the Factory, which was spinning so fast that it must surely catch fire again. As long as these people were converting steel into more steel, they were happy. They worked only for immediate infantile gratification. They spent their adult life making toys!

"What can I do against all that, Martha? The only weapon I have left is the little common sense I inherited from my grandfather who got it from his, and an enormous reserve of kicks in the ass that I don't have the right to use. . . ."

He'd aim the first one at the paper—an immense robot made up of empty heads manipulated by the Prefect from the top of his tower.

"It's funny, Martha: the paper is responsible to the Prefect, who is responsible to the workers, who are responsible to the paper which is responsible to the Factory because of the advertising it buys. And all of them pretend to be responsible to the City."

Then he told Martha what he had seen outside Esther Labrique's house.

"She's collected a band of lunatics and neurotics to stir up

195

trouble instead of doing the dishes and going to the hairdresser's. Because, alas, only the women seem able to act. A few of them still have guts, even if their heads and hearts are empty."

"You're wrong, Robert. There are still a few women with something in their heads and hearts. First, there's me. . . ."

But, Baudruche reflected, as Martha ticked off some more names, they were only women. What could they do?

His mind turned to Labrique, happy in the peace and quiet of his Library.

"Ah, Labrique is well ahead of me. He's beaten the system. He saw it sooner than I did. In a sense he's shown more courage because he'll always be able to say that he kept his hands clean, whereas I'm up to my elbows in shit."

"Robert, it also takes courage to dirty your hands, and even more to stay put than to resign."

"To stay under these conditions is to be a coward."

Baudruche put down his spoon, rested his head in his hands and stared into space. Martha looked at him anxiously. The last few days had added years to his face.

He took up his spoon and started to eat again. A good sign: he'd gotten a lot off his chest, he felt better, his courage was returning, he was ready to do battle. Reassured, Martha went out and returned with a bottle.

"It's a wine from the villages. It will do you good. We bottled it fifteen years ago. It should be ready to drink."

It was going to be a long, hard day. Baudruche would have to make short work of the ramparts. Since he was alone, he felt free to lean over the parapet and get a closer look at the solitary figure of the soldier. That is how he happened to notice that the ribbon of jam was gone from the walls. It had to be the work of that idiot, Edge. Baudruche felt a pang of anxiety. He put on his glasses. It was as he feared: the ants were on the rampage again. He checked other areas and it was the same story everywhere. They were back, and more numerous than ever.

"I must find that fool. I'll give him a piece of my mind!"

The wretch wasn't far. Baudruche could just make out his silhouette in the distance. The Commissioner started running, and when he was finally face to face with the architect, he took him by the lapels and shook him like a cherry tree. Edge was too startled to resist. The Commissioner dragged him to the nearest turret and shoved his head through a spy hole.

"Did you do that? Was it plain stupidity or was it out of contempt for Labrique?"

Edge didn't reply. Baudruche straightened up.

"Probably both. Are you all in league to destroy me and the City?"

Edge stammered that it wasn't his fault if the ants were back. It was Civilian Defense's job, not his; he had alerted them yesterday, the moment he had seen the gray patches.

"And so?" Baudruche barked.

"There's nothing to worry about, Mr. Commissioner. They're going to do something right away. They've been waiting for this."

Baudruche left the contemptible beggar and ran posthaste along the walk, down the stairs to Civilian Defense headquarters.

"Are you still here, Fisher?"

"Yes, and I'm alone, Mr. Commissioner. It's my pleasure to inform you that the five old directors have all resigned. And would you like to know why? Because just when they were about to realize all their years of effort with the first test of the deterrent, they opposed it! Can you believe it!

"We had an extraordinary session after Mr. Edge's visit. I saw that it was now or never. So we have an invasion of ants? O.K., that's what our powder is for. Those old dotards were scared stiff. They notified the Prefect they'd rather resign than see the experiment take place. I didn't waste a moment. I went straight to the Prefect and told him I would stake my reputation on the results. He said, 'go ahead!' Ah, Mr. Commissioner, what luck to be governed by a man of such wisdom and discernment! May he live a hundred years! Where would we be without him? What would happen to the City?"

Baudruche did not answer. What was the use? At least he could go to see Labrique at the Library.

Labrique looked up in astonishment.

"Oh, it's you. You scared me. I thought it might be a reader."

"Isn't that what you're here for?"

"Yes, but I'd rather they didn't come. What may I offer you? Something easy for a start? Or have you come to return the Montesquieu you borrowed?"

"Close up the Library and come with me."

"You want me to desert my post? What for?"

"I want you to come to the Church. There isn't a moment to spare. It's beginning to crumble all over."

"Let her crumble. There's nothing you can do. Besides, I'm no longer the architect. Why don't you take Edge?"

"He's hopeless; he's a fathead."

Finally Labrique gave in with a gesture of lordly condescension. "O.K. I need some fresh air anyway."

Baudruche wanted to hurry, but not Labrique. The Commissioner had to prod him up the narrow, twisting streets that led up to the Church. As they penetrated the old neighborhood, they could feel the anxiety all around them. People were talking on their doorsteps and looking up to the sky.

When the sound of falling stones reached their ears, Labrique lost the last of his nonchalance.

Baudruche commanded every man he passsed to follow him, and to alert any others he could find. A cloud of grayish dust filled the air, obscuring the Church. The stones shattered as they fell and covered everything with a thin powder. Oblivious to the danger, a large crowd had formed around the enormous edifice.

"They're mad," Labrique said.

"They're all right. They're out of the range of the falling rock."

"But the whole thing is about to cave in. Everybody should be evacuated. There isn't a moment to spare."

Baudruche barked out orders. His men gradually pushed the crowd back. Used to obeying, the people retreated without asking questions. Baudruche took a group of men into the houses nearby and explained why the inhabitants were being asked to leave. The people listened politely, complied and left with only the barest essentials, but it was obvious no one believed him. They kept looking up to the sky. . . .

"Come look, Baudruche."

The Commissioner and Labrique approached the Church. It was shuddering like a stricken beast. The architect pointed to a long crack, the same one Baudruche had noticed on his last visit. It was much larger.

"Look, it's growing under our very eyes, as if an invisible crayon were extending it in both directions. It's done for, Baudruche. Just let's hope it doesn't cause too much damage when it collapses."

"What about the two men? They must still be inside."

What could he do with them? There was no way to use them outside the Church. Too bad; two lost men. Once out of their crumbling world, they would cause only trouble.

"Bicard, go call the Department of Hospitals and tell them we need two places right away."

Through the wide-open door—the right half had fallen to the floor—Baudruche looked into the interior. Most of the ridiculous decorations had come away from the walls and were lying on the ground, gilt and painted plaster mixed with the rubble.

"See, Baudruche, now you can make out the lines of the old building. It was well built at the beginning, then they forgot the original plan. They were forever changing the poor old thing, trying to pass it off for what it wasn't, forgetting that its original purpose was to provide a refuge and gathering place for people. That's what did it in."

"I've got to find those two men."

It was beginning to look dangerous. Labrique tried to hold Baudruche back, but the Commissioner shook him off and marched down the long nave alone, a dimming figure in the swirling dust. Baudruche followed their voices for guidance. Still the same jabber, still the same phrases repeated back and forth, back and forth. They finally emerged, a white carapace covering their dark clothes, like two gesticulating statues fallen from their niches. It was a wonder they hadn't been killed by the hail of stones. Baudruche called to them. They took no more notice of him than they had the first time. But time pressed. He walked between them and pushed them apart.

"Stop talking and leave at once. The Church is about to collapse."

The two men stood still, struck dumb with surprise. Then they broke into hysterical laughter. One of them pointed at Baudruche and screamed:

"He's a madman! He says the Church is about to collapse. Doesn't he know the Church is eternal!"

Their laughter turned to fury. They denounced Baudruche, calling him a blasphemer, a heathen, and a lot of other names he didn't recognize. Undaunted, he grabbed each of them by an arm and tried to drag them out. They broke away. Baudruche seized one of them around the waist but the man clung to a pillar. The other tried to stop Baudruche by strangling him. The Commissioner gave up. Madness had given them the strength of ten. For the first time they agreed about something: both wanted to crush the sacrilegious monster. They chased him down the nave, stirring up great clouds of dust. One brandishing a halberd, the other a bent stick, they shouted in unison:

"Anathema! Anathema!"

Baudruche made it to the outside without serious injury. Why wouldn't people let him help them?

Labrique was furious with him.

"Baudruche, you're a damn fool to waste your life on those crackpots."

"You're probably right, but some things are instinctive."

As they moved away from the Church, they could see the two men standing by the battered door, shouting in triumph. That was Baudruche's last sight of them, for as they started back inside, the whole vast edifice began to tremble and sway from side to side, then collapsed in a disaster of dust and stone.

It took a long time for the dust to settle. Baudruche could make out Labrique next to him but little else. Neither looked at the other; both felt an overwhelming sadness. Finally, they dared to venture into the ruins. Labrique climbed over the piles of stones and occasionally picked up a fragment of sculpture. He looked it over carefully then put it back.

"There were some nice things here, you know."

Bicard arrived breathless.

"I talked to the Director of Hospitals, Mr. Commissioner. He has reserved two places in the ward for incurables."

"Suitable, but no longer necessary, I'm afraid."

The flying stone had perforated the houses in the immediate vicinity as if they were paper. One by one, the inhabitants returned and looked about, not understanding. One of them went up to Baudruche.

"What will we do now, without the Church?"

"Whatever you did before."

"We'll be afraid. Tell me, will they build us another one?"

"Ask the Prefect. But it would surprise me if he did."

Groups formed. First they only whispered, then they grew bolder and spoke out loud: Could the Church have fallen all by itself? It must have been undermined from outside, by the people in the lower City.

A group of women approached timidly.

"Where will we live now?"

"I'll see if there's any room left in the refugees' barracks."

They grew pale.

"You mean we will have to live with the people of the lower City? We can't, Mr. Commissioner. We'd be frightened."

Labrique tugged his sleeve.

"Come on, there's nothing you can do here."

"I'm just trying to do my job."

"Yes, but maybe not the way you should."

The architect left, complaining that he'd wasted two hours for nothing while a reader might have been trying to get into the Library. . . .

"What time is it, Bicard? My watch must be fast."

It wasn't; his lunchtime was long past. He hurried to the Hotel.

His arrival was greeted with astonishment. The Commissioner was unrecognizable—covered with a fine white powder, breathless, his clothes torn.

"Is Mrs. Poulet in?"

"Yes, Mr. Commissioner; she just went up to her room."

He ran into Posey in the second-floor hall. She was startled.

"Ah, Mr. Commissioner, you're enough to scare the rats, that's for sure!"

He moved on, unable to think how to put that fresh snippet in her place.

Elisa was sitting in a chair, dreaming.

"How are you, Elisa?"

"Fine. I'm very happy."

"I'm glad someone is. Did you see yesterday's paper?"

"No, why should I? Nothing ever happens and I have better things to think about."

Suddenly she laughed: she had just taken in the Commissioner's condition.

"Good heavens! What happened to you? You can't go around looking like that."

"I was about to tell you a very disagreeable piece of news about your husband."

"Let me brush you, clean you up, see that you're mended. . . ."

Elisa took Baudruche's hat and coat while the Commissioner explained how Emil Poulet had abandoned the City at great risk to himself. Elisa was too busy to answer in anything more than monosyllables.

He said, "You don't seem very interested."

"It's very confusing. And I'm so happy. . . ."

Patiently, Baudruche went over it again. She tried to show more concern. She was very glad for Emil; he had never adjusted well to the City. He'd be much better off down there. How soon would he be coming back? No, no, it was of no importance. She didn't need him at all.

Elisa and her happiness exasperated Baudruche. People shouldn't be thinking about happiness at a time like this. His voice went dry as he asked her if she had learned anything more about the stranger's ideas or plans.

"His plans, his ideas? I think I can guess."

"What are they?"

"He thinks only about me."

Elisa was especially trying today. All he got for his pains was that she finally remembered the stranger had given her an envelope for the Commissioner.

So he needed more money? Baudruche left and Elisa thanked him for her happiness with a kiss on both cheeks. Baudruche stormed as he went down the stairs.

He bought two sandwiches at the Hotel bar and hurried back to his office where he had summoned the men who had volunteered to serve on Emil Poulet's team. Cautiously and at great length, he gave them to understand that this trip would be full of risks, that they would prove themselves more useful to the City if they stayed here. . . . He tried every argument that might make them give up the project. It was a lost cause. Each of them had received a letter from the Prefect congratulating him on his decision: their place was there, not here.

Discouraged, Baudruche left them to their fate and sent them off with a farewell handshake. In another half hour, he had something even worse coming up: Esther's lecture. Because it threatened to be ugly, he was taking twenty of his men. It might well not be enough.

Through the window, he could see that the room was full to overflowing. Baudruche recognized a number of faces from the photographs in his files: all the troublemakers, all the do-gooders, all the City's pains-in-the-ass were there.

Esther dominated the group, both by virtue of her character and her position on the platform. At first, Baudruche couldn't hear her for the applause. When things had calmed down a little, he heard her say:

"That's why I asked you women to come here. It's for yesterday's oppressed to come to the aid of today's."

She covered everything, criticized everything, except them. Only they saw clearly, only they were reasonable, only they wanted peace. Why, she herself had already been tested and made to suffer for it. What was her crime? That she had spent her life fighting the selfishness of the City's inhabitants, that she had wanted to see their neighbors, the rats, find their rightful place in the sun. Her ideas had run counter to her husband's and he had avenged himself in a most despicable and cowardly manner. The room reverberated with indignation. The name of Hector Labrique was on everyone's lips.

Esther made a sweeping gesture. She couldn't tell them what he had done; they must respect her womanly modesty. But they were free to imagine what a jealous man was capable of. What she could tell them, in fact it was her duty to tell them, was that he had an accomplice, a highly place accomplice, whose name was Baudruche. . . .

The atmosphere in the room grew stormy and filled with threats. Several women rose and clenched their fists at an imaginary adversary.

Esther continued, her voice rising, her gestures becoming more belligerent. Her final moment was an apogee of pathos. Stepping back to the wall, Esther struck a touching pose of resignation, head bent, one hand covering her breast. There was an almost religious silence. Then the entire audience rose in a delirium. Baudruche could hear his name and Labrique's on every side— the suggestions that they be hanged, drowned, drawn and quartered. The women seized placards scattered about the room and started painting slogans on them. Baudruche caught sight of one that coupled his name with insults.

Placards on high, the women flung open the door and prepared to fan out into the City.

It was the moment Baudruche had been waiting for. He blew his whistle and dashed after them, his men in his wake. The crowd that had gathered outside scattered at the threat of violence. Baudruche's men were now face to face with the Women's League. The men tried to seize the placards. The shock troops of women went in swinging. The intellectuals, both noisier and cleverer than their sisters, bit and clawed their opponents from the rear. At last, the forces of law got the upper hand and Baudruche's men cleared the hall, arresting thirty of the league's most ferocious fighters. Among these were its president, on whom Baudruche claimed the honor of affixing handcuffs.

Five of his men sought first-aid treatment at the nearest pharmacy. Then the group, with Baudruche at its head, marched in triumph to police headquarters.

"Lock them up for the night. Inform the parents of minors if there are any, and the husbands, if any were mad enough to marry these hellions, and keep a close watch over Esther Labrique. We may get her on charges of sedition and incitement to crime and violence."

The stranger was on the ramparts, conversing with the soldier.

"What's new?"

"Nothing much since yesterday when some guys came with scrubbing brushes and cleaned the jam off the walls. They had a hard time of it. What was that big noise I heard awhile back?"

"It was the Church falling down."

"Why did they let it do that?"

"Because they weren't using it anymore and also because they thought it would hold up a lot longer."

"I haven't been to church since I was a kid, but I don't like that all the same. Church is where I took communion. You should have seen me with my armband and my candle! My mother was bawling and my father gave her hell. I went back later, but then it was to pinch coppers from the collection box with a corset stay tipped with glue. You know the trick? But one day the priest caught me and pulled my ears. What happened to the priest in your Church?"

"The Church fell on him."

"Jesus, that's terrible!"

"What happened down here last night? They say they heard shouting and singing. Was there a brawl?"

"The place was full of workers dressed the way they used to, in velvet trousers and wide red sashes. They were arguing and bawling and singing. They carried red flags and lots of posters that said 'We need food.' Their wives and kids were standing behind. They didn't look very pleasant, I can tell you! Then they all walked up to a regiment that was waiting for them, guns at the ready. The soldiers were dressed, like the soldiers in my father's time—with kepis, epaulettes and short spats. Very sharp! When the commanding officer saw the mob coming at them with their mean faces and flags and posters, he ordered the soldiers to fire.

"When the prolos heard that, they seemed to waver. They stopped; some of them picked up pebbles off the ground, others shouted:

" 'Don't shoot, boys. We aren't Prussians!'

"The soldiers looked at each other. They didn't know what to do. Then one of them cried out:

" 'Aim at the sky!'

"They all followed suit. Naturally, the mob felt better. They went up to the soldiers and explained that they didn't have enough to eat. The soldiers understood.

"It was suppertime. The soldiers took out their pots and started cooking and everybody ate together, me included. It was beef and beans. Like every night, they said.

"After that, they went off in separate directions. As they were leaving, the soldiers said it wasn't worth getting them out of their barracks for a thing like that—that it wasn't their job. What do you think?"

"What do *you* think?" the stranger asked.

"I think they were right. Our job is war. And that wasn't war. I don't know what you call a situation like that. Politics, maybe? No, it wasn't even politics. It was just guys who were hungry which made them a little mean. People have got to understand that. Besides, even if it was politics, it was none of their business. A soldier isn't supposed to get involved in politics—especially when he's holding a gun."

Things were going from bad to worse around the Factory. The rats had taken over whole blocks. The moving men couldn't keep up with the work. So the tenants moved out, leaving their possessions behind. Sometimes they carried a suitcase or two, surreptitiously, like thieves. They were afraid.

Strange noises came out of the apartments. There were people in the stairways who tried to pick fights. Women didn't dare go out alone for fear of the rats' advances.

A few of the inhabitants summoned the courage to complain at the delegation. The President received them warmly, made all sorts of excuses, explained that it must have been a rat in his cups—weren't there drunks everywhere, even among the inhabitants? They had only to point him out and the President would see that he was punished. The inhabitants left, proud and happy over their reception. But soon after, they were conscious of being followed by the same people they'd complained about. So they rushed home, took the stairs four at a time, pulled out their keys with trembling fingers.

There was not enough time to close the door; a foot slid between door and jamb. Neighbors then heard sounds of furniture being shoved around, beatings, bodies falling, children's screams.

There were no further complaints to the President. The next day, the door was half gnawed away, a stone crashed through the window. Then they hurriedly packed two suitcases and left.

Baudruche wondered how many apartments had been taken over by rats. And how many more of them were in the sewers. Nobody knew. The worst of it was that they seemed to be reproducing much faster since the City had started feeding them. Their offspring were everywhere, in every corner, in alleys, sitting in rows on the doorsills, or inside the apartments, sharpening their young teeth on the furniture.

"Mr. High Commissioner, I've been waiting to congratulate you on the splendid group of assistants you assigned to Mr. Poulet! They are indeed worthy of their chief. But I hope you will put a little pressure on them should the need arise. You know, we're not asking for anything out of the ordinary; we're a humble people and we need only an ordinary structure just so long as it's large enough. We'd prefer it to be simpler than Mr. Poulet's design if that would speed up the project."

Baudruche whiffed a discreet smell of blackmail in the air, which might grow stronger in the days to come. The President took two carefully folded sheets from a drawer and handed them to the Commissioner.

"You see, Mr. Commissioner, I've kept my word. Here are the first two copies of *The Rodent,* one for you and one for the

Prefect. At last we have a competitor for that infamous *Liberated Rat.*"

Baudruche unfolded the paper and gave it a quick glance. It was even worse than he'd feared. It was almost identical to *The Liberated Rat* in ideas, style and violence. It attacked the halfhearted policies of the City (it was not the fault of the Prefect but of his entourage). There was high praise for those inhabitants of the City who, despite the handicap of a badly oriented education, expressed feelings of friendship toward their brothers. . . . Nevertheless, the City's population must change: it was an "old people," rotten, mean. Everything must be turned inside out to allow for the infusion of a new spirit, new blood, new ideas—that's what brothers were for.

What particularly intrigued Baudruche was that although many of the articles were in the same rough, elementary style as *The Liberated Rat,* some, such as the editorial aimed at Baudruche, were not. That editorial raised his suspicions. There was something in the way the phrases were turned, in certain expressions that reminded him of articles in the City's own newspaper. It smelled of Canard's pen, especially the page dedicated to gossip about the City's daily life.

Baudruche was particularly struck by the lines about a certain E.P., the wife of a petty official who had deserted the conjugal bed to become the High Commissioner's mistress, and who was supported in lavish style out of the City's coffers.

That was too much. It was one thing for Canard to vent his malice, but that he should know where Elisa's money came from was too much. Clearly, there were leaks at the Prefecture. Furious, he thrust the article under the President's eyes.

"Did you read that? You allow such stuff to be printed! It's slander!"

"Unfortunately, I didn't have time to read the entire paper. I can't do everything. . . . You know how it is, Mr. Commissioner."

The President scanned the article.

"I agree with you, Mr. Commissioner; it's shameful. If we had the time, I'd have the entire edition destroyed. But, alas, it has already been distributed. However, I'll do what I can. I'll find the guilty party and see that he's punished."

"But that's not the whole of it: this sheet bears a strange resemblance to *The Liberated Rat*—the same violence, the same bad faith. And it's better written, hence more dangerous."

"How else can we do it, Mr. Commissioner? We have no choice. If we're to fight *The Liberated Rat* effectively, we must use the same weapons. Otherwise we make no inroads on its readership. Only when we've finally done in that scurrilous sheet can we adopt a more correct tone. I don't like it any better than you do, Mr. Commissioner. I will even confess that it's what kept me from reading the whole paper. In our jobs, we are often forced to lend ourselves to things we really don't approve of, isn't that so, Mr. Commissioner?"

Baudruche made quick work of the distance between legation and Factory. *The Rodent*'s distribution must have blanketed the City, for it was already in the hands of the Factory guards. But they were no less deferential than before. No question about it: the President had things well under control.

"Get cracking, Miss Bourrot, we're late!

"It is my belief, Mr. Prefect, that rather than resort to means whose effect we cannot foresee, it would be wiser to return to Mr. Labrique's economical and proven solution.

"I also wish to call your attention to the enclosed first issue of *The Rodent*. You will see that our capital, our printing presses and our typesetters have been placed at the service of a sheet every bit as belligerent and one-sided as *The Liberated Rat*. The simplest solution, obviously, would be to withdraw our subsidy and reclaim the presses, but this decision is up to you. We could at least forbid the sale, distribution and perhaps even the reading of this paper within the City.

"Have we covered everything, Miss Bourrot? The Factory, the Women's League, the occupation of the apartments? Well, then, just wind it up with the usual. . . ."

Martha and Labrique were already at supper and Sophie had been sent off to bed when the Commissioner finally opened the door.

"Labrique, I am pleased to inform you that I've just sent your wife to the clink."

"For once you've done something useful."

14

BAUDRUCHE spent an agitated night. For the second time in a row, he dreamed that he had strangled the Prefect. He woke up with his hands around Martha's neck. Laughing, she protested that she didn't deserve to be killed after putting up with him all these years.

As he sat drinking his coffee, he announced that henceforth they would have to sleep in separate rooms. Who knows? Another night he might go even further . . . He said this with some constraint, for it was painful to him. She tried to talk him out of it, saying she wouldn't mind dying as long as it was in his arms. But Baudruche held to his decision and both were sad as he left. It was like a little divorce which neither of them wanted, but that's what life had done to them.

Baudruche was in more than his usual hurry: the test was coming off in the afternoon. Reluctantly, Leponte let his workers off early, since all the City's other departments were doing it. On the other hand, all the stores and cafés were open: who could turn down such an opportunity with so many people on the loose? Schools were closed; the children had been given a lecture on progress, science and the admiration due men capable of achieving what they were about to witness.

Baudruche arrived before the main gate. An enormous set of bleachers draped with bunting filled the area. That was where, with the touch of a button, Fisher was to set off the explosion. Baudruche climbed the stairs. As he reached the top, he caught sight of Edge and Fisher leaning over the ramparts. The two men turned and saluted.

Baudruche leaned out to examine the surface of the walls. Scaffolding had been hung from the top to support the mysterious powder which had been enclosed in long, sausage-like tubes. Wires were strung every which way. What a gigantic piece of work! The scaffolding ringed the entire City, and it had all been done without setting foot outside the City walls. And what it must have cost! The answer would be drowned in a sea of numbers. Incomprehensible calculations divided up among dozens of offices, sections, departments, ministries, so that no one would understand, not even those responsible for it.

And the ants were back, more numerous than ever, covering large stretches of the sentry walk. Baudruche stamped on them.

A letter from the Prefect was waiting for him at the office—four single-spaced pages. Baudruche had to take deep breaths every few paragraphs to keep going. The Prefect flattered him and thanked him for his devotion and zeal, but also warned him that he was still influenced by opinions long since outmoded. He was wrong to question the effectiveness of the powder of deterrence. The possession of this weapon would reassure the population and give it back its self-confidence. Moreover, how could he doubt that a powder of such power would eradicate a few ants?

The Prefect fully understood the Commissioner's reaction to *The Rodent* but he counseled patience. Its verbal violence (hardly dangerous in itself) was tempered by its satiric intent.

In any case, it was unthinkable that they try to prevent the printing or distribution of the paper. "Everyone has the right to read and publish what he wishes. You cannot refuse to others what you permit yourself. After all, we do have our own paper, Mr. Commissioner!"

A little further along, Baudruche was scolded for his handling of the Women's League. Had Baudruche been motivated by a personal grudge to destroy a movement that was serving the City's policies—and with great courage? As for Esther Labrique, a trial was out of the question. It would create a scandal and might well disturb the present good relations between City and rats.

The last lines were extremely friendly. Baudruche mustn't go to so much trouble. He need only follow the Prefect's general directives. That's what the Prefect was there for: to do his thinking for him.

"Miss Bourrot, please telephone the jail and tell them to release Esther Labrique at once. It appears she's a national heroine."

The door which Labrique was obliged to unlock a few hours each day had opened. A man came in and asked politely if he might look around. Labrique assented, pleased that he didn't have to disturb himself from his reading. After a while, the man came back with a book he wanted to take out.

"Sir, unfortunately the book you wish to borrow may not be exhibited, loaned or read. I'm sorry, it's not my fault. It's an order from the Prefect. Look at this list! It's endless. It begins with Pliny the Elder and finishes with *Phantom of the Opera*. There's your book: *The Pied Piper of Hamelin*."

"Why all these prohibitions?"

"Because all these books treat a taboo subject: rodents. Pliny speaks of cities destroyed by them; then there is La Fontaine who tells the story of a city rat who invites a country rat to come to the city and share with him a city dweller's provisions.

. . . You have to be sick to dream up stories like that. That La Fontaine had a perverted mind. . . . *The Wind in the Willows, Stuart Little* . . ."

"Well, can I take it anyway?"

"Why not? I'm here to see that books are taken out and read, not forbidden."

The machines were beginning to clutter up the streets. People were throwing their old ones out the window. They only had room for one—and they had to have the new one.

When the machine hit the ground, the sound of the crashing metal drew a circle of rats. Pretending indifference, they stopped and looked it over, examined it for cracks and dents, and if its condition seemed good enough, one of them picked it up and carried it home. The inhabitants smiled pityingly at the idea of anyone wanting what they had rejected.

Baudruche ate his lunch on the run. He'd been running all morning, assigning the police and taking every possible precaution to minimize the hazards of the test.

"Martha, their damn fireworks could burn us to cinders!"

"But what about the Fire Department, Robert?"

"Of course they've been alerted, all my men have. But they think it's going to be a lark. They're only mad because they didn't get the afternoon off."

"You'll be needing them tonight. There'll be a lot of drunks around."

"Just so long as they aren't incinerated drunks."

The President greeted Baudruche with a wide smile.

"I have good news for you!" and showed him the latest edition of *The Rodent*. "Read it for yourself, Mr. Commissioner. On the right, where it says, 'A correction.'"

Baudruche put on his glasses. The heading read: "Commissioner Baudruche Protests" and the story: "Justifiably

216

shocked by the tenor of a news item in yesterday's column 'City Gossip,' Commissioner Baudruche addressed a heated protest to our President, which the latter conveyed to us. It was most unfortunate that we stated as fact something for which we had no positive proof, to the effect that Commissioner Baudruche was supporting his mistress, Mrs. Elisa P——— at the City's expense. We have no reason to doubt our amiable Commissioner's word or his denial of our imputation. It appears that the funds are entirely his own. We wish to offer our sincerest apologies to the Commissioner and pledge that similar mistakes will not be repeated. . . ."

"I hope you are pleased, Mr. Commissioner. And do notice that the correction is in the middle of the front page, whereas the inaccurate story was barely visible on the seventh. You don't often see corrections like that! We are absolved of our sin. No, no, don't try to thank me. It was the least we could do. You've done so much for us already!"

The last refugee found himself climbing the rampart stairs two hours before the usual time. He leaned over the parapet:

"Watch out! It's about to happen!"

"What is, when?"

"The explosion. The powder."

"I know all about explosions and powder."

"You don't know about this one, and they don't either. They have no ideas what it might do."

"Why don't they relax and use the old powder? It did plenty of damage in its day."

"I'm afraid they're going to damage themselves, without meaning to. They're a bunch of children. You should go somewhere safe, before they put the match to their fuse."

"Where can I go? There's no shelter anywhere. Besides, my time isn't up."

"How long have you got?"

"A few days."

"Then we've got to hurry if we're going to use you."

"To do what?"

"You'll see. You said a soldier's job is to do what he's told and not ask any questions."

Baudruche sat down in the Director's office.

"What's new, Mr. Leponte?"

There was a suggestion of anxiety in the Director's face.

Leponte answered with difficulty: "Nothing really. Lots of work, as is usual at this time of year. We hope to show an increase in sales of two point thirty-five percent over last year."

So that was where the shoe pinched! Baudruche had only to add a gentle squeeze. . . .

"Only two point thirty-five percent, Mr. Leponte? But you were quoting a much larger figure only yesterday. And that enormous advertising campaign! It doesn't look very good, does it? Advertising doesn't come cheap, you know. I'm afraid you're in for a considerable deficit this year."

Leponte hung his head.

"I'm afraid so too, Mr. Commissioner."

Baudruche added a little more pressure.

"You had high hopes for the ads in *The Rodent* and *The Liberated Rat?*"

"I have to admit they were a grave disappointment to me. We had figures and percentages that were beyond question. This is the first time they've failed us. It's a terrible thing to have to admit, but we haven't received a single order, not one, from our new neighbors."

"Do you read the paper, Mr. Leponte?"

"Faithfully, every evening—the advertisements and the financial page."

Baudruche took out the fourth edition of the City paper he had stuffed in his pocket an hour before.

"You should glance at the other news from time to time. For instance, look at this picture on the front page. . . . Yes, there: the rats removing a machine."

"A machine? Machines in the streets? What are they doing there?"

"Don't you ever look around the City?"

"Seldom, Mr. Commissioner. I'm so preoccupied I don't notice much. . . . I have so many problems racing through my head. But that doesn't explain why the rats are removing the machine or what it's doing there in the first place."

"I can clear up the mystery in a few words. From one point of view, your advertising campaign was a great success: you did bust the secondhand market. But since people couldn't re-sell their machines, they got rid of them by throwing them out the window. And the rats took possession of them. Why should they go out and buy what we give them for free?"

Leponte looked crushed.

"Is it possible that I've made a mistake?"

"It's unthinkable and irrational, Mr. Leponte, but unfortunately the proof is there."

Baudruche contemplated his work: Leponte, head in his hands, elbows on the table, prostrated.

Suddenly, Leponte sat up like a Jack-in-the-box.

"Eureka! as my colleague Archimedes said. I've got it, Mr. Commissioner! The best idea yet. It means success, financial triumph—but I'll need your help. Listen: help me collect all last year's models that are now lying around the streets. As you know, our current model is exactly the same as last year's, except for a slight change in the cabinet. So I'll change the cabinet. . . . There'll have to be small adjustments in the books, a little fiddling here and there, but I'll take care of that. Then we sell them as new models! It means a financial windfall for the Factory, especially since there's nothing to stop us from continuing year after year. . . ."

"I don't like fraud, Mr. Leponte, whether public or private."

Baudruche rose to his feet. Leponte threw himself across his path.

"Mr. Commissioner, you haven't taken the report. Miss Foyle! Miss Foyle!"

Baudruche had opened the door.

"Don't bother, Mr. Leponte. I haven't time."

When Baudruche reached the courtyard, he noticed that the guardhouse was empty; it looked abandoned. Could it be? In fact, the entire area looked different: the rats had disappeared; there was not a rat in the streets, not one in the windows. All the shutters were closed, doors shut and the rats' flea market was deserted. They must all have withdrawn into their houses. Even the delegation headquarters were shut tight.

The rats didn't trust the explosion. They had no appetite for unnecessary dangers. How clever of them! Baudruche picked up speed. He must be at the gate at Zero Hour, for there might be trouble. As he raced along, he noticed rows of bright little eyes in sewers and basement windows, watching, waiting, safe in the dark. . . .

Elisa was annoyed. Her lover had refused to accompany her to the explosion. He pretended he wasn't interested and that it might be dangerous as well. It made her laugh. He always had to know more than anyone else, more even than the newspaper which said there was absolutely nothing to fear.

There was an air of celebration throughout the City; streamers and garlands hung from the trees in anticipation of the ball later that night. Turning down Prefect Avenue, Elisa noticed that more and more people looked at her with respect and admiration. In the men's eyes she read desire; in the women's, jealousy.

"That's her!" a boy said to his girl, pointing to Elisa and his newspaper at the same time.

Intrigued, Elisa bought a copy at a newsstand but couldn't find what the boy was referring to. Farther along, she saw another paper in a child's hand—one she had never seen before. Her first name and the first letter of her last name jumped at her from the front page. She took the paper from the child, gave him a penny and raced off with it to a nearby bench.

It was gratifying, even flattering, but why hadn't they printed her full name? How would people know it was her? She must mention it to the Commissioner—after thanking him for the article, of course. She put the paper in her bag and set off again.

The crowd was getting thicker and thicker. She was having difficulty squeezing through when a woman pointed her out to two of Baudruche's men near the gate. Payne and Revere came running and, to her astonishment, led her to the official stand where they found her a place among the members of the Academy of Moral Sciences. They knew the chief would be grateful to them, since it was now virtually official.

She sat and waited, surrounded by men in strange uniforms. At last she saw Baudruche in the distance. What better time to thank him? She leaped up from her chair and, waving her arm, cried out, "Yoo-hoo! I'm here!" To her great disappointment, Baudruche didn't seem to notice. She sat down in confusion.

The Director of Civilian Defense appeared, walking through the narrow path the police forced through the crowd. Fisher climbed to the top of a high wooden platform built just for him. Baudruche watched him from his vantage point by the main gate. Fisher pulled some sheets of paper from his pocket and walked up to a microphone. Elisa heard little, as most of the members of the Academy of Moral Sciences were deaf and preferred discussing their health. Over their voices, she caught words like progress, democracy, science, the future—enough to make her think she wasn't missing much. Anyway, she could read it in the next morning's paper.

A wave of applause indicated that the speech was over. She saw Fisher move away and push a button to his right. Elisa's heart beat faster; she was watching the top of the main gate, as was Baudruche. With the roar of an exploding rocket, a huge, blinding, multicolored flame leaped into the sky and a shower of sparks fell outside the walls. The crowd roared with joy and wonder as the fire sizzled along its preordained route around the vast enclosure.

Fisher was only half satisfied; something wasn't quite right. True, the walls had proved indestructible, but out of some incomprehensible contrariness, the flame had moved toward the left instead of the right, as expected.

The audience looked at the giant fireworks in the sky and decided that all that money they'd paid in taxes had not been in vain. Good-bye, fear. The City was still strongest because it had the know-how. Then, spontaneously, the national hymn rose from every throat:

> "Children of this City with its glorious past,
> Should the enemy ever defy our borders . . ."

The first verse came on strong, then the voices gradually died out; only those too old to sing knew how the rest of the song went. The flame returned, as lively and luminous as when it started, and flickered out as it reached the main gate. Baudruche let out a sigh of relief. The City had survived.

Then a thick, black, nauseating smoke slowly wafted into the sky, forming a huge crown above the City. Darker than the clouds stagnating overhead, the miasma plunged the town into semidarkness. Baudruche gave orders to turn on the street lights.

Everyone raced for the rampart stairs and fanned out on the sentry walk to look over the ramparts. The ants had gone. Down in the moat, they could just make out the piles of corpses. Cries of joy went up.

The crowd's enthusiasm focused on Fisher as he climbed down from his aerie. A group of muscular young men lifted him to their shoulders and a roar went up: "Hurray for Fisher!" and "Hurray for the Prefect" and "On to the Prefecture!"

A procession formed and started up Prefect Avenue, with Director Fisher borne like a banner. The procession made its way to the large square in front of the Prefecture to the strains of the national hymn whose first verse started over and over again, augmented by onlookers who joined as the people filed by. Shouts of "The Prefect!", "The Prefect!" rose from the crowd. Thousands of hands shook the iron gate in front of the Prefecture. Baudruche struggled to restrain the mob for fear the gates would cave in.

The shouts grew louder, calling for the Prefect to appear. Newsboys inched through the crowd with the evening's last edition. They'd made quick work of it: all the details of the ceremony and the explosion were there. Of course it had all been printed ahead of time. The shouts now came in rhythmic, imperative waves: "We want the Pre-fect!" "We want the Pre-fect!"

The sea of eyes fixed on the tower saw a light turn on, out-lining a silhouette with its arm outstretched. It was he. Just as quickly, the light turned off and the silhouette disappeared. At that same moment, every light in the City went out.

Was it a bad joke? Sabotage? Incompetence? These possibili-ties raced through Baudruche's mind as he ran into the Prefec-ture to telephone the electric power plant. What was going on? The Director of the plant had no idea. Ever since the explosion, something had gone haywire with the generators. Unforeseeable side effects from the test. But no fear, it would be repaired. How long would it take? No knowing, but at a minimum . . .

Outside, the crowd's enthusiasm had collapsed. Euphoria does not thrive on darkness: people see things that aren't there.

Suddenly there came the sound of heavy raindrops. Could it be true? The rain they'd been waiting for so long had finally come! But a moment later, they realized it was a kind of black mud which spattered their clothes. The crowd broke up and started running in all directions. The shops closed their doors against the invading mob. People squeezed under any available shelter. Fear spread like a plague; people lost each other, un-able to see. Some women fell and were trampled underfoot.

Baudruche felt what was happening, but was powerless to act. Only one shelter was available to him—the Prefecture—but he wasn't allowed to open its door. Standing under the portico, he watched as the heavens opened and poured down a liquid mud, at long last released from the gray clouds that had so long hung over the City like a threat.

Elisa had no desire to join the mob in front of the Prefecture and was returning home by way of Prefect Avenue when the lights went out and the first drops of rain fell. "My white suit!" she shrieked as she felt the sticky spots. In search of shelter she tried the doors of several stores, but they had all shut tight in fear of thieves. But the Hotel wasn't far away. She started running; the rain was coming down harder and harder. Finally she reached the Hotel entrance, covered with mud, her suit ruined.

She took off her shoes which were oozing mud and went up to her room in her stockinged feet. She decided to try number 23. He was stretched out on his bed, reading by the light of a candle. It was always the same! He was indifferent to everything. The world could go to pieces . . .

"Have you seen what's happening outside?"

Without taking his eyes off his book, he answered, "Sure. It's raining."

"That's not what I mean. Look at my suit; it's a wreck!"

The man looked up from his book and saw the black spots.

"Say, that's weird."

The rain was falling even harder now and coming in the open window. The man got up and closed it, and the drops beat against the panes, leaving dark circles as big as saucers. They overlapped, converged, covering the entire window with a thick mud which closed off the room from what little light remained outside.

The man resumed his reading, but Elisa didn't return to her room. She was afraid to be alone. She took off her spattered clothes, lay down next to her lover and covered herself with a quilt. She was shivering.

He kept on reading, as oblivious to her as to what was going on outside. He was exasperating. She broke in:

"What are you reading?"

"An old legend, *The Pied Piper of Hamelin.*"

"What's it about?"

"It's the story of a man who gets all the rats to leave a city. They follow when he plays his flute."

"Are you going to get the rats to leave the City that way?"

He laughed. "They're not that stupid anymore."

She put her arm around his neck.

"I want you to pay attention to me."

He removed her arm.

"I want to read."

Just then, the rain stopped. She got up, wrapped in the quilt, and opened the window. The silent street below came back to life, reverberating with the sound of running feet. In the dim light, the street looked like an endless stretch of gray mud. There were shapes of the same dirty gray, sliding, falling, getting up again, some disappearing altogether in the mud. Suddenly the air filled with hysterical cries of "The rats!" "The rats!" There were shrill cries, then others that sounded like cries of pain, then galloping feet and long small shapes wiggling through the muck. A terrible fear gripped her and she returned to the bed.

"It's ghastly! What is going on? You must do something!"

Her lover put down his book with a weary sigh.

"What do you want me to do?"

"I don't know, but I'm frightened."

"You think that will change anything?"

She curled up against him and at last he put his arms around her. Her panic gave way to violent desire. Only one thing could calm her . . .

Baudruche heard the same sounds under the portico of the Prefecture where he had found shelter with a few of his men.

"You hear that! Go do what you can."

"What are our orders?"

"No orders. Just do what I said—the best you can."

225

His men went off and Baudruche was left alone.

The rats crept out of the shadows and bit people's ankles. Trying to defend themselves, the people slipped in the sticky mud and fell. The rats went to work with glee. One of Baudruche's men heard screams, ran to the rescue and tried to wrest the rat off a writhing body, but the rat slid from between his hands and ran off with a little cry of triumph.

In the tightly closed Public Library, Labrique was making the rounds, a candle in one hand and old Pholio's cane to feel his way in the other. He knew that rats loved paper.

The rats were trying to force the doors of the shops; more often than not, they succeeded. Unable to break the windows, they went after the wooden frame of Linon Taffeta's door. With a crash of broken glass, the door caved in. The rats swept in, grabbed the flashlight with which Madame Taffeta had helplessly watched their invasion and set about clearing the shelves. The petrified saleswomen watched, huddled in a corner of the store.

Most of the shops along Prefect Avenue suffered the same fate. Used to living in the dark, the rats moved about with ease. Clutching at shelves or perched on counters and chairs, they set up a chain to speed up the emptying of the stores. Each rat had been given his assignment and knew exactly what he was to do. Everywhere, it was bite, gnaw, steal. . . . The proprietors stood about, rigid and speechless with fright. The whole City was at the rats' mercy.

Baudruche felt in his pockets for his pad of cigarette papers and a few shreds of tobacco, then rolled a cigarette as calmly as if he were sitting of an evening in front of his fire. He lit it, threw the match in the mud, then hands in his pockets and hat down over his eyes, headed for his office.

Suddenly all the lights went on again, blinding everybody with the unaccustomed brightness.

The power plant was back in commission. Here and there, scattered lights shone in the houses, and once again the streetlights defined the thoroughfares. On every side came sounds of hurried scampering and sliding. Put to rout by the lights, the rats were going home. Baudruche hurried down the almost-deserted streets. Occasionally he crossed paths with a mud-covered citizen trying to reach his house.

The guard was still standing by the entrance. Looking up, Baudruche saw that the windows seemed to be intact: the rats had respected his building. Inside the courtyard, a glance through the interior windows indicated that everybody was at work in spite of the late hour. They would have been crazy to try to leave.

Miss Bourrot was stammering with emotion. "This is terrible! What are we going to do, Mr. Commissioner?"

"Why, the report, of course!"

Baudruche telephoned Martha to reassure her then, still spattered with mud, started his dictation. With his accustomed calm and precision, he informed the Prefect on all the essentials: his conversation with the President, the explosion, and, of course, what he knew of the invasion and sacking of the City.

". . . the looting was considerable and the damage will be serious. It is of course too early to give anything but an approximate idea of the extent.

"I trust you will understand, Mr. Prefect, if I forgo a report on such problems as the Rathouse and your desire to give official recognition to the Women's League. Tonight, I cannot help but think them of secondary importance.

"The Weather Bureau is unable to make any predictions, in view of the atmospheric perturbations caused by the test.

"No enemy has appeared on the horizon.

"Respectfully yours, etc."

Baudruche opened a closet and took out a strong walking stick.

The Commissioner felt less discouraged than usual when he reached home. He was finally doing something. Perhaps he and his men had put up a weak defense, but at least they had indicated the right direction to take. He had floundered home without falling, thanks to his stick, although the mud must have been at least eight inches thick—too thick to run off into the sewers. The streetlights were a blessing, not only because they had put the rats to rout, but because it was now possible to navigate without colliding with the wreckage of abandoned machines, furniture and whatever else the rats had dropped in their frantic flight.

Never had they eaten so late. Everything was out of kilter. Martha had reassured him that all was well and that the rats had respected his house. No question about it: the President had his people under tight control.

"Anything new?" Labrique asked the Commissioner when he had finally changed out of his muddy clothes.

"Nothing much. Just the usual. . . ."

"Well, I have some news for you. I had a reader at the Library today. A man who is staying at the Hotel—a charming guy. Your mistress's lover."

15

~~~~~~~~~~~~~~~~~~~~~~

O N T H E ramparts, the sentries were talking.

"Did you get bitten?"

"No, but I saw some people who were."

"By the rats, of course."

"What makes you so sure, Beagel?"

"Who else, Shell?"

"I saw people who were bitten and they thought it was **the** rats too. But when I asked them if they had really seen **them,** they said, 'No, how could you? It was too dark.' So I told them maybe it wasn't the rats, that you shouldn't talk that way if **you** weren't sure, you shouldn't accuse the rats that way without proof. That made them think twice, and they said maybe it wasn't the rats after all. I told them what I thought—and I'm not the only one who thinks so—that it was a plot, and the rats weren't real rats but agents in disguise."

"You really think so, Shell?"

"I'm not absolutely sure, but it's likely, it's even more **than** likely: it's logical. Think it through. How else do you explain the blackout? It was a reactionary racist plot because they're mad that we're getting along with the rats."

"You do have ideas, Shell!"

"Listen, I'm not the only one. There are others, and at the very top too. You know what? My wife's cousin who works at the paper was saying the same thing last night. There are still a few of us who haven't been brainwashed."

"Was there much damage at your house?"

"Sure, but the government's going to have to pay for it. After all, they were responsible."

"Hey, look, Shell! I can see now the light's getting stronger. I told you: he's still there."

Beagel pointed to the soldier who was just emerging from the shadows.

"I thought for sure he'd been done in like the ants."

"No, he's still alive. See, he's moving."

"Does that mean the powder won't destroy everything?"

"Of course it destroys everything or they wouldn't have made it. Listen: the first one died; this is another one who's come back."

"Just so long as there aren't two of them at the same time!"

Martha barely closed an eye that night in her worry over her husband, herself, everything. She had finally dropped off when she was awakened by the sound of Baudruche stirring in the next room. She opened the door; he was standing in the middle of the room.

"What are you doing, Robert?"

"As you see, I'm getting up."

"But it isn't time. It's barely daylight."

"This day will never be long enough for me."

She put on her dressing gown and went down in the silent house to heat up some coffee.

"Find me my boots, Martha—the ones I used to wear for hunting when we lived in the villages. . . ."

Baudruche sank up to his calves in the mud. He had to hold tight to the railing as he climbed the ramparts. He leaned over. It was hard to see anything. Yes, the walls were still there, unharmed, but who knew what might be lying under that layer of mud? It would be impossible to tell until later. He left.

The inhabitants were timidly opening their shutters. A few picked their way down the street in rubber boots; those who had none went barefoot. Groups formed, people talked in hushed voices, trying to fathom what had happened. They were sure the rats weren't responsible: they lived on good terms with their new neighbors, with never a sharp word, no fighting, nothing. A very few—those who had abandoned their homes rather than live next door to rats—complained in low voices. But nobody knew what had happened in the vicinity of the Factory. It was probably the work of troublemakers who wouldn't accept the rats. They must have been plotting; otherwise how could you explain it? The proof was clear when they began to discover the bodies of rats in the mud.

Baudruche heard enough to know that, once again, the inhabitants had let him down. What in God's name was it going to take to open their eyes!

Miss Bourrot had not arrived yet; it was still too early. Baudruche went through the mail and saw that there was a long letter from the Prefect. You had to say that for him: he was a worker! Why didn't he ever take some time off?

Baudruche opened the letter: the same tone, the same bilge. More than ever, the Commissioner was showered with praise and covered with flowers, but as always with a few thorns hidden among the roses. The Prefect was sorry that Baudruche had not exercised better control over his men since, unfortunately, it appeared that they were in part responsible for the evening's incidents—starting with provocations, then brutality and ending in murder. Little wonder if the rats had resorted to a few excesses. The Prefect counted on Baudruche to make amends when he made his daily visit to the President, in the interests of both their people. However, he counseled against disciplinary action for fear it might throw too much light on their role.

On the other hand, he asked Baudruche's help in the urgent task of quelling the population's animosity toward their neighbors, which threatened to undo all his efforts toward mutual understanding. He had already instructed the newspaper to that effect.

The first order of business was to compensate last night's victims, especially those shopkeepers who had been looted. The Prefect suggested they be granted a tax reduction of 11 percent for the year. Later, an approximate evaluation of the damage should be made in case their neighbors' government saw fit to assume some of the responsibility at some future date. These measures would of necessity force an immediate tax increase on the machine.

Baudruche went to Leponte's office.

"I have come to requisition all the workers in the Factory. They are needed to clean the streets. It's imperative."

"They won't do it, Mr. Commissioner. You are forgetting union rules."

"I'll take care of that."

"But what will we do? This is our busiest season."

"Close the Factory."

Impossible! The Commissioner had obviously gone mad. Leponte tried to argue, but to no avail. Baudruche simply looked at his watch and said, "We are in a hurry, Mr. Leponte, we are in a hurry."

Sick at heart, Leponte set off the siren; all the workers spilled out of the shops and into the courtyard. Baudruche opened the window and, leaning out, explained at length what he had said briefly to Leponte. The men were silent and motionless, except for shaking their heads in refusal. Finally, one man stepped forward and looked up at Baudruche. He was the union representative at the Factory. He was very sorry but it couldn't be done. They hadn't spent all these years fighting for their rights—one of which was to work only at their specialty—to give them up now, just like that, because a little dirty water had fallen out of the sky. . . .

"I'm coming down," Baudruche said.

For fifteen minutes, he pleaded and argued. He understood the union representative's position, but this was an emergency. The City was paralyzed. The Sanitation Department was overwhelmed. Every able-bodied man was needed to help. The man shook his head: he still wasn't convinced. It set a dangerous precedent; who would guarantee that the requisition would end when the work was done?

"I will," Baudruche said.

He reminded the man that the Baudruches' carpentry shop had always played fair with the unions. Why, his grandfather had helped set up the first union shop and had always discussed everything with the shop stewards. They had thrashed things out, face to face, man to man, as Robert Baudruche was doing now.

"All right," the shop steward said at last, and shook hands with Baudruche.

The workers filed out of the Factory as Leponte watched mesmerized from the window. Everything was awry: the Commissioner was beyond his depth and it foreshadowed the most serious consequences. Mechanics, fitters, specialists and even foremen were reduced to degrading work! Demoralized, Leponte returned to his desk, trying not to look at the productivity chart which seemed to point an accusing finger at him.

Baudruche was waiting on a bench in the square in front of the Prefecture. He wanted to be on hand to direct the first efforts, here, in the very heart of the City. He dug the tip of his cane into the mud. It had begun to harden. They must work quickly or the job would become increasingly difficult.

His eyes roamed around the square. The Prefecture and the neighboring buildings were all the same dirty gray. It would take giants to clean them. Better to wait for rain—that is, if it ever rained again. A newsboy walked past and Baudruche called out to him. The evening edition was just out. He bought one and opened it.

The front page was what he expected: a shameful collection of adulterated, mutilated news. Nothing had happened the previous night but a few minor incidents of no importance. Furious, he turned to the next page. There was a long article by Canard about the occupation of the buildings. It appeared that he had solved the problem—or so the heading read. Baudruche sighed. Canard had studied the problem closely, particularly in the area around the Factory where it existed in its most critical form. The rats were being patient; the concessions by the inhabitants had been infinitesimal—a few private individuals had given up a few wretched accommodations in the City's poorest section. One could hardly be surprised if, victimized by the police, the rats lost patience and had taken the little they needed to survive from the inhabitants' greedy hands. "They must find room," Canard stated; "they cannot wait for concessions which inevitaby will come too late."

It was all perfectly clear to Canard: the City's inhabitants should give up certain sections in the southern part of the City which the rats would take over. Those ejected would relocate where they could—in the northern area.

The first workers arrived with their shovels and wheelbarrows. The pavement began to emerge. Baudruche could leave now. He returned to his office, but Miss Bourrot barely allowed him time to take off his coat.

"Mr. Commissioner, Inspector Bicard is waiting to see you. He has something very important to tell you."

234

Bicard came in, overcome with emotion.

"Mr. Commissioner, I have news for you this time. And what news! The stranger . . . the lone man . . . the last refugee . . . I know what he's up to."

"What have you found out?"

"I was supervising the mud detail by the Public Gardens when I happened to look through the fence and saw our man blowing into a small tube. He was surrounded by a crowd of children who were listening to him, although I couldn't hear anything."

"What the hell do I care?"

"But you told me, the other day . . ."

"The other day was the other day; today is today, and you have better things to do than look through the Public Gardens fence. Get back on the job and don't waste your time on any more crap like this or you'll go to a nice job at the Factory."

"But won't we do anything about this man?"

"What do you want us to do?"

"I don't really know. To begin with, do we allow blowing in a tube?"

Bicard left, deflated. "Miss Bourrot, tell Mr. Newman, the Editor-in-Chief, to come over here right away and then look up Canard's address in the telephone book."

"It's Twenty-two Chestnut Street."

"That's in the north, isn't it?"

"Yes, Mr. Commissioner."

Mr. Newman arrived looking contrite, the paper folded in his hand.

"Mr. Commissioner, it's my mistake and I take full responsibility. I never thought Canard would be so irresponsible. But what can I do? I haven't the time to read each and every article before the paper goes to press."

Baudruche was surprised at Newman's attitude: he seemed honestly upset. Was it possible he still had a trace of conscience and common sense? That he realized how treasonous Canard's idea was? Evacuate the southern section to their hereditary enemy, indeed!

"Mr. Newman, you will start by firing Canard, I hope."

"I shall see that it's done right away."

". . . and see to it also that an article is printed in the same place on the same page, stating that the opinions in the preceding article represented only those of the author and in no way those of the publisher."

"It's already done, Mr. Commissioner. Here it is; I've brought you a copy."

Newman gave Baudruche a scrap of paper. It concerned a regrettable paragraph on page 7. Baudruche picked up the newspaper again, scanned page 7 and found the key to the mystery. It was discreetly hidden under the heading: "Just passing along what I heard . . ." a grab bag of City gossip. It read:

"People are saying that the reason for sending Emil Poulet to our neighbors is not so strange when you consider that he is the husband of the beautiful Elisa—in whom one of the City's top men has been showing considerable interest. Husbands can be an embarrassment . . . and there are protectors with long arms . . ."

So that was it. Now it was clear. If he hadn't written this slanderous paragraph, Canard would have escaped his richly deserved punishment. Baudruche looked up:

"Good. I'm counting on you, Mr. Newman. I'm terribly sorry about this but you must admit it's necessary."

"I agree with you, Mr. Commissioner. Besides, it's an absolute rule: the newspaper must never attack members of the government. Still, it's sad to have to give up such an intelligent colleague. Did you read his article on page two this morning? Inspired solution, don't you think? So simple, yet somebody had to think of it. . . ."

"Where do you live, Mr. Newman?"

"On Prince's Road, Mr. Commissioner."

"That's in the north, isn't it?"

Miss Bourrot rushed into the office.

"Mr. Commissioner, they want you in Prefect Square right away. There's been a new incident with the rats."

Baudruche found himself among a crowd of idle workmen in the middle of the square. Their wheelbarrows were full, but they weren't dumping them.

"What's going on here?"

"What's going on is that they don't like it down there in the sewer. Getting all this muck . . . they plain don't like it."

"It's none of your business what they like. Get back to work."

The workmen shook their heads.

"No, we can't. They're prolos just like us. We don't do nothing against our class."

Baudruche tried to explain the importance of the previous day's events. Timid but stubborn, they answered that there was no proof that the rats had been guilty of the incident. It was useless to go on: Baudruche was talking into the wind. Yet the mud had to be cleared away and there was no time to lose. It couldn't be piled anywhere in the City, nor could it be thrown out beyond the walls because nobody dared go out. There was only one solution if they were going to be so stupid. They would have to throw mud from the top of the ramparts into the moat. Baudruche explained it to the men. Many were reluctant to take on such heavy work, but in the end, class solidarity carried the day.

Baudruche's men arrived from every direction to tell him that the same situation was developing everywhere. He told them about his new plan and ordered them to commandeer all the government trucks in the City. They must be loaded, then driven to the base of the walls where a pulley would lift the mud to the top of the walls and dump it into the moat. It was very simple. It was also sad: this sinister, nauseating muck was going to fill the moat where flowers and wild grasses still grew.

"Why not go out anyway?" Elisa asked herself as she looked at the street scene through the restaurant windows. The danger was well past and the City seemed to have come back to life. It might be fun to see the streets after what they'd been through. She asked her lover to go with her, but he refused.

So she went by herself. It was amusing, seeing all those men working around her. And weren't they efficient! Well, not always. A workman dropped the contents of his shovel on the sidewalk and spattered Elisa's shoes.

"Can't you be more careful?"

Everybody knows there's nothing more difficult than getting spots off suede.

My, but Prefect Avenue was sad! Everywhere, shattered glass, stores in a mess, broken furniture, empty shop windows. Really, if the rats did all that, it wasn't very nice. Why didn't the Commissioner put a stop to it? After all, that's what he was there for. She would have told him so except that it would make him so irritable. And she needed him. . . .

She stopped in front of Linon Taffeta's. It was unbelievable! The door had been bashed in. But when she saw the long table covered with piles of clothes on sale she couldn't resist. She fingered, rummaged, rumpled, selected. Things were marked 25, 30, 40 percent off! She filled eleven boxes. A trip to the cleaners and everything would be like new. It was just around the corner. She had three salesgirls help her carry.

What a disappointment! Miss Carbone had been overwhelmed with work since early morning. Naturally, she wasn't going to say no to Mrs. Poulet, but it would take six months, maybe even longer. In addition, she couldn't guarantee the results. They knew nothing about this mud, nor if it could be cleaned.

Elisa went back to Taffeta's. No: sale garments were not returnable, not even in her case. She had the lot carried to the Hotel where she opened the boxes and carefully examined each garment. It was horrible! Linon Taffeta should have warned her. Having nothing else to do, she cried.

The rats had reemerged from their holes. They entered into conversations with passersby, at first shyly, then when they saw they were well received, with more openness. It was sad, what had happened the night before. Why pick on them when they hadn't said boo to a soul? Everybody agreed: it was all the fault of Baudruche's men. Not Baudruche's fault, of course. But his men were just a bunch of swine, in the pay of the reactionaries who were supposed to have long since gone but were all the more dangerous for being secret and underhanded.

The City felt a surge of happiness. They had feared that the rats would be angry. But not at all! It was such good news that everyone drank to it in the bistros, toasting the Prefect's health, the President's health, Baudruche's health, and to understanding between peoples. And the rats gave advice to the poor men forced to do the work of a chain gang, to remove all that sticky mud that didn't really bother anybody.

The rats' flea market had spread to several more streets and was jammed. Self-interest and snob appeal, both, had drawn the crowds. It was the smart thing to do—to make your purchases from the flea market. Today the inhabitants were there out of necessity. Some had to replace broken furniture, others, stolen articles, or clothes that had simply disappeared. Some had only the clothes on their backs. So they came, still mud-splattered, looking through baskets, through piles on the tables and even on the sidewalks, hoping to find something fit to wear. There was certainly no lack of choice. . . .

The rats granted massive reductions in prices, even over those marked on the merchandise: 50 to 80 percent. The label might be that of a well-known store, but at such prices, who cared? The flea market was much more interesting than the shops on Prefect

Avenue, and much better stocked. No question about it, the rats knew a thing or two. On the bargain tables, things were even cheaper. Not that they were giving them away . . . how could they, those poor people? But they gave such reductions it was embarrassing. Dresses, coats, underwear, furs, shoes, often from the best houses, could be had for almost nothing.

From time to time, an inhabitant recognized a jacket or bedspread that had disappeared from his own looted apartment. But how can you tell one jacket from another jacket, or one bedspread from another bedspread? That's what the new owner said to the man who dared confront him. A few insults were exchanged, but it never went further than that. A band of rats always turned up in time to separate the adversaries. What was the point of fighting over a jacket when there were so many others so much handsomer and for practically nothing? So, the inhabitant went his way, mollified.

It was like a big village fair. With a little money and a scrap of know-how, you could make a fortune in two hours: pictures, rare books, watches and jewelry were scattered all over the sidewalk or offered from hand to hand at ridiculous prices. You always left richer than you came. Couldn't you really hug those rats? They weren't nearly as bad as people said. And it was whispered that the rats were very accommodating when a woman didn't have enough money for a dress. All she had to do was go with the seller to a neighboring house to try it on. . . .

Baudruche launched his attack, knowing his cause to be hopeless. The President didn't try to deny everything (after all, they were both reasonable men . . . he wasn't afraid to admit what was true). He admitted that there had been some looting and vandalism (they weren't all saints, any more than the City's inhabitants), but they weren't the only ones guilty; the inhabitants themselves also had troublemaking elements who had indulged themselves a little too freely. And for all that the rats had stolen a few things here and there, there was a much more serious factor: they had not fomented the disorder. It wasn't only his opinion: it was shared by a large segment of the population.

"Mr. Commissioner, I'm afraid you need to conduct a purge among your people."

Baudruche boldly denied the President's accusations and maintained that the only ones responsible for the disorder, the only ones involved in the looting, were the rats. The President looked at him pityingly.

"And the dead rats who were found almost everywhere in the City? I suppose they committed suicide?"

"My men were seriously bitten."

"Ours defended themselves before dying, Mr. Commissioner. We are a brave people. Believe me, I am very serious: you must purge the City, for its own sake as well as yours. Oh, for the moment, you have nothing to fear in that respect: I know your worth, but in the end, the agitators may end up believing that you support those who are doing such harm to my people. Do you understand what I'm getting at?"

Yes, the Commissioner saw all too clearly what the President was getting at: he wanted to disband Baudruche's men because they were too devoted to him and replace them with a new group picked at random. Wooden swords, straw rifles. On that point, Baudruche wasn't going to give up. He answered sharply that he knew of no disturbing element in the City, and that he was fully confident of his men.

The President looked doubtful. "As you like, Mr. Commissioner. I'm telling you this as a friend, and because it would be very unfortunate if we ever had to ask you to answer for crimes committed by people you were supposed to control."

When Baudruche brought up the subject of looting, the President suggested that a commission be formed to investigate, a commission made up in equal parts of inhabitants and rats, selected by the Prefect and himself.

Again, Baudruche understood. The investigation would conclude that Baudruche's men were wholly responsible, that he

241

had lost control over them, that they had acted in defiance of his orders. He would be forced to agree to their dismissal, and with their disappearance would vanish the City's last hope.

Better to shut up and abandon all hope of reparations. Baudruche renounced his claims, for which the President thanked him in the name of both their people.

"And while I have you here, Mr. Commissioner, tell me, between ourselves, what has Mr. Poulet actually built in the past?"

"Not much, to tell you the truth. It was our idea that we should abandon the old conceptions and methods that no longer correspond to the new attitudes in the City. That is why, as you know, the Prefect preferred to pass over Mr. Labrique, for he represented a generation whose art and techniques are now hopelessly old-fashioned."

"Ah, now I understand. But I want to remind you that our ambitions are most modest. All we want is something solid and well built, in the manner of your own official buildings."

"What you mean is that perhaps Mr. Poulet is not exactly right for the job?"

"I didn't dare say it. . . ."

"I hope you will pardon us for our mistake. Our intentions were of the best."

"It's easy to make mistakes when you try too hard."

"Then why don't you send Emil Poulet and his team back to us?"

"Not so fast, Mr. Commissioner, not so fast! They might think it was occasioned by personal animosity, or a lack of confidence. . . . We will wait until they are replaced. They will be very disappointed, I know, because they have no desire to leave us."

"I'd like to be sure about that," Baudruche snapped back.

"And you shall be," the President said, taking a packet of postcards out of his pocket. "Read these, Mr. Commissioner."

"What are they?"

"This is their correspondence. I told them you wanted to hear from them, and I'm happy to say they all responded."

Baudruche took the packet. It contained a dozen postcards on which were printed identical sentences with the heading "Cross out unnecessary phrases."

Card for International Correspondence

~~I am sick~~
I am in good health
I like it here
~~I want to go home~~
Having wonderful time
~~Having terrible time~~
Hurrah for the Prefect!
Hurrah for the President!
Hurrah for the High Commissioner!

The people are very
friendly
~~The people aren't friendly~~
~~I need~~ . . . . . .
I don't need
anything

}Cross out if you do not agree

Signed: Emil POULET

"This is the only kind of correspondence authorized between our country and the City. I wish to point out that we don't have censorship. We despise such base police methods."

"But these cards are all identical. Each one has the same sentences crossed out. How come?"

"How come? Because all the men are of the same mind. I have to admit I admire such unanimity of opinion."

"I want to see letters, real letters. . . ."

"If it were up to me, you'd have them tomorrow. But we too have laws and regulations, and I don't think that you, Mr. Commissioner, with your well-known civic conscience, would ask me to relax them. And may I add that I would not be in the least offended if we were to receive the same kind of correspondence from our people now living among yours. I am not an enemy of your people, Mr. Commissioner, and I can prove it to you. Only a few moments ago, I had a visit from that blackguard, Canard. Guess what he wanted! He wanted to be an editor on *The Rodent!* I don't think he knew I was aware of that insulting paragraph in your newspaper. I confronted him with it and told him plainly that I thought his dismissal entirely justified.

"Your City is too soft on people like him. We would have been much harsher. Well, he has been amply punished and his disgrace is complete. Do you know where he has gone? To *The Liberated Rat!* That filthy sheet! He's found the right niche this time."

The last refugee was heading toward the ramparts. He leaned out and the soldier addressed him:

"What were they up to yesterday? Those were some firecrackers! It was like Bastille Day. I used to set off firecrackers when I was a kid even though it was against the law. Little Louis and I used to set them off between the legs of our local cop."

"Did they get burned?"

"Not really; besides, he had only one to burn; the other was wood. He'd have to come tell my father. Then they'd sit down together and have a glass of wine. . . . You know, you almost scared me when you told me about their new powder. But it wasn't so bad. It was like a big flare."

"But it was no joke. You saw what fell afterward?"

"Sure, I saw. It wasn't exactly spring water. And it stank, I can tell you. The black rain didn't reach me. It got only as far as the ramparts and quit. But what a stink! I'm not all that sensitive, but I sure was relieved it was gone this morning."

"I wish that were all there was to it. The smell wasn't the trouble; it was the rats who came out of their sewers by the thousands."

"Well, if you don't want rats around, you have to keep a clean house. Mud attracts them."

"Come in!" Elisa called out.

Baudruche appeared at the door, covered with flakes of dried mud.

"What's happened to you, Mr. Commissioner? Has another church collapsed?"

"No, this fell on me in the street."

"You don't need to tell me, Commissioner. Nobody dares go out; it's dirt and disorder wherever you look. You must do something, Commissioner. The sidewalks are filthy, the workmen are rude, the shopkeepers take advantage of you. . . . It can't go on like this. People are even saying that maybe the rats can put things to rights."

"If this continues, I wouldn't be surprised. But I've come to bring you news of your husband. I have a letter from him."

"He wrote to you?"

"Not to me, to you."

Baudruche gave Elisa the card from Emil. She hesitated before taking it.

"What does he want?"

"Just to say how he is."

"I'm not really interested. Emil—you understand, Commissioner?—is the past. I need to forget it if I'm to live. . . . He isn't coming back, is he?"

"I'm doing everything I can to see that he does. I have to admit I'm a little worried about him."

Elisa finally took the card and started reading.

"Is this all? He couldn't even write me a real letter? Why do you want to make him come back? He says he's very happy down there: 'having wonderful time, people are friendly. . . .' What more do you want?"

Maybe, after all, it was better this way. Her stupidity protected her from everything.

"Any news about our man?"

"Yes indeed, excellent news. He's just fine."

"I'm delighted. Anything else?"

"No, nothing. He goes out alone."

"Try to find out why he plays the flute in the Public Gardens."

"Oh, is that worth reporting?"

She was really too much, but what could he do? He was about to go when Elisa remembered that she needed money. Her lover also needed money, as Baudruche learned from the letter Elisa gave him.

She carefully counted out the bills, then she looked up.

"What about Emil's salary? You could give it to me if you're having any trouble getting it to him."

"I'd need an authorization signed by him. Tell me, Elisa, how exactly does a flute sound?"

"It's delightful!" She whistled briefly. . . . "A little like that. But you have to be able to hear it."

Baudruche left. This business of the flute was curious: funny that Bicard couldn't hear it. Was he pulling his leg? He'd better not. . . .

Miss Bourrot looked at the clock. The Commissioner was certainly lucky to have a devoted secretary! Little Miss Niquel would never have shown such devotion. . . . He'd been gone three-quarters of an hour and there she was, still sitting at her typewriter, the door locked, trying to finish the report, while the lights in the windows around her went out one by one. She adjusted her glasses and resumed.

I am beginning to be able to assess yesterday's costs. I won't mince words: they are not comforting. All our storehouses were looted: the amount of food missing is considerable, and the condition of what remains is disastrous. The contents of the vandalized sacks were trampled underfoot and covered with mud. I am trying at this moment to salvage what I can. A detailed inventory is attached to this report.

We must now face up to the practical consequences of the disaster: it will be necessary to ration our supplies, unless of course you decide to suspend our commitments to our neighbors. It is my belief, Mr. Prefect, that you can take this decision with a clear conscience in view of the devastation they caused.

Also, I feel it is useless to ask the paper to conduct a campaign to moderate whatever animosity the population may feel toward the rats as a result of yesterday's events. The campaign would be pointless, since the police report no trace of even verbal resentment on the part of the City's inhabitants.

The Weather Bureau predicts no change in the weather as a result of the returning cloud cover over the City.

Miss Bourrot carefully reread the report. She wanted it to be faultless, or it would be like an act of treason against the Commissioner. She folded the pages, slipped them into an envelope, sealed it and tucked it inside her blouse. Then, as on every evening, she burned her shorthand notes.

Baudruche kept to the middle of the street, for the chunks of dried mud kept falling onto the sidewalk. It wasn't dangerous, just annoying. It turned you a dirty gray from head to foot —rat color. Martha was watching for him from the window. That woman was always anxious. Nobody was going to abduct him! Labrique was already there, shuffling the cards. As though Baudruche had time to waste on cards!

"Labrique, come into my study. I want a couple of words with you."

"Robert, there isn't time. Dinner is ready. You can tell Hector anything you like after dinner."

"He isn't hungry, nor are you. Dinner can wait."

Labrique sat down opposite him in the study. "What do you want? Can't you leave people in peace after office hours?"

"The way you spend your day, you can't be all that tired. Listen, Labrique, this time it's serious. You've got to make me a plan, a few drawings, I don't care what, for that damn Rathouse. Anything to keep them quiet. . . ."

"I'd be doing you a bad turn, and besides, I want nothing to do with it. I've already told you."

"Labrique, I've got to get Emil Poulet and his team out of there."

"That's their tough luck. They had no business going."

247

"You're a heartless man, Labrique."

"Not toward everybody."

The Commissioner went on pleading his case, but Labrique didn't even answer.

They went into the dining room. Sophie was yawning with hunger in front of her empty plate. Baudruche had insisted she eat with them despite the late hour. The little girl amused him. But he had to get back at Labrique.

"Hector, I have a note for you from the Prefecture."

"What does it say?"

"It's a bill for cleaning off the jam you smeared on the ramparts."

"Tell them to go to hell."

"You tell them yourself. Another thing: you may expect the return of your wife any day now, lock, stock and barrel. It's her right. Wherever you are is the conjugal domicile. You can't lock the door on her."

"Don't worry. She won't come."

"Why?"

"I've set rat traps."

Labrique was impossible, always flaunting his agility with the comeback, always cutting him off. All the blankets were on his side of the bed. . . . To spite him, Baudruche refused to play cards. When Hector had gone, the Commissioner fell back on Sophie.

"What did you do today, Sophie? Did you go to school?"

"No, I went to the Public Gardens."

"Why the Public Gardens?"

"Because there's a man there who plays the flute."

That's all he could get out of her.

16

‸‸‸‸‸‸‸‸

‶'D O N ' T   L E A N on it that way, Shell. You'll make another piece fall."

"I didn't make it fall. You did."

"That's why I'm telling you to be more careful."

"What's the matter with these walls, anyway?"

"I'm wondering if they're not having a dizzy spell or something. It's normal at their age."

"Want me to tell you what I think? I think it's the explosion the other day that's attacking them."

"You're sick, Shell. You can't know more than the people who set it off. There was nothing to be afraid of inside the City. The danger was outside. So why should it do anything to the walls?"

"Listen, Beagel. There's a funny noise at the foot of the ramparts. It sounds like waves."

"Waves? You're nuts! There's no water around here—only the river, and it's far away."

"I'm not kidding. Listen."

Beagel strained his ears. It was true: it sounded like waves breaking against rocks.

"I'm scared."

"Why? You won't drown. Even if it is the sea, we're way above it."

"But they might come by ship and we wouldn't hear them. We wouldn't have time to get away. Stand up. You try to see."

They both stood up and cautiously walked up to the parapet.

"See anything, Beagel?"

"No, only the soldier."

"What's he doing?"

"Can't really tell. He looks as if he were fighting, but he's all alone. Now he's moving away. He's disappearing."

"Well, that proves it isn't the sea. He can't walk on water."

"Have you finished your inspection already, Mr. Edge?"

"Actually, it can't be done this morning, Mr. Commissioner. It's too dangerous."

"How come?"

"The stones are disintegrating. One could have a bad fall."

He explained in detail the walls' condition and how collapse could be imminent.

"Then who will do the inspection?"

"I don't know, but it won't be me."

"Yes, it will. Come on, up you go. You first and I'll follow."

Edge started up, turning every so often to repeat, "I tell you, this is madness. It's dangerous."

Baudruche was still unconvinced when he reached the top of the ramparts. They looked the same as they had the day before.

"Mr. Commissioner, come a little farther ahead."

They reached the spot where Beagel and Shell had spent their watch. Stones were missing from the parapet; some were on the ground at their feet. Baudruche picked up one of them; it felt like a sponge.

"What does this mean, Mr. Edge?"

"I have no idea, Mr. Commissioner. I am an architect, not a mineralogist."

"You are neither."

"I beg your pardon, Mr. Commissioner; I can show you my diploma. But I'm not staying here another minute. The whole thing is ready to go. All it needs is a flick of the wrist."

Matching his actions to his words, Edge sent a piece flying into the moat. He pivoted clumsily, teetering on the edge of the walk. Baudruche just had time to catch him by the leg.

"Get going, if it's all that dangerous."

Edge moved off, picking his way carefully. Baudruche gave a start: he'd just felt a sharp prick, like a burning sensation on his ankle. He pulled up his trouser leg and saw a dozen large red ants. He shook them off and crushed them with his foot. He noticed that the ground ahead, which was still covered with a layer of dried mud, was heaving as if it were alive. He broke off a piece with his heel: red ants were swarming under the crust. He stamped, crushed, killed, making a reddish goo, then a new wave of insects arrived to eat the corpses. Discouraged, he gave up.

Baudruche leaned out over the parapet. The ants were climbing everywhere. He looked on the City side; they were going down the interior wall.

Baudruche's eyes scanned the rooftops covered with mud. Whenever a small piece fell, a cloud of dust rose from the ground, covering the passersby. How long would this go on? What could he do about it? Nothing. Only rain . . . but no rain came.

The sound of loud voices reached Baudruche's ears. The first workmen had arrived to work the pulleys. Baudruche ordered them back: they weren't to throw mud over the ramparts any longer; it was too dangerous. Better a little mud in the City than accidents. They were to convey this information to the rest of the gang.

The workers were happy; at last they were done with this de-

251

grading job. A good thing the Commissioner had come to see for himself how distasteful it was.

Baudruche put a piece of the stone in his pocket and went down the stairs.

The mud was almost dry on the houses but it was still like glue on the ground. The sidewalks and pavement were clean; that had been done with dispatch. The mud had been shoveled into wheelbarrows and piled in long rows along the gutters where it waited for trucks to come and take it away. Now it would have to stay there. No sewers, no moat. Nor was it likely to fly up into the sky and change back into the gray clouds that hovered over the City.

In this gray cityscape, Baudruche was just another vague silhouette. Since he was unrecognized, he took the opportunity to listen in on one of the lines of people outside the shops. They'd been forming in queues since the preceding night. Nobody quite knew how the news of an impending shortage had gotten around. Shortage of what? Nobody knew. So, for fear of running short of something, they wanted enough of everything.

Rationing would be very moderate, the evening papers informed its readers. There would be limits on the sale of bread, rice, potatoes, dried vegetables, meat, fats, wine, but only until the following summer when they would be able to restock. All other goods would be unrationed. Within the next few days, similar restrictions would be placed on clothing and unessentials such as string and library paste. They consoled themselves by reading the ads for the machine and a comic strip on the life of the Prefect.

Baudruche rapped on the Library door. No answer. He grew anxious and banged with his fists. The door opened a crack.

"The Library isn't open yet. Not until ten o'clock. Oh, it's you? Come in. I'm not obliged to open until ten and you are six minutes early. I don't like to be disturbed when I'm reading."

"You're reading? Reading at a time like this!"

"What else is there for me to do?"

Baudruche didn't reply. He took the piece of stone from his pocket and placed it in front of Labrique. The Librarian examined it in every light and weighed it in his palm.

"I guess it isn't only people who suffer mysterious illnesses; stones do too. This stone is sick, Baudruche. I've never seen it before. It isn't the only one, is it? You have more?"

Baudruche indicated he had many more. Labrique dropped the stone on the floor and it broke into fragments.

"That stone's completely disintegrated! Where did you find it?"

"It's a piece of the ramparts."

Yes, they'd really done it with their explosion. Why didn't they try another test in the sewers? They would have to tear down all the infected parts of the walls to keep it from spreading to the healthy parts; then it would have to be rebuilt. An enormous piece of work. But otherwise everything would be lost. Unless, of course, the sickness stopped of itself. But how could you tell? Nobody had ever seen anything like it.

Labrique followed his friend to the door.

"Believe me, Baudruche, you can't do anything with those fools."

As he was walking, Baudruche knew that nothing could be done about the walls. It would take most of the men in the City to work fast enough to hold the disease in check. And where would they find new stone? People now knew only concrete and cement: that's what all the new houses were made of. The quarries where the stone had come from were far away. No, it was out of the question. They might be able to fill the worst cavities with the remains of the Church and of a few other negligible old buildings, but that would be impossible too. To get the necessary number of men, the Factory would have to shut down, and that the Prefect would never allow. "You can't do anything with those fools." Labrique made him laugh.

It was in the cards that Labrique wouldn't have a moment's peace that morning. Yet another visitor had come after Baudruche. They talked at length; actually, he did the talking. It was because the man had launched him on a subject that interested and even obsessed him: Baudruche. His visitor seemed like a trustworthy fellow. A free man, a loner, a monster—like himself.

He already knew a lot about the Commissioner through Elisa Poulet (he had a nerve, quoting his sources!), but her honesty was almost as undependable as her intelligence. That's why he had wanted to talk to Labrique, Baudruche's oldest and closest friend.

Who was Baudruche? Good heavens, in the old days, he looked like anybody else except for a few unusual qualities, and a little more character. Now he seemed to split the clouds, the way the Church had done not so long ago. He was isolated in the middle of a square, just as the Church had been. And, like the Church, he was of a different time.

As for the Prefect and the Commissioner, everything should have separated them: they were born to follow a collision course until one of them was eliminated. But it hadn't happened because, unfortunately, the latter had scruples unknown to the former. The antagonists were ill-matched. More than that: there was no contest because one of them refused to fight.

"Perhaps you visited our Church before it collapsed? Did you notice the fine piece of sculpture directly under the steeple? A Saint George and the Dragon with his sword halfway down the beast's throat? Well, that's what was supposed to happen, except that our Saint George doesn't want to fight the Dragon, because to him the Dragon represents stability, traditional order and most of all legality, to which he has sworn his fealty. So, in our case, we have a Saint George groveling at the feet of a contemptuous Dragon.

"Would you like to talk to the Commissioner here? It's fine with me, except that I have the impression he's not eager to meet you. It could be compromising. . . . You know, the Prefect might not like it. But I'll give him the message."

"Where have you been?" Elisa said. "I've been sitting here waiting for half an hour."

"If you were so hungry, why didn't you go ahead and eat?"

"I can't eat when you're not here. . . ."

"That's too bad, because that way you may someday die of starvation."

She was at a loss to figure out what he meant, but didn't dare ask for fear he'd think her stupid. For the moment, at least, neither was likely to die of hunger. Baidroume had reassured them. He was coping with the difficulties of rationing, they wouldn't be without anything yet, and he would do everything in his power to see that it continued that way. The Hotel's guests came first. . . . He only hoped no one would come nosing into his affairs, otherwise he couldn't guarantee anything. He counted on Mrs. Poulet to pass the word along to the Commissioner. It would be in her own interest.

She would be only too glad. What a shame! Why couldn't they let people work in peace? In any event, he could count on her.

Baidroume thanked her, bowed deeply—he had to go because he had a great deal on his mind: a large banquet to plan for the next day. What, they hadn't heard? A dinner in the City for members of the government and the top officials of the neighboring state. The Women's League was assuming the cost to show its gratitude for the Prefect's patronage.

"Good day, Mr. Edge."

"Good day, Mr. Fisher. My compliments! What a spectacle! What reassurance for the City! What a marvelous piece of work!"

"Oh, you know, I didn't do it alone. I was lucky enough to have quite a good team. And in the final analysis, it is really a question of talent. Others might use another word, but they undoubtedly exaggerate. What it comes down to is specialization. A first-class brain, oriented in the right direction, is capable of anything—with an ease that astonishes even its owner. But one is always a little surprised when the thing one is surest about works. . . . How is the architecture going, Mr. Edge?"

"We're far behind, I'm afraid. We are hemmed in. Our work could be constructive (forgive the pun, my dear friend), but we're smothered in a mass of degrading tasks—chiefly the maintenance of a pile of old stones that serve no purpose."

"You are referring to the ramparts?"

"Oh, they have their uses, I won't argue that. They were our only defense—a pathetic one at best—against the enemy. But what use are they now?"

"My friend, their use is as a testing ground for our explosives. That alone makes them worth maintaining."

"The top parts seem to be a little the worse for wear. They've been invaded by ants again, but not the same ones you reduced to dust. These are a pretty red, very numerous and seem quite aggressive."

"In that case, our next explosion will not be just a minor test. Confidentially, we are preparing another one, using a considerably more advanced powder whose power is beyond our present knowledge. You know, I even hope the enemy comes, for I'd be very disappointed to have to retire before I witnessed the crowning achievement of so many years of arduous and inventive work."

On his way to the President, Baudruche made a small detour via the Public Gardens.

He could just make out a crowd of children with a single figure standing above them. The man was playing a flute, but Baudruche could hear nothing above the children's singing.

As he came up to the group, a couple of the children recognized him, stopped singing and whispered his name to a neighbor. Gradually the singing stopped and the man removed the flute from his mouth. Embarrassed, Baudruche left.

On a sudden impulse he turned down a side street leading to a section of old houses the rats had taken over.

The flea market had expanded to almost every street. Everything that couldn't be found elsewhere was here. Food and clothing were the big sellers now.

Suddenly, on impulse, Baudruche found himself buying three packages of tobacco, a half bottle of his favorite aperitif and a pair of gloves—the thick, warm kind Martha always bought at Manformen.

"Why, Mr. High Commissioner, you've been shopping! I hope the prices were right."

"It's not a question of price," Baudruche said as he took his accustomed seat before the President, "but where they came from. Can you explain to me how your compatriots are able to offer City merchandise in broad daylight when its sale is strictly controlled?"

"City merchandise, you say?"

"Look for yourself. These gloves are from my usual store, then I have this half bottle of Picard and three packages of tobacco."

The President examined each in turn.

"You frightened me, Mr. Commissioner! For a moment I thought it was some sort of black market run by highly placed City inhabitants and some of our own delinquents. Thank heaven it isn't so! These things were made by us. Look at the labels!"

Baudruche put on his glasses. To be sure, the gloves, the bottle and the tobacco each bore a tiny inscription indicating they were imported.

"We are proud and happy to be able to offer the City real competition—to the point where you could make this mistake. I'm sure you're as happy as I, for I gather you are beginning to have a few shortages in the City."

"Only temporary."

"Of course, Mr. Commissioner. But meanwhile, we are here to fill the gap, to come to the aid of your faltering economy. What we offer is what we've learned to do without. Everything is for export. It's a question of life or death for our people."

There was nothing left for Baudruche but to present his solution to the business of the Rathouse, and leave.

"Here is the key to one of the City's public buildings, the Museum of Man. I place it in your hands at the request of the Prefect; he doesn't want you to have to wait any longer."

"But that's perfect! Please extend our deepest thanks to the Prefect; he must be equally relieved to see this problem resolved."

"You will no longer need Emil Poulet and his team, so you can now return them to us. The City has great need of them."

"Alas, Mr. Commissioner, alas! That is a very painful subject. *The Rodent* has just appeared with the story. Please read it. I'd rather you learned it from the paper than from me."

The headline ran across the whole front page: "Unusually Mild Verdict: Only Poulet Condemned to Death."

The Commissioner leaped from his chair. "What does this mean?"

"Read it, Mr. Commissioner, read it."

"I haven't time. Tell me in a few words."

"Emil Poulet and his gang were convicted of espionage and sabotage. They confessed of their own free will. Their trial was conducted in the most correct manner, observing all the rights of the accused. We had to force them to accept lawyers: they insisted they weren't worthy. So, as you see here, the jury showed great clemency. Only Emil Poulet, the worst offender, was given the penalty all should have received. We are not a cruel people: the sentence was executed immediately. After all, what is more painful for a condemned man than a long wait between the judgment and its implementation? The execution was not public; we despise that kind of spectacle. He did not suffer: the hanging was over quickly. We are experienced. . . ."

"But that's murder!"

"No, Mr. Commissioner, the word is justice. I understand how under the strain of emotion and surprise, such an untoward expression might have slipped from your tongue, and I won't hold it against you, even though it recalls certain particularly painful memories to us—all those corpses lying about the City streets while you were celebrating. . . ."

"You are going to liberate Poulet's companions?"

"Of course, Mr. Commissioner, as soon as they have served out their sentences. We no longer condemn men to prison sentences but to mandatory terms in camps for political reeducation. At the end of fifteen years, we send them back new men with healthy minds, like yours and mine—that is, if they wish to return to the City. We prefer reform to punishment."

"But Emil's death . . ."

"We had to make an example of him in order to warn the City's inhabitants against disrupting the good relations between us. I am just as disturbed as you are. . . . Let's forget it; it's too sad. I didn't show you the newspaper just to inform you of this unfortunate development. Look again: it has some news I know will please you. . . . There, on the first page."

"I don't see anything," Baudruche answered, his eyes riveted to the picture of the hanged man.

"See, under *The Rodent*'s masthead, in the small type: 'Merged with *The Liberated Rat*.' I've absorbed it; it's been swallowed, eliminated. Their wretched staff will sink under the weight of our editors. The size of the type is proof positive of the position they will henceforth hold. We did consent to keep their motto: 'We'll keep nibbling; we'll get them in the end!' But that's all. Didn't I tell you I'd get rid of the sheet that dared insult you? By the way, we will inaugurate our new headquarters tomorrow with the banquet the Women's League

259

is giving in our honor. That Esther Labrique . . . What a woman! What energy! What a heart! How proud you must be . . . There aren't only Emil Poulets in the City. . . . Oh, I almost forgot: I've been sent a package containing Emil Poulet's personal effects. Do you wish to give them to the widow yourself or do you prefer I send them over?"

Baudruche walked out unsteadily. His glance fell on Canard in the cheering crowd outside the entrance, waving the new edition of *The Rodent* over their heads. Canard sidled up to him:

"Have you a few words for *The Rodent*, Mr. Commissioner?"

The stranger was leaning out over the parapet, taking care not to disturb the loose stones.

"Hey, soldier, catch!"

He threw down a package which fell into the soldier's outstretched hands.

"What is it?"

"Food. Hide it."

"Why? Don't I have the right to eat?"

"I don't think they think so. When people don't think they have enough, they always think other people have too much. And food is getting tight."

"All they have to do is get it from outside."

"That would mean leaving the City and they'd rather die of hunger."

"Why don't they eat the rats? That's what they always do when a city's under siege. But what's going on in there? The other day it was raining mud; now it's stones from the wall."

"Yes, the wall's beginning to disintegrate. They really did it in with their explosion. I can't even let Posey come here anymore; she might break her neck."

"If I can't see a girl now and then, I'll go nuts. There's nothing to do here; it's so boring. I can't wait for my discharge!

Thank God it's coming soon. If I'd known about Posey, I would have deserted last night and stayed with them."

"Stayed where?"

"In a country I'd seen only in the movies. It was pretty wild the way it happened. I was sound asleep when I was awakened by a big splash of water in the face. It was the sea. A wave had broken over me. Then, right over there, I saw a dinghy with a bunch of sailors.

"This naval officer jumped out and came up to me and asked me who I was, what I was doing here, and why he couldn't go into the City. I told him what I knew. He asked me to come aboard the big boat and tell him more.

"They rowed me out to the big boat, and I told him everything I knew about the City and the civilians in there, what I'd done and how I got here. I could see the captain was getting more and more depressed. He said if he'd known that, he wouldn't have come.

"I ate with the sailors, and afterward we drank some rum together, and I began to feel the boat roll and pitch. I just had time to run to the side and lean out. Afterward, I went to bed in one of their hanging contraptions. Finally the sea calmed down and I heard somebody call out:

" 'Shore leave!'

"There was this island bathed in sun, with sand, palm trees, women . . . unbelievable! They showed almost everything. And no complications, no beating around the bush. They'd had it up to here with sailors. It took me only an hour to find a real dish. . . . But we had to get back in the boat. That night, the captain asked me if I didn't want to stay with them.

" 'You can be a marine. There aren't any anymore.'

"I sure hesitated, I can tell you, but something wouldn't let me. I told him my place is over there. He shook my hand and said I was right. He took me up on deck. We were right near the City.

"The dinghy brought me back here and I jumped off. It's better here; at least it doesn't move around."

The stranger moved away. Long stretches of the sentry walk were without parapets. He walked with great care, but even so, loose stones kept rolling down the sides of the walls.

Baudruche cleared his throat.

"Elisa, I have some bad news for you.

"Oh, I'm getting used to it: the dust, the restrictions, the black market. There's nothing in the stores anymore; you have to go to the flea market. At least the rats know how to cope. I haven't been yet; it's supposed to be very picturesque. Have you, Mr. Commissioner?"

"Yes, once or twice . . . but that's not what this is about. The paper is going to announce tonight . . ."

"Oh, I don't bother with that anymore. There's never anything interesting in it."

"The paper is going to announce that your husband is not coming back."

"I told you that, Commissioner, but you wouldn't believe me. Let him stay."

This was beginning to get on his nerves. Suddenly Baudruche blurted out:

"He's not coming back because he's dead."

Elisa's face brightened.

"You mean I'm a widow!"

"Nothing gets by you, does it?"

"How did it happen?"

"He was convicted of espionage and sabotage—obviously untrue."

"Untrue? What a shame! I could have been a hero's widow. Of course it's sad for him, but you must admit it simplifies my life."

"I thought you'd adjusted well to his existence."

"Not so well, Commissioner. Between you and me, I was

262

feeling a little guilty. Now I don't have to anymore. But there is one inconvenience: I will have to wear black and where am I going to find it? And at what a price!"

Dazed, Baudruche got up and made for the door. Elisa caught him by the arm.

"You've got to understand, Commissioner. I can't go around like this; it wouldn't be correct."

He took out his wallet, pulled out a handful of bills, thrust them in her hands and fled.

She caught up with him in the hall.

"Tell me, Commissioner, what about my widow's pension? About how much will it be?"

"Let's get on with it, Miss Bourrot; we're almost there."

Baudruche had expressed his distress over the fate of the Poulet mission and his hope that the Prefect would use his ample leverage to force the release of the team. Now he was trying once again to convey his general anxiety.

"Without going so far as to encourage the population to acts of violence or war, I think the time has come to make our people understand what has been happening in the City. In my view, the situation is becoming more disturbing with every passing day.

"I have just learned that the Women's League has decided to hold a banquet for the benefit of our government and a number of representatives from our neighboring state. I think it would be wise to find some plausible pretext to forbid this ill-timed demonstration, as it might appear as an insult to the memory of Emil Poulet, his colleagues and the City's entire past.

"That's all I can say. I can't go beyond that."

Miss Bourrot looked up.

"Is it as bad as that, Mr. Commissioner?"

"Much worse, I'm afraid, Miss Bourrot."

"I'm not worried. I feel confident so long as you're here."

Baudruche left without a word. Her confidence gave him

a pain. As he reached his own door, he heard a newsboy shouting:

"Read all about it! Eighth and last edition. . . . Traitors convicted!"

He took out his key and opened the door. Labrique was sitting talking to Martha in the dining room. He raised his head when the Commissioner entered the room.

"Know what? My reader came again—the man from the Hotel. He'd like to see you, privately—at the Library, for instance. He wants to talk to you about the City's problems."

"Maybe."

He had spoken too soon. He should have said "no" outright.

17

〜〜〜〜〜〜〜〜

"HELP! HELP!"

Beagel was stretched out his full length on the sentry walk. Stones were falling into the moat and on the pavement, City side. He felt someone grab his legs.

"Please don't hurt me!"

"Why should I hurt you? I just don't want you disturbing the stones."

"Oh, it's you, Shell?"

"Who did you think it was?"

"I thought the enemy had climbed up the walls."

"But what were you doing there on the ground?"

"It's too dangerous to stay upright. And anyway, you can see everything this way since there's no parapet anymore."

"You're right. There's no point taking needless risks."

"You can lie down next to me. There aren't any ants."

Shell stretched out cautiously next to his comrade.

"Look at him, Shell. What's he making all those motions for?"

"Who?"

"The soldier, you stupid jerk! Can't you see him in front of his fire, moving his arms around? Look, he's signaling for them to come."

"Who?"

"The enemy, you pinhead! Who else? He's calling to them. It's a good thing we're here to see this. I always told you it would end this way."

"Signaling the enemy! . . . But those guys are all buddy-buddy."

"And you can bet they're well paid! But they won't be paying this one much longer."

Beagel stood up.

"What are you doing, Beagel?"

"I'm going to kill the snake! Hand me a rock."

Shell gave him a few small stones off the wall and Beagel threw them at the soldier.

"They're too small; they don't go far enough; I can't reach him. Give me a bigger one. . . . We're heroes, Shell! We'll be decorated and promoted to chief sentry."

"But that's dangerous what you're doing. He might get angry and climb up the wall."

"We can escape down the stairs. Give me another one, Shell."

"You're going to strain your back."

A large section of wall fell away. Shell and Beagel watched as part of it rolled down into the moat and the rest fell on the street side. The soldier turned around and called out, "More!" and continued walking back and forth and beckoning with his arms. Finally, tired from his efforts, he stretched out by his fire. On the other side of the walls, a few lights appeared in the windows. One of them opened and a voice called out:

"Come back to bed, Ernest. It's not them yet; it's only the falling rock."

266

Baudruche arrived at the walls earlier than usual. He had let Edge off, since it was now a waste of the architect's time. There wasn't anything that could be done.

He tapped the stones in front of him with his thick walking stick. Little by little, the sickness had spread to all the stones. Then he reached a stretch where there had been so many rock slides that the walk was reduced to a narrow ridge. He had to smile: if he were still a child, he'd have risked it on all fours.

Less brave now, he turned back, went down the nearest stairs and climbed up the next one. Things were no better there. Large sections of the parapet were gone; what spy holes remained looked like gaping wounds. Most of the turrets had fallen into the still-soft mud of the moat. The last paving stones on the walk were coming loose and cracking.

And everything everywhere was swarming with ants. Baudruche leaned out over the outside wall; they were scurrying up, much faster than their predecessors, and so much larger. A number of them had infiltrated the lower cracks and from there, from hole to hole and passage to passage, had worked their way through the rotten stone until they reached the other side.

Baudruche turned around and saw a mirror image of the scene on the City side. Thin columns of millions of small shiny bodies extended from the bottom of the walls to the first houses. Baudruche went down.

His attention was drawn to a sizable bump made by a mass of swarming ants on top of a mound of dried mud. Curious, he scattered them with the tip of his stick and saw that they had been feasting on a dead rat. Undiscouraged by the interference, the ants returned to the attack.

He stood watching them. No doubt about it, they would win in the end. Yes, one day they'd be Number One. What could one rat do against a thousand ants?

"Mr. Commissioner! If it isn't too much trouble . . . would you come and see?"

A woman was pointing to her house a few feet away. He followed her and, as he entered, the sound of a child screaming assaulted his ears.

"What's the matter?"

She had left to do her shopping, as she did every day, but she'd been late coming home because the lines were even longer than usual. When she returned, she was greeted by this terrible screaming. She ran to the crib and saw that her baby was covered with large red ants—the same kind that were on the ramparts. The child was trying to fight them off. The mother tried to pluck them off with her fingers, but they resisted with all the strength of their tiny jaws. The child was now safe in the kitchen.

"But listen to him," she said, "he won't stop screaming."

Yes, she had called the doctor but there'd been similar cases nearby, and the neighborhood doctor was running from one to the next.

Baudruche looked closely at the child. It was covered with ugly sores and dried blood. The ants had attacked its eyelids, its eyes; its nose was partly eaten away. He couldn't bear the sight.

"After I called the doctor, I came back into the room with my broom and killed them all, every last one. Come and look."

Already new ants were coming in through the cracks in the closed window. They set about eating the corpses of their kin, on the floor, along the wall, in the empty crib.

"Where is your telephone, madam?"

The number of the nearest fire station was on the dial. He called. The captain was categorical: the best he could do was try to drown them. He'd be there right away. The woman wanted to save her furniture, her most precious belongings.

Her neighbors made a chain as the firemen directed the water through the window. The woman was running around in circles. She stopped, hesitated for a moment—there were so many people around—then decided she had to open her secret cupboard. She had mislaid the key, so she pulled on the door with all her strength until it suddenly gave way. An avalanche of flour, dried beans, sugar, crackers poured forth, carrying bottles of oil and pots of jam in its wake. As bottles and pots broke, an agitated red blotch spread over the mess. Baudruche looked inside the cupboard; the interior was infested with ants. At that moment, a stream of water hit the Commissioner's head, carrying his hat with it. The water pressure doubled. Soaked to the skin, the women sought refuge on the hall stairs, taking the screaming baby with them. Baudruche walked out to the street to contemplate the scene.

A river was flowing into the street. The current carried bits of food, ants, small objects, then the water turned dark as it mixed with the dried mud on the ground. The river grew as neighboring houses were hosed down. All ground-floor apartments were evacuated. But once they had cleaned out the apartments, what then? They couldn't keep on drowning them forever. No, the solution wasn't there but, as usual, on the other side of the walls. Baudruche hailed a fireman and pointed to the walls behind him now alive with ants.

"Give them a hosing down, will you?"

The fireman dutifully aimed his hose at the ramparts. Large pieces of stone flew off in all directions.

"Hey, stop! It's wrecking the walls!"

Attacked at their base, the walls threatened to cave in in whole sections, endangering the houses opposite.

The Commissioner ordered the firemen to stop all hosing. The water drained out of the apartments; the ants seemed to have disappeared. Baudruche called his office for reports. Ants had invaded the houses near the walls in several parts of town. He gave orders that they try the same remedy.

The doctor finally arrived to examine the child who was now reduced to whimpers. He ordered it removed to the Hospital along with three other babies who had undergone the same ordeal.

The woman returned to her devastated home with empty arms. She looked at her furniture in the street outside, the bedding floating in the muck. Her neighbors were whispering. She'd been hoarding food! Henceforth, she'd be ostracized.

"Just go back and market again, little one," an old woman cackled as she passed by.

The neighbors dispersed without speaking to her. When they had gone, the woman fell sobbing into Baudruche's arms. Automatically, he took out his wallet and handed her a few bills, but she refused them with outraged pride.

"You mustn't let it happen again, Mr. Commissioner! Are they going to do another explosion?"

Baudruche walked away. If only he could do something about the stupidity! This everlasting stupidity that the people had been clinging to for so long. These people could have been alerted to the danger; their natural instincts hadn't rotted away completely.

In his irritation, he kept poking at the mudbanks with his cane—and in the process damaging the mudbanks he himself had ordered made. He leaned down. No, he wasn't mistaken: the mudbank enclosed an endless passageway. He stooped down to listen and heard the sound of scurrying feet. He stood up, ran along the mudbank and pierced it at random until he heard a small cry. Touché!

Baudruche looked around him. Thank heavens the street was deserted. People would have thought he'd gone mad.

The mudbanks lined almost every street in the City. The rats must have burrowed through them to establish a secret network of tunnels—connecting basements and sewers to the delegation at the other end of the City. A whole impregnable underground city was beginning to take shape, forming numberless roots and muddy tentacles reaching into the City—his City.

Baudruche was very late returning to his office. He immediately asked for the Prefect's letter and read it through at a glance. The Prefect found Baudruche's assertions about Emil Poulet's trial and subsequent fate gratuitous. Why should the rats want to kill or imprison people who were devoted to them? Obviously the men were guilty and the Prefect was gratified that they had been suitably punished. But one important question remained. Whom were they working for? There must still be a hidden but powerful opposition to the Prefect's policies. The Prefect was astonished that Baudruche had failed to find any trace. "I must have the guilty men, Mr. Commissioner."

"You don't need me anymore, Mr. Commissioner? Can I go to lunch now?"

Baudruche raised his head at the sound of Miss Bourrot's voice. He looked at the clock. It was well past noon. He had no time to waste, for the dread banquet was taking place in a half hour and Baudruche was eager to be on hand. He walked down to the courtyard where the men he had chosen for the assignment awaited him.

The Museum of Man was a large, square, handsome building set in a small garden surrounded by a low iron fence. It had been designed to instruct the City's inhabitants on their origins, their habits and characteristics—that which distinguished them from the animals. At the beginning, a few visitors had come to look around, cast a vacant eye on the glass cases and left soon after, unimpressed. Ever since, a lone guard had meticulously dusted each object and document once a year and returned to sleep in his chair by the entrance. Now the building belonged to the rats.

Baudruche ordered his men to disperse discreetly around the garden. If they heard him whistle, they were to run back. He kept Revere and Payne by his side.

The three men stood on the sidewalk opposite the entrance, watching and waiting. Baudruche's eyes wandered over the facade of the building and was shocked to see that a new flag had replaced the City's. Those rats wasted no time!

Suddenly, the door opened wide and two hundred rats

crossed the garden and took up positions around the iron fence as if to protect the building. Where had they come from? No one had seen a group of such size enter the Museum that morning or the night before. Baudruche guessed they had dug a passage between the building and the sewers. But why this deployment of forces, and all these precautions? "Not a good sign," Baudruche said to himself.

"Hi, Mr. Commissioner!"

Baudruche turned at the sound of the voice. It was Posey, a large basket in her arms which she was delivering for the head table's repast. Baudruche was surprised. Didn't she work upstairs and not in the kitchens? She laughed at his question: she had simply offered to help the baker's assistants. Besides, it was fun and the banquet had made a lot of extra work for the Hotel. She had only to provide for the representatives of the new government and the board of the Women's League. The other tables, those for the league's rank and file and the lower echelons of the neighboring government, would be taken care of by the rats themselves.

Baudruche kept his eyes on the entrance where two fat rats now emerged—he remembered them from the old ex-Social Progress—and took their place. They were soon joined by two women, one of them small and thin with glasses, the other large and powerfully built—two militants who had given him special trouble at Esther Labrique's lecture.

The rest of the women arrived alone or in groups. They exchanged a few words with the guards and went in. Finally, a woman appeared who was of particular interest to Baudruche. She entered into a discussion with the two guards and they motioned her away. The Commissioner swore under his breath: the guards had refused to recognize Delilah Spier as one of their own. She was Baudruche's best female agent and represented his only chance to find out what was going to be said or done at the banquet. After all, the building and its garden were on foreign soil, hence forbidden to him. Once again, things were going against him.

Finally, Esther Labrique and her band of faithfuls arrived. She threw him a disdainful look, passed through the gate and the doors closed.

The rats kept to their stations along the fence, making it impossible for Baudruche to see what was happening behind the windows. Then he had an idea. He alerted Revere and Payne and entered the house next door.

He climbed to the third floor, rang, gave his name, entered and asked permission to take up his position by the window. With his binoculars Baudruche could just make out what was going on in the banquet room. He could see the head table on the platform, the other tables lined up at right angles to it. At the center, Esther Labrique and the President sat in state. They were talking to each other and making friendly gestures. Perhaps Esther was plotting a splendid revenge for the Commissioner's humiliation and her husband's abandonment. As wife of the President, she would cut quite a figure in the City. That is, if the President would consent. . . . Baudruche was quite certain he wouldn't refuse.

Then the scandal would be official: a monstrous couple, legally united, making a frightful example for the City, an example which inevitably would be followed. When that day came, the racial problem would be resolved for all time.

Esther got up, spoke, sat down again. The President got to his feet, replied, and sat down. Everybody was eating greedily; the more their hunger was appeased, the more Baudruche felt his own pangs.

His eyes moved to the rats policing the Museum who were distributing copies of *The Rodent* to passersby. A crowd formed in front of the iron fence. Baudruche looked back toward the banquet. Something was wrong. The guests at the head table were getting to their feet, then falling down and writing on the floor, while rats and women from the other tables ran to them. He could hear sounds of commotion. He left abruptly, hurried down to the street and blew his whistle.

Baudruche could no longer see but he heard much more clearly. There were assorted sounds of scuffling, small squeaks from the rats and shrieks from the women (which could mean anything . . .). His men looked at him questioningly, then asked timidly if they weren't to do something. Baudruche had to remind them that the Museum and its surrounding garden were no longer part of the City; they couldn't enter legally without an invitation from the rats, which they didn't have.

Revere spoke up.

"There are women in there. Things don't seem to be going well, and we can't let them fend for themselves."

Baudruche looked unconvinced. Besides, the women in there weren't much to his liking. Revere continued:

"I'd like to do something, Mr. Commissioner. They are our women after all, and there are others there besides rats."

Some of his colleagues seemed to agree with Revere, even Payne, who was the most circumspect of the lot. A number of them broke away and went over to the fence to try to discuss matters. Baudruche hesitated, but he didn't dare call them back. He just didn't want to be identified with what they were doing.

Still undecided, Baudruche listened to the arguments flying back and forth. The inhabitants were warning his men against violating foreign territory. They wanted no provocations, nothing that might endanger the peace. Insults began to fly.

A dozen women had joined the men and were even more vehement in upholding legalities and respect for the law. Some hurled insults at Baudruche's men while the more wily tried to take them by the arm. Baudruche still hesitated. He had no desire to risk a confrontation on such dangerous ground just to arrest a couple of hundred lunatics. He blew on his whistle and summoned his men back while the crowd applauded.

The noise inside the Museum of Man was getting shriller. Suddenly a voice could be heard calling for help. This was too much for Baudruche.

"Let's go," he said to his men.

As if obeying a command, the whole crowd lay down in front of the fence, causing great amusement among the rats. As Baudruche's men advanced, hands clutched at their legs in an attempt to trip them. Others were bitten on the ankles and calves. Blows were exchanged. For a second time, Baudruche called his men back.

The crowd on the ground rose to its feet and began to shout rhythmically: "Baudruche is with us!" "Baudruche is with us!" New screams came from inside the Museum, among them more appeals for help.

"Shoot into the sky!" he told his men.

At the sound of the rifle fire, the crowd dispersed; the rats panicked and fought their way back to the sewers.

"Let's go!" Baudruche shouted.

He strode toward the Museum entrance, his men at his heels. There was no sound from inside. Baudruche rang, knocked and finally ordered his men to break in the door. He rushed into the banquet room; it looked deserted. The tables were overturned, broken dishes and bottles littered the floor. He stepped up to the head table. There on the floor lay the inert bodies of the President, Esther Labrique and all the government members and the league's board. A vast silence had set in in the wake of the earlier commotion. Then his ears picked up a small noise that seemed to be coming from the basement. He grabbed a few of his men and ran for the stairs.

It was very dark. He flipped a light switch, but nothing happened. Baudruche took out a small flashlight and moved forward. Muffled cries came from a distance. He saw some rats grappling a few women in front of an open trapdoor, but by the time he arrived, they were gone and the trapdoor shut tight. He tried to open it but it was locked from below. That must be where the underground world of the sewers began.

Baudruche went back upstairs. The men he had left behind seemed to be playing some kind of game which stopped abruptly as he came near. The small circle broke up, revealing Canard a little the worse for wear. One of his eyes was badly swollen and his clothes were torn. When he saw Baudruche, he cried out:

"Mr. Commissioner, I protest! I've been the victim of police brutality not worthy of a civilized people. . . ."

Revere didn't give Baudruche time to answer.

"He was hiding behind a table, trembling. He was emotionally disturbed."

"They hit me savagely, several times. They said they were delighted to find me alone in a corner. All because I told the truth in *The Rodent* and these gentlemen weren't pleased."

"Mr. Commissioner, his present condition is due to the fact that he fell as he tried to get up—even after we came to his assistance. Isn't that right, Payne?"

"That's God's truth, Mr. Commissioner."

Canard shouted:

"Mr. Commissioner, I'm going to lodge a complaint for premeditated assault and battery. They even threatened my life."

"All right, lodge your complaint, Mr. Canard. Meanwhile, I'd like a word with you."

Baudruche led the journalist away where they could sit down.

"Tell me what happened."

It was Borgia-like. Every member of the rats' government and of the board of the Women's League, its president, secretary, treasurer—everybody had been poisoned. The bodies were there; the Commissioner had only to count them.

"What happened to the other women? There were at least two hundred. . . ."

Canard hesitated.

"They chose to escape with the rats when they saw you running in with your brutes!"

"Watch your language or I'll have you arrested for insulting the forces of law and order. . . ."

"It's perfectly understandable. They had everything to fear from your people. You have only to see what they did to me."

"But what about your rats? They must have done something? From what I know about them, they were doing more than lighting the ladies' cigarettes."

"I am ready to testify that all those women fled of their own free will. We'll find out the truth about this outrage!"

Reluctantly, Baudruche let him go. Why hadn't his men hit harder? Baudruche stepped up to the platform and contemplated Esther's body and those of her companions. They must have suffered. They were still clutching their stomachs. A gang of deranged, stupid women, but Revere was right: they were women. He looked at the President, uglier in death than in life, his wide-open eyes staring at him with hatred. Baudruche gave Revere his orders: in their flight, the rats had been reluctant to abandon their dead; let them be. But the women were to be carried to their homes. And he instructed him to remove all food left at the head table, and take samples from the other tables. Then Baudruche left, alone.

He directed his steps toward the Hotel, climbed to the second floor and opened the door to the small room reserved for the staff. Posey was there.

"What a pleasant surprise, Mr. Commissioner! Are you looking for Mrs. Poulet?"

"No, I want to see you. It's serious."

"Oh, I'm so sorry but my heart belongs to another."

"Don't be an idiot and answer my questions. What was the food you brought to the Museum of Man this noon?"

"It was what we prepared here at the Hotel for the rats."

"You haven't answered my question. What was it?"

"You know, the chef really worried over that menu. He wanted it to look good but not to cost too much. So, I told him to leave it to me, that I knew what rats ate because I'd seen

277

them around the villages. So I made up the dishes from what was in the garbage cans. With a little parsley and sauceboats of swill, it looked very appetizing. I could have eaten it myself!"

"Stop joking and tell me the truth. What else was in those dishes?"

"Ah, I'm glad you reminded me. . . . I was afraid it might taste a little flat so I added some seasoning. Mayonnaise and mustard are hard to find and very expensive with the rationing and black market. So I added a powder I found in a cupboard and I didn't stint. They must have liked it. . . ."

"What was the powder?"

"I don't remember too well. I think maybe it was rat poison."

Exactly as Baudruche had guessed: Posey was the culprit. He could have kissed her! He looked at her sternly.

"Do you realize that you are a murderer? And you didn't kill only rats? You killed a dozen women too. . . ."

"Oh, those fanatics in the league? Women who sleep with rats . . . you call them women?"

"Yes, they were women all the same."

"Well, they didn't have to go. They got what they deserved."

"You know this could get you into a lot of trouble?"

"Trouble? I know you'll take care of it. Otherwise I certainly wouldn't have told you about it."

Baudruche took two sandwiches from the Hotel bar and stuffed them in his pocket. He was in a hurry. He wanted to see Leponte. The Director was beginning to seem far less offensive than the other people Baudruche had to deal with.

"What's new, Mr. Leponte?"

"Nothing good. Productivity is down. I'm working with a reduced labor force, and you should see the state my workers were in when you returned them to me! Our plant doctors can't keep up with it. I'm missing forty-three point seven percent of my employees."

"But nobody did anything to them."

"Then how do you explain the accidents on the job, Mr. Commissioner? And the overwork? Look at this report from our head doctor: it lists cramps, blisters, loss of appetite, lumbago, head colds, coughs, chilblain, sties, debility, nervous depression. . . . There are words even I don't understand. I can't know the vocabularies of every profession. He even lists sunstroke!"

"Sunstroke! Here? That's quite impossible, Mr. Leponte."

"It's not only possible; it's a fact. I have the doctor's certificate to prove it. They're specialists too, health technicians, and if you're going to question a specialist's word, where will it end? There is even the likelihood that all work will have to cease. That would be our ruin, Mr. Commissioner! And all because of some mud that wasn't bothering anybody."

"Mr. Leponte, I specialize in mud as you do in production. Therefore my decisions on that subject are beyond discussion."

"Forgive me, Mr. Commissioner. But that isn't all. You see this pile of papers on my desk? That means money going out—a fortune, an immense fortune! And all of it is legitimate. I have to play fair with my workers. There's sick leave, compensation for underproduction, for transfers, for excessive labor, for overtime, for soap, nail brushes, deodorant . . ."

"Is that all, Mr. Leponte?"

"No, Mr. Commissioner: there are also unemployment benefits, reemployment . . ."

Leponte continued, his myopic eyes bent over his papers. Baudruche got up and left.

Without intending to, he found himself in front of the Library. He opened the door and went in. Labrique looked up.

"Have you finally made your decison, Baudruche?"

"What decision? What do you mean?"

"To take action."

"Is your fellow here?"

"No, but he's coming. Well, I gather you put on quite a show awhile ago?"

"I did what I could and what I thought I should."

"At last! I'm not exactly against it, you know. . . ."

"I don't like it. It could make trouble for the City—and for me especially."

"It had to happen sooner or later. It can't go on like this and you know it. You don't know what your next move is and that's why you're here. Isn't that so, Baudruche?"

The Commissioner shrugged, sank deeper into his chair and refused to reply. That damn Labrique! Always talking about things he knew nothing about. He saw everything from the top of his ladder. Let him stay in his book nook, far removed from the City, from its problems, from everything. What can you know of the world if you retire from it?

The door opened without a sound. The stranger entered and locked the door behind him.

The stranger was gone now and Baudruche didn't have the strength to get out of his chair. He felt even more dejected than when he had arrived. The man hadn't been completely wrong. He saw things clearly, but only the darker side. Couldn't one try to do better? To salvage something? He'd been pretty contemptuous of the City's inhabitants.

Labrique coughed. "What is your decision, Baudruche?"

"I don't know. I have to think first."

"Nothing can be done without you, and you can't do anything without him. Don't think too hard. Time is running out. It's even later than you think."

Baudruche got up without speaking and headed for the door.

He almost ran to his office. It was terribly late. The streetlights were already on, making halos in the swirls of dust.

When he had finished his report to the Prefect, he asked Miss Bourrot to get him copies of both the City paper and *The Rodent*. It was important that he read everything tonight.

He stuffed the papers in his overcoat pocket and read them as soon as he arrived home. Both were full of the day's big event at the Museum of Man. The paper described it in vague, somewhat embarrased terms, full of "It is possible that" and "It is thought that." Nothing was certain. Baudruche's role was barely suggested. However, his men's actions were made much of. They had been out of control, some should be summarily removed; they were the ones responsible for the day's tragedy; they were fomenting a reign of terror. The proof was the way the women fled at their approach. They had preferred refuge among the rats rather than fall into the hands of these "Praetorian Guards."

The wind is shifting, Baudruche. It's not a frontal attack yet, but they're watching you. . . . He opened *The Rodent*. There, the tone was definitely more vitriolic and Baudruche was mentioned by name. It expressed surprise that the Prefect would grant such responsibilities to a man whose loyalty was questionable. There were two series of pictures across the middle of the page. One showed photographs of the former members of the rat government, with the caption "The Victims"; the other, the faces of the new President and his ministers, captioned "The Avengers."

"They look meaner than their predecessors, Labrique."

"Yes, and it doesn't bode good for the future."

Martha came in to announce dinner.

Baudruche slapped his friend on the shoulder.

"Come, widower, time to eat!"

Labrique stirred.

"Yes, and what's extraordinary about that woman is that she's a bigger nuisance dead than alive."

18

"'IS SOMETHING wrong, Robert? You don't look well this morning. Didn't you sleep last night?"

"I couldn't digest my dinner. You're feeding me too much heavy food, Martha."

"Don't lie to me, Robert. Tell me what's bothering you?"

"It's too hard to explain. Read about it in the newspapers."

"I have, but they don't tell me everything."

"What they say is already more than enough."

"You're in for a bad time?"

"No doubt about it."

"How do you think it will end?"

"Badly, whatever happens."

He left under Martha's sad and watchful gaze. She hadn't dared ask him more.

Labrique and the man had been very unfair to him. They said he had missed a great opportunity. They called that a great opportunity! Like telling a thief that he's just passsed up a jewelry store. What was against the law was against the law. You couldn't get around that, and he wasn't about to change his ideas on that subject. They'd asked him: what if somebody had killed the Prefect? Well, he'd have gone after the killer and seen to it he was punished. If anyone had even considered such a crime, he would have looked him up. They'd laughed at him. But nobody was going to stop him from doing what was right. Besides, the rats were too solidly entrenched in the City. The inhabitants' attitude was past changing. They'd been contaminated by the rats.

How would it end? He didn't know but he refused to accept the man's prophecy. That the rats' encroachment would continue was unfortunately certain, but to go from there to assume that . . . That was a long jump. Baudruche had refused to accept it: it was impossible, impossible. But what if it wasn't. On second thought, it had a certain logic: the rats would establish their dominion over the City—a form of protectorate. They would control everything: all the services, all the ministries, all the forces of law and order, even the Prefecture.

Nor would they stop there: the population would be only too happy to serve, because everything that could possibly remind them of their past—museums, monuments, books, education, freedom—would have been destroyed. The children would be raised to serve the rats. They would be taught that they had no other function. The girls would consider themselves lucky to find a place in one of the rats' harems. It would be their ultimate ambition, just as the men's would be to submit to their tasks.

Work would be very different from what it was now. No more paid vacations, no shortened workweek, no more sick leave. Work or drop dead. They would have to feed the master race and it had a large appetite. The slaves would never be done working, nor would there ever be enough slaves. They'd find ways to make the women produce the most children possible in order to have more slaves. . . . No, that couldn't be; it couldn't come to that. Something had to happen . . . but what?

He had arrived in front of the main gate. The guards stood

well away from it to avoid the falling stone. He passed the big board with the official bulletins nobody read anymore, and climbed the stairs. It had become a pilgrimage.

The soldier was throwing dead wood on the fire. They had almost forgotten his presence in the City, or that he was patiently waiting at his post. But Baudruche knew his time was almost up. The last refugee had told him that.

Baudruche turned and looked at the City. Up the street where he had been the day before, he noticed a crowd in a state of great agitation. People were arguing on the sidewalks, others were carrying bundles and suitcases, still more were moving furniture. It was where the first invasion of ants had occurred. From the looks of things, they must have returned. He took the nearest staircase and went down.

The place was in an uproar. He was immediately surrounded by a circle of people all talking at once. All he could make out was that they had called the Fire Department.

The captain of the fire brigade arrived with a covey of red trucks. The colonel would be there in a moment. The situation must be pretty serious if he was coming himself. The firemen leaped from their trucks and attached their hoses. They were watched with gratitude not unmixed with fear. The captain informed Baudruche that this invasion was much worse than the previous day's. This time, the ants were taking over whole buildings.

Baudruche made a quick visit to the buildings. The task seemed insuperable: each room would have to be completely inundated, and even that wouldn't take care of all the ants. He heard footsteps behind him on the stairs: the colonel had made his appearance. He had assessed the disaster and now told Baudruche what could be accomplished. It wasn't much.

"Mr. Commissioner, the only solution is cohabitation. Perhaps the inhabitants will get used to it."

"You are joking of course, Colonel."

"I never joke on the job, Mr. High Commissioner. We haven't

enough hose and not nearly enough water, for the same situation obtains in other peripheral sections of the City."

"So what do we do?"

"Burn the buildings, Mr. Commissioner."

Firemen? Burn buildings? Clearly, madness was abroad in the land. Yet, it was either that or, by tomorrow, the same ants would cross the next street and invade still more houses. Baudruche thought of the nearby warehouses that contained the City's food reserves. They must be saved at all costs. He gave in.

The colonel opened the window and shouted to his men to turn off the hoses and set fire to the houses. The firemen looked at each other blankly. The colonel explained his reasons and ordered them to attach their hoses to gasoline trucks. He returned to the street. The crowd took issue with the colonel, in spite of the fear his uniform inspired. Did he really mean to burn down their homes, their furniture, above all their machines which they hadn't had time to remove? The colonel tried to argue but their resentment increased. The newspaper was right: there was a secret reactionary party working to subvert the City and drive them to panic in order to seize power. But they weren't going to give in so easily. Fists started to fly and the frightened colonel called for help.

The captain heard him and ordered the firemen to train their hoses on the crowd around the colonel. Baudruche, who had witnessed the scene from a third-floor window, rushed down. The people had taken to their heels, cursing the reactionaries and all uniforms. Some spoke of asking the rats to intervene. The High Commissioner's attitude did not inspire confidence. They discussed him in small groups, some defending him, others not. A few broke away and came to discuss matters with the Commissioner.

But the moment Baudruche left, the arguments started up again. The evicted took issue with the firemen and the drivers of the gasoline trucks who had stepped down from their cabs. They mustn't do it; where were they going to live? Their apartments were all they had, and most of them hadn't finished paying for them. The colonel was unmoved; he gave out orders; the people screamed. At least let them save their machines! They bolted up the stairs as the firemen started to spray gasoline through the windows. Time was short and the machines were heavy; it took four men to lift one. They helped each other throw them out the window. The firemen were barely able to jump out of the way before the machines fell on the sidewalk with a thud, spraying them with muddy water.

Everybody rushed down the stairs. The colonel announced he was about to set a match to the first house. The man he had given the order to hesitated. The crowd pressed around him, pleading. He couldn't bring himself to do it. Silently, his colleagues surrounded him. The colonel decided it was too risky to insist further and left with his men. He should have had written instructions at the very least, something to protect him. It could mean the colonel's dismissal or even a court martial. And with his retirement only two years off? He and his men left.

The crowd crowed with joy, but their enthusiasm collapsed quickly. Where were they to go? Baudruche should have solved the problem, but it didn't look as though he were going to. So they loaded up their wheelbarrows with everything that wasn't ruined by the mud, hoisted the children on top and set off aimlessly toward the center of town.

Occasionally, a man knocked on a door to ask for asylum. They weren't demanding; anything would do—a corner in the attic, in the garage. But nobody had room. Doors were closed in their faces, shutters clattered shut. Nobody wanted these kinds of people.

The long file of victims circled the City's center. There was no hope there; that was where the rich lived. Maybe they'd find something farther off, in the working-class district where the proletarian heart beat. The interminable line of wheelbarrows, groaning women and whining children wound down Poitiers

Avenue. Once again the men knocked on doors, called to people in their houses, stopped passersby in the streets. Their tone was different here: less submissive, more familiar, sometimes even assertive. They felt at home here. And they were at home, but the results were no better: nobody had any room. The weary procession came to a stop. The men sat down where they could, on the sidewalks, on mounds of mud, while their women went off to beg for milk to feed their crying children. Nobody knew where to go. They were beginning to get hungry, and if things weren't better soon, they'd have to take down their mattresses and sleep in the streets.

Some rats approached the line and engaged the people in conversation. They were very sympathetic: they too were on the bottom rung of society, and it was precisely because they were both have-nots that they should come to each other's aid. Some of the rat females appeared with glasses of milk and crackers. Faces brightened. No, they had not been abandoned altogether. The paper—and *The Rodent* even more—was right: these were their openhearted brothers. They chattered together and slapped each other on the back. The rats made funny faces at the children which made them laugh. People began to smile again, even to laugh.

The rats invited them to follow: they were only a stone's throw from their own neighborhood. The rat homes were not exactly palaces, but they could always squeeze in one more. The men went back for their wheelbarrows and pushed them to the section near the Factory. The rats came out of their houses to invite them in—a far cry from their previous experience.

Miss Bourrot was in a state.

"They were looking for you everywhere, Mr. Commissioner."

"I ran into Fisher who is still boasting about his explosion. But tell me, why isn't there any smoke rising from the southern part of town? I gave orders that the houses be burned."

"The colonel of the fire brigade said the people wouldn't let him. And that's not all. The homeless are everywhere, causing terrible congestion with their wheelbarrows. They don't know where to go."

"They had only to come to me, as agreed. I'll see to their relocation."

"That's what your men told them, but they didn't want to."

"Where are they now?"

"Last seen, they were on their way toward the Factory."

Baudruche took a few of his men and set off at a run. They mustn't go in that direction: he knew only too well what awaited them there.

But by the time he arrived, the buildings were already being organized. Providentially, the rats had been sent extra hands. All the homeless had been herded into the largest courtyard and all exits closed off.

First, they were given a thorough examination, their biceps tested, their mouths opened and investigated. Groups formed to discuss them. Then, alone or in families, they were directed onto a platform. Figures were called out, an occasional arm shot up, then a rat came to claim his possession. It was explained that this rat would be responsible for their shelter. They thanked him profusely and followed: he was too kind, they hated to be a nuisance, they would take up as little room as possible and make every effort not to upset their normal homelife. They were immediately reassured: the rats showed them into an attic, a corner of the basement, an outhouse, where they threw their mattresses on the floor. It wasn't precisely what they had hoped for, but it was better than nothing.

"What about the rent?" they asked timidly.

Those wonderful people didn't want any rent. The women and girls had only to lend a helping hand during the day; the men would be asked to perform simple tasks suitable to their superior strength. There was plenty of work; the choice would be up to them. There was coal to bring up, wood to cut, walls to wash down, furniture, bundles and trunks to move. And the flea market required a lot of work. Once the men were occupied, it would be even easier to find work for the women: to start with, what came easiest, work their sex had destined them for. If they resisted, they were threatened. And if that wasn't enough, or if they fought back, the rats called their own females to explain that here one didn't defy the males' orders. So, well pinned down, the most recalcitrant were forced to submit, sometimes under their children's terror-stricken gaze. Meanwhile, the husband was filling bags of coal in the basement.

Once the act was over, the women sobbed and moaned. The females consoled them with slaps and packed them off to work. There was the cooking to do, the housework, the children to clean up. At last the rats had help, an intelligent pair of hands that knew how to make those complicated machines work. The record player played as the mistress of the house stretched out comfortably to watch the woman polish the floor. The children were sent off to play with the little rats in the courtyard. The rat children had a favorite game, "rats and Baudruche's men," which always ended with Baudruche's men groveling in a corner, crying over their bites.

The men sometimes complained when they came home dirty and exhausted, but then they were dragged into a corner; they would be sure not to complain again—if they were still capable of it.

Baudruche returned to his office, sad and worn out. If they had only executed his orders, this new misfortune could have been avoided.

"We'll never see those people again," he said to himself, climbing the stairs to his office.

Baudruche took the Prefect's letter from Miss Bourrot's hand but this time he opened it slowly. It appeared that he had been wrong to get excited over a few houses in the southern part of town. Further along, the Prefect returned to the fact that Baudruche had failed to control his men. Public opinion was right: his ranks needed weeding out. The Commissioner was advised to begin the purge without delay. The Prefect proposed to recruit a militia of his own, capable of inspiring greater confidence. Baudruche knew what that meant: the Prefect was going to disarm him the better to have him at his mercy.

He telephoned the commissariats in the outlying regions to find out what was happening with the ants. The news was reassuring except for the southern part of town. They must have thought they'd won a victory there, for they were continuing their advance, moving faster and faster.

Baudruche walked over to the wall map of the City. The smallest street, the meanest house were there. A large blue area in the inner city was growing day by day. Baudruche sighed, picked out a red pencil and crosshatched an area to the right of the main gate. He must go back there and find out what was going on.

He set off with a handful of men. As they were walking, Revere reported that a man who worked for the Prefecture had tried to recruit him for the Prefect's new personal guard.

"He said you were going to have to lay off some of your men. Is that true, Mr. Commissioner?"

"Were you the only one propositioned?"

"No, Smith, Muller and Hernandez were too."

"What did you tell him?"

"To fuck off, but some of the others asked for time to think it over. The conditions are better, they say promotions are faster, there's better job security. . . ."

"You tell them that as long as I'm around, no one will be fired except for bad performance on the job."

"Gladly, Mr. Commissioner. A lot of men were beginning to worry."

Baudruche had decided he would not allow himself to be disarmed as long as he still had options. The Prefect could "invite" Baudruche to lay his men off, but he couldn't force him to. But he could try to detach as many as possible, which was apparently what he had set about to do.

"I'd better look out for myself," Baudruche muttered under his breath. He had reached the ant-infested district. The insects had crossed yet another street and were moving in on a new group of houses. With fire and water eliminated, there was only one solution. It was simple, it was foolproof, it posed no danger for the City.

Yes, it was simple. All that was necessary was to put things back the way they'd been, get rid of the mud clogging the moat, open the canal that connected the moat with the river and let it fill with water once again, remembering to keep a passage clear in front of each gate. It could easily be done and would take very few men. But there was a "but." They would have to leave the City, go beyond the walls, and that the City's inhabitants would never dare do.

"And I can't kick them in the ass. There are too many of them."

He must talk to the Prefect. Until then, there was nothing to do but try to slow down the invasion with whatever expedient came to hand. That's what he told everybody who came to ask his advice. Then, with a feeling of helplessness, he left for the Museum of Man where the new President was expecting him.

A small female with the shadow of a moustache asked him to come in: the President was at his disposal.

Baudruche examined him quickly. He was thinner than his predecessor, meaner and more ferocious. His instincts were clearly discernible in his eyes. The Commissioner began—half-heartedly—with a frontal attack on the question of the women of the league.

"But, Mr. Commissioner, why did you frighten them? Put yourself in their place: for an hour, they watched you agitating on the sidewalk, knowing full well your sentiments toward the league; then they witnessed with horror the cowardly assassination of their board and our government; then they saw you charge in at the head of your men. Their panic is perfectly understandable. They preferred to find refuge with us, and I doubt very much they will risk returning to the City so long as this tense atmosphere prevails."

Baudruche broke in:

"These women were inhabitants of the City. They were calling for help and it was my duty to come to their rescue."

"In the City, yes. Here, no. You seem to forget they were under our protection, Mr. Commissioner."

"You have a funny way of protecting women."

"It's as good as yours. At least they weren't afraid of us, as we've proved to you. You look skeptical, Mr. Commissioner. Do you doubt my word? It is your right. But I have one hundred and ninety-nine written testimonials to the truth."

The President handed Baudruche a thick packet of postcards. They were identical to those from Emil Poulet and his team and the same phrases were crossed out.

"I know what your cards are worth!"

"Mr. Commissioner, you are pleading a lost cause. Let's move on to the next subject: the assassination of the members of our government."

"Assassination? What assassination?"

"Don't you find it curious that the only table with the poisoned food was the one prepared by your people?"

"That's not surprising. It simply proves that our inhabitants' food is bad for rats' stomachs—which I never doubted. I feared for that banquet. Something told me it would come to grief."

"What about the Women's League? Their stomachs don't tolerate the City's food either?"

"There is absolutely no proof that they were poisoned, and I don't believe it for a moment. But I do assume they were murdered. How and by whom is for you to say."

"Why should we kill women who were supporting our cause? No, let's drop it, Mr. Commissioner. Neither of us has any time to waste. I have prepared a note which I would like you to read before I send it to the Prefect. It lists our demands as a result of the recent calamity."

Baudruche took the paper and put on his glasses. It was insane—beyond his wildest fears!

The President's demands included:

1. An official apology from the Prefect, and reparations in kind for the violation of territorial rights committed by the High Commissioner at the head of his armed forces.

2. A serious investigation [the word "serious" was underlined] of the poisoning, which must bear results, to be followed by the delivery of the guilty party or parties.

3. Disarmament of Baudruche's men, as much for the security of the City's inhabitants as for the rats'.

4. The right of their people to move freely above ground and to set up armed patrols to prevent a repetition of disorders like the one of the preceding day.

5. The High Commissioner's resignation.

Baudruche forced a laugh.

"This is pure folly!"

"In what way, Mr. Commissioner? Our demands are entirely reasonable. They prove that, in spite of recent events, our goodwill and desire for collaboration remain intact. It is a bare minimum, so that our people—who are naturally horrified by provocations and assassinations—do not escape my control and abandon themselves to other excesses for which I wouldn't dare hold them to account. You, Mr. Commissioner, should know what it means when a people flaunt authority and discipline?

"As to your resignation, it is in your best interest, Mr. Commissioner. Better to resign than be dismissed, don't you think? And the way things are going . . ."

"Are you trying to make fun of me?"

"I wouldn't dream of it, Mr. Commissioner. I speak the language of reason. And I wish to remind you that in spite of our hardening attitude—which cannot have surprised you—we continue to hold the same friendly feelings toward you. The proof is in the current issue of *The Rodent*. Here, take it and read it. You'll see that we ask only to prove the sentiments I've described. We appeal to your population to open their homes to our nationals and do unto us as we've done unto you, as it were: doors wide open to the rats. We showed the way when we welcomed those poor wanderers everybody else was turning away. We welcomed them; it made things a little tight, but that's all. And we stand ready to welcome still more."

"I will oppose that with everything in my power."

"Is that your view of individual liberty, Mr. Commissioner?"

"I think we have nothing more to say to each other."

"Not today, Mr. Commissioner."

Baudruche got up, purple with rage, and left, gripping his thick cane. If only he could have smashed everything in there, but there were too many of them. . . .

He strode back to his office, head buried in his shoulders. He wasn't going to the Factory that night. The machines, Leponte, advertising, productivity—they could all go to hell. The house was on fire and he didn't know how to put it out or even to save the furniture. Furniture? Yes, furniture. What were these people but furniture and things without shape or brains to throw themselves this way into the lion's mouth as if they were going to a ball?

The last refugee climbed the disintegrating rampart stairs and called out from one of the few remaining spy holes.

"Soldier, what's new?"

The soldier barely raised his head, shrugged and resumed his original position. The man threw him a package. The soldier was too busy crossing out the days on his pocket calendar to get up and claim it. The stranger repeated:

"Soldier, what's new?"

"Two to go."

That's all he could get out of him. Before leaving, he gave a last look at the deserted plain. It wasn't very lively out there either. But in the distance, there was still a small ray of sunshine.

"Let's keep moving, Miss Bourrot. Don't look at me with those fish eyes. Continue."

One by one, Baudruche answered the points the President had raised. But the Commissioner chose to refrain from comment on the subject of his resignation.

He warned, though, that the new President was following a much harder line than his predecessor. "Mr. Prefect, the City is in danger. The enemy we have been awaiting from the outside has not and will not come. He has erupted from inside the City and is gradually taking over."

Then he asked the Prefect for permission to return the City to the way it was before the appearance of the first rat and first ant. "I will do it in such a manner that our neighbors will show fear and respect, retire to their side of the border and return to us alive those members of our population who have disappeared. In order to carry out this project, I ask you to close down the Factory for a brief period so that I can mobilize the workers to clear the moat and permit the water to return. This will solve the problem of the ants in no time. . . ."

"That's all, Miss Bourrot. End with the usual. . . ."

Baudruche took his coat and cane and left, forgetting for the first time in his life to say good night to his secretary. As he walked along, he reflected on what he had just done. Never before had he dared talk this way to the Prefect. But he knew he was right. If it made the Prefect angry, so much for him! He wasn't man enough to ask for Baudruche's resignation—not as long as even one of Baudruche's men remained faithful. But how long would that last?

Head down, lost in thought in the midst of the dust and enveloping night, he failed to notice the girl who now accosted him.

"Want to come with me, ratty?"

Labrique complained that Baudruche was starving him. He took the Commissioner aside and whispered:

"I saw our man. The soldier has only two days to go."

"It isn't much," Baudruche sighed.

"He also wants you to know he's fed up to here with Elisa."

"So am I," Baudruche replied.

19

BAUDRUCHE went to the ramparts even though it was a pointless exercise. He crushed a few ants with the delight of a sadistic child, then went into one of the few turrets still standing and looked through a spy hole. The plain was even darker today. The sunshine seemed to be retreating farther and farther; the clouds were encroaching on the horizon. There were no reflections on the river; darkness enveloped the nearer villages. Perhaps it was better so. He didn't want to see them anymore. It was too painful—the pitiful blackened walls where he had once been so happy.

Ah, with what envy he had once looked at the walls of the City! It had been the goal of all his ambitions: to leave the village and go to the City. He used to talk to Martha about it all the time, although she was less eager to leave the village than he. Weren't they happy where they were? Yes, of course; he didn't want to contradict her, but—yes—he thought they could be even happier. That had proved untrue, for happiness had gradually forsaken them. It wasn't really their fault: it was simply the way life was. Oh, he wasn't admitting defeat yet! You were defeated only when you stopped fighting, and nothing would prevent him from fighting as he always had, and to the very end. But there it was: he was fighting without spirit, without conviction, for now he knew his private struggle had no future.

He left the turret, turned on his heels and walked to the spot over the main gate. No need to worry: he was still there. He still had two days. No, not even two days. His stint would be over the next evening. Though why shouldn't he stay on a few extra days? It wasn't so bad, sitting there doing nothing. After all, Baudruche was hanging on.

He turned and looked toward the City. The muddy roofs were still visible, but everything below was hidden in the swirling dust. Like a finger pointing into the sky, the tower of City Hall dominated the scene. For a moment, he thought he saw a bright eye watching him from the middle of its facade. But it was only the illuminated face of the clock.

He went down the stairs. The guards were still standing by the main gate, armed now with large brooms with which to fend off the ants. He noticed that the big bulletin board for the official notices had been devoured. Oh, well, it was just a lot of worthless bureaucratic junk anyway. . . .

The Commissioner followed the deserted streets to the first inhabited houses. People were milling about in the street. As soon as he was recognized, they flocked around him and fired him with questions. Couldn't he do something? He answered "no" with a mixture of shame and embarrassment. All he could suggest was that they send a delegation to his office and tell him how many were without homes, by families, and the minimum space each would need. He would do everything he could to find them lodgings, probably in the temporary barracks occupied by the refugees from the villages.

One man spoke up timidly. He said maybe it wasn't necessary for the Commissioner to go to all that trouble, that the others had easily found shelter in the Factory district with the rats. . . . Baudruche tried to argue, but they stopped talking and fixed their eyes on the ground. So he left, and when he turned after a few steps, they were looking at him with distrust.

As if they'd been waiting for his departure, the rats converged on the scene the minute his back was turned, and went through the same motions as on the previous day. Today's procession was still longer as it headed for the Factory; it completely filled the courtyard. The moment the last evacuee passed under the porte cochère, the door was locked and the arrivals shoved into different lots: the solidly built men who appeared to be in good health were put in one corner, the others were pushed aside. Then the rats picked out the young, vigorous-looking women and lumped the older ones together with the useless men. Lastly, the children were herded together and led into another courtyard. Suddenly, a window on the fifth floor flew open and a man leaned out, shouting:

"Get out of here! It's a trap!"

The crowd stiffened and looked up at him. A ripple of fear ran through them; they wavered, and a few tried to push toward the entrance. They were turned back with cudgels and well-placed bites. Screams went up, as much from fear as pain. Their angry voices reached into the neighboring streets where the flea market was in full swing. Some City inhabitants inquired about the cause of the noise and were told that the people in the courtyard were rehearsing some songs. The inhabitants asked no further questions; they had become accustomed to the strange way the rats sang. And besides, why get involved in things that didn't concern them?

The body of the man who had shouted teetered on the window ledge and fell to the pavement. A few of the evacuees tried to reach him, but the rats pushed them away, tapping their foreheads to indicate that the man had lost his mind. Other rats prodded the useless evacuees toward a flight of stairs that led to the basement and from there to the sewers. Tomorrow there'd be a large stock of new used clothing to throw on the market.

That done, the auction began. This time, more force was

301

needed to get the evacuees up on the improvised platform, but only the first called up made a show of resistance. Those who followed were threatened into docility. The auction speeded up; there were so many to dispose of. Only the best specimens were bought singly; the rest were sold in lots. It wasn't easy to get rid of them. Prices were well below the previous day's which discouraged speculation. If still more arrived, the bottom might fall out of the market.

Baudruche's first act on returning to his office was to open the Prefect's letter. Not that he didn't know exactly what it would say. The Prefect gave in when he was no longer the strongest. The man was good only for tyrannizing the weak. Why hadn't Baudruche seen this sooner?

All the President's demands were met, and more: Baudruche must agree to the disarming of his men in order to avoid clashes with the new militia under the rats' control. The Prefect was very relaxed about whether they had found those guilty of the poisoning; they would always be able to find someone to pin it on—if the President pressed his demands. Also, he knew he could trust Baudruche to arrive at suitable reparations for the unfortunate violation of territory at the Museum of Man. So far as the ants were concerned, Baudruche had only to be patient: the new powder would be tested within a few days. He twitted Baudruche for wanting to clean up the moat, in view of the fact that no one in the City would be willing to go outside the ramparts. Even if they were, he would oppose it. It would mark a return to the Middle Ages. If the moat had been abandoned, it was for a good reason.

The Commissioner's resignation was lightly brushed aside. The Prefect held him in too high esteem even to contemplate such a thing. . . . What a faker! Let the ranks of his men be decimated and it would be a very different story. . . .

The last paragraph was a long and amiable sermon on how Baudruche must rid himself of his old-fashioned, bellicose ideas. He should thank the Lord that the conscience of his people and their leaders had been awakened; differences were resolved not by arms but through negotiation.

Baudruche boldly crumpled the pages in his hand, tore them to shreds and threw them in the wastebasket. He remained seated a long time, unable to face the pile of papers on his desk.

"Miss Bourrot!"

She opened the door a crack. "You called me, Mr. Commissioner?"

"Obviously, since you are there. Have you heard anything about my men leaving my service?"

"Yes, Mr. Commissioner. They're going into the Prefect's."

"Couldn't you have told me sooner?"

"You haven't given me a chance."

"You only talk nonsense; this is important. Have there been many?"

"About a dozen. The list is there on your desk."

"Hand it to me. Why do you look at me like that? Do I have a spot on my nose?"

She fled, visibly upset. Baudruche glanced at the list. Every name hurt. He saw their faces; he had thought they were attached to him. Money! They hadn't been able to resist the money. And perhaps the fear of making a mistake by sticking by the Commissioner. Pitiful. The whole thing was pitiful. Bastards? Not even that—just pathetic. He crumpled the list as if it were no more than an unpleasant memory and tossed it into the wastebasket. The door opened again.

"What is it now? I said I didn't want to be disturbed under any conditions. . . ."

"I know, Mr. Commissioner, but Mr. Labrique is here."

"Why didn't you tell me sooner? Show him in!"

Labrique entered, his hands in his pockets.

"Do you see your fellow again tonight?"

Labrique looked at his watch. "Yes, he may even be on his way there now."

"Well, then, get going. If you don't find him at the Library,

303

try to see him before tonight. Tell him it's O.K. and everything will be ready at the agreed time."

"My poor friend, this is hard on you, isn't it?"

"Mind your own business and don't be late for dinner."

The stranger was on his way back from the ramparts. He had thrown the package to the soldier, but the latter was as non-committal as the day before. All he could get out of him was:

"It's almost over."

Dinner at the Baudruches' was almost gay. Each felt so sad that he did his best to seem happy. They even came close to laughter, and once the table was cleared, Baudruche himself got out the cards.

In the hall of the second floor at the Hotel, Elisa was shaking the door of number 23. He had dined before her, or so she had been told, obviously to avoid her. There was no answer. But she was certain he was in his room. His key wasn't hanging on its hook. She said in a loud whisper:

"Open the door. I have something to tell you."

Still no answer. She raised her voice; it grew insistent. At last she heard someone move inside the room. He was finally going to open up. No, he stayed on the other side of the door and said just loud enough for her to hear:

"Beat it!"

The game was almost over at the Commissioner's. And he'd won. He'd beaten that cad, Labrique, at his own game by cheating better than he. Labrique looked at him indulgently. Throwing his cards on the table, he smiled.

"At last you're beginning to learn how to play!"

20

‹‹‹‹‹‹‹‹‹‹‹‹‹‹‹‹

N O O N E had ever seen the Commissioner arrive so early.
The building was still dark. Baudruche tried the door to the
office. It was locked. He found his key in the bottom of his
pocket among some shreds of tobacco. He went in, removed his
hat and coat, threw himself on the couch and took four sheets
of paper from his jacket pocket. He had spent a large part of
the night on them.

He reread the pages carefully, made some corrections and
rose abruptly at the sound of footsteps in the courtyard. He
looked out the window and saw that it was Revere. He called
down:

"Come up right away. I want to speak to you."

Revere entered, bewildered and out of breath.

"What's going on, Mr. Commissioner?"

"You'll know soon enough. For the moment, it's none of
your business or anybody else's. I want you to post yourself at
the entrance and tell anyone who comes to the door to wait
in the courtyard. Each time you see someone you trust, tell him

to go guard an exit. I want the entire building sealed. People can come in but they can't leave. If anybody asks you why, tell them what you know, which is nothing."

Revere left. Baudruche sank into his leather chair. He needed a moment's relaxation, for the night had been brief. He had pretended to be asleep for Martha's sake, but actually he had been checking over in his mind all the things he must anticipate. Anything could happen and nothing must go wrong. Everything rested on him. He scratched his head and cracked his knuckles with anxiety. There was a noise in the hall. He opened the door; it was the Prefect's messenger.

"You can give it to me, boy."

"To you, Mr. Commissioner?"

"Isn't the letter addressed to me?"

"Yes it is, but I'm not used to . . ."

"Well, you'll get used to it, if it becomes necessary. We all need to change our ways from time to time."

The messenger left without further word. Everything was all mixed up. He ran into Miss Bourrot on the stairs.

"You have the letter?"

"Not anymore. I gave it to the Commissioner."

"He's here already?"

She sped up the stairs and knocked gently before opening the door.

"You're here, Mr. Commissioner!"

"No, it's my ghost, my double. Actually I'm off fishing."

"But . . . why?"

"Why what? Do I have to give an account of myself every time?"

She tiptoed back to her office. Didn't she count for anything in this place? After all these years in the Commissioner's service, he was treating her like scum! She opened the window and noticed that the courtyard was filling with people. Baudruche's men were standing around in small groups, probably discussing the same subject that consumed her. She hoped that at least nobody knew any more than she did. That, she could never forgive him.

"Miss Bourrot!"

She ran to the door.

"You called me, Mr. Commissioner?"

"Get me a dozen stenographers and have them bring their typewriters with them."

She wanted so badly to ask him why . . . but she soon returned with a troop of girls.

"Take whatever place you can find. I want each of you to type eight copies of what I'm about to dictate. No, don't leave, Miss Bourrot. I need you too. Now, take this down: 'General Instructions.' "

Baudruche gathered up all the pages and told his secretary:

"Lock up all these girls in an office. They are not to leave before I return this evening. Give them lunch on the house."

The girls filed out in a flurry of whispers. Baudruche went over to the window. The courtyard was now full. Baudruche saw Revere giving orders to close the main door. Apparently everybody had arrived so Baudruche started down the stairs.

"Is anyone missing, Revere?"

"Yes, Mr. Commissioner, about a dozen men. I don't think they'll be coming. They've gone over to the other side."

"Well, we'll get along without them perfectly well."

Baudruche stood on the stoop and addressed his men.

"Today, you don't go to your usual stations. I want you to form into squadrons of six men, each squadron to be commanded by an officer. Payne, come here. . . . Take these sheets of paper and dole them out to the head of each group."

Baudruche looked at his watch. Time was running out. He ordered the main door opened and, walking at the head of his men, directed his steps toward the Hotel.

The stranger had left a short while before. As soon as he reached Prefect Avenue, he leaned against a wall, took the flute out of its case and put it to his lips. Passersby looked with curiosity at this man blowing into a pipe from which no sound came. Some women approached him and stood around in a circle. From every window in the vicinity, children's heads emerged. They recognized the flute player, galloped down the stairs and pushed through the women to get near him. He played a moment longer, looked up, and seeing that there were no more children at the windows, moved on. People walking by joined the crowd out of distrust for what they didn't understand. They tried to get nearer to the man but the children pushed them away. The adults heckled the man with the flute, but he paid them no heed. The crowd grew larger and more threatening; a few stopped to pick up stones off the street. Baudruche's men arrived at that moment. The Commissioner ordered the crowd to break up and everyone dispersed. He placed his men in two long rows on either side of the children to guard them. The man with the flute moved up Prefect Avenue, his followers constantly growing in numbers.

The mob of children and women kept on marching, protected by Baudruche's men who were instructed to let the children in and keep the men out. Hours went by, the procession always growing. There wasn't a house where the flute wasn't heard by those who could hear it. Baudruche's eyes darted right and left. Up to now, everything had gone as planned. A few incidents but nothing serious. Payne, who was walking at his side, asked:

"Is it going all right, Mr. Commissioner?"

"I'd say so . . . if it lasts. Have you seen any of the Prefect's men?"

"Yes, several, but they all left."

Some of the men who had latched on tired of following this bizarre procession. They understood neither its purpose nor its goal. Where were these kids going, trailing after that nut? What was the Commissioner doing in the middle of this carnival? The rats' patrol was disturbed by the sight of the procession but kept out of its way. It was too well guarded.

The endless column headed toward the northern part of the City, filed down all the major arteries, turned east and rejoined Prefect Avenue. Hanging from their windows, some laughed, others looked alarmed. Had the City gone mad?

The column of children had reached the area of the Factory. They had difficulty getting through the mob obstructing the narrow streets where the flea market was in progress. Baudruche's men cleared a path as the man kept blowing on his instrument. Baudruche prodded the man with the flute.

"Let's move on. It's no good here."

The procession moved on, a crowd of rats in its wake. Suddenly the siren went off at the Prefecture. Baudruche looked at his watch: it was closing time at the Factory.

"Get moving!" Baudruche shouted from the curb, motioning his men to go faster.

The Commissioner was getting anxious. He moved to the end of the line, turning frequently to gauge the size of the crowd following behind. A group of ugly-looking rats were in the lead, and behind them, the workers from the Factory drawn by a mixture of fear and curiosity.

They finally reached the main gate. Baudruche ran to the head of the line and ordered the guards to open the gates. The crowd began to mill around. It had just dawned on the rats and the City's inhabitants what was happening. They rushed to the gates to prevent anyone from passing through.

Baudruche gave three blows on his whistle. His men went into action and charged on the rats and inhabitants obstructing the gates. Baudruche ran to the top of the ramparts to observe the scene. As far as the eye could see, Prefect Avenue was jammed with people. At the farthest end, he could just make out gray shapes moving in the clouds of dust. Dominating everything was the tower of the Prefecture whose eye had just been lit.

At his feet, fights had started to break out. He could hear screams of pain and anger. He was proud of his men; they were doing a good job. The noise abated and gradually stopped altogether. People were fleeing in all directions. As the dust began to settle, he could see the gleam of his men's helmets and the long column of children resuming their march.

The women who had accompanied the children now climbed the stairs and lined up on either side of Baudruche along the sentry walk. Clinging as best they could to what remained of the parapet, they sat with legs dangling over the side, looking straight ahead. Suddenly there was a great commotion. The mob of rats and inhabitants who had regrouped in the distance let out a roar when they saw the children start through the gates. Forgetting their fear of the plain, a group of them massed outside the gates, closing off the exit.

The soldier had gotten up to watch the scene. Baudruche gave the signal; he picked up his rifle, shouldered his bag and equipment and walked up to the gate. A great cry went up:

"They're here! They've come back!"

The crowd fell back, knocking over the children as they fled. The soldier continued walking slowly forward, the crowd melting before him. Baudruche saw him go through the gate, then he turned to watch the other side; the soldier headed up Prefect Avenue.

The children regrouped. Again, the man with the flute put the instrument to his lips and, slightly in the lead, approached the main gate.

From the top of the ramparts, Baudruche watched the man with the flute come out of the other side of the gates, the children behind him in tight ranks. The long column trailed off into the distance. Shouting with joy, the women waved handkerchiefs and scarves at the retreating children. The band of light still shining on the horizon started to spread over the sky. Baudruche had to blink his eyes. The light crept over the plain until it reached the blackened ramparts. Clouds churned on the horizon and advanced toward the City in great billows. Baudruche put on his glasses. Now he could see flocks of birds circling over the heads of the children. Dipping and wheeling, they accompanied the column as far as the eye could see, then they all disappeared into the horizon and the light went out. A vast silence fell on the plain and the ramparts. The women's joy subsided. They were crying now, and filed past Baudruche toward the stairs. The Commissioner was left alone. He tried to distinguish the burned-out vestiges of the nearest villages, but he could see nothing. His eyes smarted. It wasn't emotion, of course; probably the sunshine of a moment ago. He walked down the stairs.

His men surrounded him, not daring to speak, torn between joy at their success and the fear of having done something wrong. The Commissioner's eyes were fixed on the ground. Bodies of rats lay scattered about in the dust, the ants already feasting on them. Baudruche called out to the guards:

"Close the gates!"

He blew on his whistle to summon his men. Three abreast with Baudruche in the lead, they started up Prefect Avenue.

Far away, in the northern part of town, an armed man pushed open the door of an office marked "Demobilization." A solitary official occupied the office. At the sight of the soldier, he jumped to his feet.

"You've come at last! We were waiting for you so we could close down."

Elisa had been drawn into the crowd heading toward the main gate. As she watched the children, she suddenly remembered Sophie. She ran to a telephone and called Martha.

"Is Sophie with you?"

"No, my dear, she left with the others."

"Where have they gone?"

"Away."

Elisa stormed and ranted, cursing the Commissioner. Martha hung up. It wasn't so much that Elisa minded being separated from her child—she was a stranger to her at best—but she had it in for Baudruche. He had spoiled everything. He had allowed her a glimpse of another life and had thrown her into the arms of a nobody, without money, and mad besides. And this man had left her like a cad, without a word of farewell, without a present, without taking his baggage—except for his stupid instrument. Was it possible he might have left something of value in his room? She dashed down the stairs and into the empty lobby. The key to room 23 was hanging on its hook. She took it, ran back up the stairs and opened the door. Everything seemed to be in place. She looked through all his drawers but found nothing of value—only papers and some books. She rummaged through his closet but it contained only useless men's clothing. She went into the bathroom. Nothing remotely interesting except for a bottle of eau de cologne—half empty—which she tucked under her arm. Then she saw the green suitcase she had never managed to open, still standing in its corner. She picked it up and took it with her.

Back in her room, she tried to force the lock but to no avail. She took a pair of strong scissors and started snipping at the stitching. When she finally got it open, she almost fell over backward. Never in her life had she dared dream of so much money. She couldn't believe her eyes. What a miser, offering her only junk when he had all this!

She stuffed a handful of bills into her bag, locked the suitcase in her closet and slipped the key inside her blouse. She looked at her watch. There was still time; the luxury shops on Prefect Avenue wouldn't be closed yet. Night had fallen and the streetlights barely penetrated the swirling dust. She ran to the jewelry shop.

"I want the ring in the window." She pointed to the most expensive one she saw.

She paid up very nonchalantly, shuffling her wad of bills under the shopkeeper's astonished gaze. Once outside, she stopped by the shop window to let the light play on the ring on her finger. A rat who was passing by stooped to pick up something at her feet. Frightened, she walked quickly away. The rat followed. She ran. He ran, stopping to stoop down from time to time. Suddenly she noticed that her handbag was open and the bills were scattering behind her. The Hotel was now but a few steps away. She ran even faster. A hand grabbed her leg and she fell headfirst in the dust. The rat pressed his knee to her back and snatched her bag. He let out two shrill whistles; two rats ran up. Elisa felt herself being seized, lifted up off the ground and carried away. She tried to cry out but a hand had closed over her mouth.

"Free your prisoners, Miss Bourrot, and let's get down to work!

"Mr. Prefect:

"During the course of the night, my agent at the Hotel advised me that the last refugee was making plans that could well disturb the City's peace. I summoned all my men to prepare for any eventuality.

"I encountered the stranger as he was leaving the Hotel. He started to play his instrument on Prefect Avenue. To my great surprise, children poured out of all the neighboring houses and joined him. When I saw how large the crowd was growing, I had my men surround the children so that their demonstration could not disturb the peace. I took no measures against the man since there is no regulation forbidding the playing of a flute on City streets.

"The only regulation that could be invoked concerned the flow of traffic. Therefore I made certain that wherever the procession went, space was left for traffic.

"During the course of the day, the procession filed down every street in the City, growing all the while. When it reached the main gates, the stranger indicated a desire to leave the City, as did all the children following him. Since no regulation forbade it, I ordered the doors opened. A crowd of rats and City inhabitants who had been following us tried to stand in the way.

"I ordered my men to intervene in order to protect the rights of City inhabitants. I am sure you will be gratified to know, Mr. Prefect, that they were successful in their mission and that the stranger and the children were permitted to carry out their desire to leave the City.

"You will be no less gratified to learn that at that moment the soldier who sat so long in front of the main gates causing you such distress entered the City. I later learned that he went immediately to demobilization headquarters where he surrendered his weapon, uniform and equipment—all in perfect condition. He was issued civilian clothing, and has become a simple City inhabitant like any other.

"In closing, I wish to remark, Mr. Prefect, that during the whole of his stay in the City, the stranger scrupulously kept his word that he would violate no law or regulation in force in the City.

"With this report, which will be my last, I take the liberty of including my letter of resignation. My sole reason is the state of my health. For some time, I have been suffering palpitations and heartburn which prohibit the normal exercise of my functions. . . ."

Miss Bourrot raised her head.

"It isn't true, Mr. Commissioner! You're not leaving us?"

"As I've told you before, Miss Bourrot, I don't like to be interrupted when I'm dictating. Continue please.

"The Weather Bureau predicts stable weather without sun due to the presence of clouds over the City. Sentry duties having been interrupted, I have nothing to report on what may have happened last night outside the City.

"Respectfully yours, etc.

"Well, that's done. What was it you wished to say to me?"

"You can't be serious, Mr. Commissioner. You must be joking about your resignation?"

"Have you ever caught me joking about the City's affairs?

314

Good night, Miss Bourrot. Here is my office key. You will give it to my successor."

"Shall we play a hand, Labrique?"

"What's the use? You're stronger than I am now."

Small screeches penetrated through the door. Baudruche got up, put his ear to the door and recognized a sound he knew only too well—that of teeth gnawing on wood. He came back and picked up the andiron by the fireplace.

"The first one who enters . . ."